THE
LOST

VALARAII RISING TRILOGY

KRISTEN JOHNSON

Jan-Carol
Publishing, Inc

"every story needs a book"

The Lost
Valaraii Rising Trilogy
Book 2
Kristen Johnson
Published June 2025
Broken Crow Ridge
Imprint of Jan-Carol Publishing, Inc.
All rights reserved
Copyright © 2025 Kristen Johnson
Cover design: Tara Sizemore

ISBN: 978-1-962561-73-0
Library of Congress Control Number: 2025940990

You may contact the publisher:
Jan-Carol Publishing, Inc.
PO Box 701
Johnson City, TN 37605
publisher@jancarolpublishing.com
www.jancarolpublishing.com

For my daughter, Emma Grace.

Be kind...of a badass. I love you.

Valaraii Rising Trilogy

The Forgotten
Book 1

The Lost
Book 2

THE LOST

Author's Note

I have been blessed in my life with the presence of strong women, and it was these women who allowed me to dream and believe I could be a warrior like Syllē. It was also because of these women that my books, including the one you are holding right now, were written. My list of these women is beautifully long.

There were my grandmothers, who always graciously stood up for themselves but weren't afraid to go "nuclear" if the situation demanded, and my mother who grabbed breast cancer by the throat and drop-kicked it out of her life. There was my Aunt Mary, who was always such a joy to be around even when her horse-crazy niece begged to go riding on Spartacus in the middle of a cold Pennsylvania day, and my Great-Great-Aunt Marj who always found the time to write and remind me that I had potential.

There was also my AP U.S. History teacher whom students and administration called "The Battle Axe," because she refused to accept anything less than your utter respect. My dear friend Vickie, who called me religiously after my breast cancer diagnosis and has no fear of being blunt or standing up for herself and others. My colleague, April—who was at that time making her own kefir—decided to bring me smoothies and parfaits every morning to school after she heard I had breast cancer, and she is not the only coworker to show me such amazing support. Most recently, Evelyn Hammonds showed me compassion, humor, and such strength as well as an amazing knack for calling a spade a spade with no apologies. I love and admire that kind of gumption.

My list could fill an entire book, actually; and the stories could fill an entire library. So, as my favorite sweatshirt says, "Here's to strong women. May we know them. May we be them. May we raise them."

GUIDE TO THE
PEOPLES AND PLACES OF MITHTERRA

(Thank you, Emmajyn, for the suggestion.)

Note: I have included how phonetically the various names sound to me in my book. You, dear reader, are perfectly welcome to pronounce them as you like.

The Realms:

Dwarven:

Shara (Shar-ah): greatest of all dwarf kingdoms and founded by the legendary King Asger. It was destroyed by Merilik, and its last king's (Farin) fate is still unknown.

Exulias (Ex-zoo-lee-as): created by the remnants of the Shara dwarves in the twin mountains not far from the Rudu Mountains. It is ruled by Tarin, son of Farin, and is a constant focus of Merilik. The Dark Lord wants this kingdom, especially its ruler, exterminated.

Banruhm (Ban-room): ruled by Farin's brother Modun and Sappha, whose sons are Nerun and Trygve. It is located in the White Mountains.

Verrum (Ver-room): ancient dwarf kingdom adjacent to the wereling settlement in the Perdarus Range. It has been long abandoned by dwarves, per the treaty between Asger and the wereling Queen, Shasha. Unfortunately, it has made an excellent prison complex for the Drēor Therendē'al.

Elven:

Kuaryll (Cue-ah-rill): ruled by Athenéal and Thorunmilé. It is located in a beautiful forest, a three days' fast ride from Exulias, which to many of the dwarves is way too close for comfort.

Elathnora (EE-lath-nor-ah): southernmost kingdom of elves and adjacent to the Moaning Bog. It is ruled by two brothers, Raemir and Cathir.

Aelgalad (Ale-ga-laud): ruled by King Thallen and Queen Azrul, who was slaughtered by Thallen's brother Glaucis. The pair have two sons, Thranulas and Granulas. It was surrounded by a great lake, but Merilik has blocked the river and drained the lake, imprisoning Aelgalad's citizens within the walls of the kingdom. For several hundred years, this once thriving elven kingdom has been laid siege to by Merilik, and it is very close to falling.

Calarta (Caw-lar-taw): the hidden kingdom. Ruled by Arterius and Genna, parents of the Princess Esmerelle. The road to the kingdom was hidden ages ago by a dense fog and almost no one has been able to find their way through to Calarta. It was allied with Norolin, the northern kingdom of humans, founded by Arterius's brother on the shores of the great sea, Thalassen.

Main Characters:

Syllē (sill-lay), a.k.a. Sylēmar (sill-ay-mar): one of only 13 remaining Valaraii (Vah-lar-ray) or children of the Lēas (Lay-as). She was sent to Mith Terra to combat the forces of Merilik but hadn't been too successful, as she had been entombed for several hundred years when the twins found her in Book 1. Adopted into the Exulian clan, Syllē is determined to not only save her new family from Merilik's extermination plans but also have a little revenge of her own on the Dark Lord.

Tarin (Tair-in): son of Farin (Fair-in) and ruler of Exulias. He is haunted by the memory of leaving his father behind on the day Shara fell and refuses to be called "King" because of it. He is grumpy, suspicious of all (outsiders especially), and brave. He has accepted Syllē into his kingdom mainly out of a sense of duty to his father, who gave Syllē a Sharan crystal as a symbol of their friendship.

Trygve (Trig-vee): Tarin's cousin and captain of the Guard for Exulias. He has lived with Tarin for most of his life now and has designated himself as Tarin's personal bodyguard. He is extremely loyal to his cousin and hates and deeply distrusts elves and humans, but especially elves.

Hil: Tarin's sister and the healer for the Exulias clan. She is also a formidable warrior and staunchly loyal to her brother. Of Farin's children, she is definitely the most reasonable and willing to work with and accept help from outsiders. Her twins are Tarin's heirs and the ones who discovered and released Syllē from her tomb.

Finn: The oldest of Hil's twins, but most wouldn't guess that, as Finn is an extreme prankster and prefers laughing and having fun to anything else, strong warrior though he is. He also has an innate ability to read Syllē's moods and know when she needs him.

Kwin: The youngest of Hil's twins by only three minutes, he is more reserved and quieter than his brother, which is why most people think he is older. A strong warrior like his brother, Kwin reacts more cautiously in situations, preferring to think things through and then act.

Athenéal (A-theen-ay-el) and Thorunmilé (Thor-un-mill-ay): the king and queen of Kuaryll and longtime unknown allies to the dwarves of Exulias. Neither would be considered great warriors. Their powers lie in visions and the wisdom to interpret and act on those visions.

Halicyon (Ha-lee-cee-on): one of Syllē's oldest friends and a formidable warrior, he has had his own tragedies—the murder of his wife and loss of his infant son. While Therendē'al's plan to turn Halicyon Drēor was unsuccessful, it did come terribly close to working. Focusing on keeping the remnants of the dwarves safe from Merilik kept Halicyon walking in the light... barely.

Falinor (Fæl-eh-nor): one of the greatest elven warriors in MithTerra, he was chosen by High Queen Sedivar to train and protect Sylēmar so the young child could eventually grow into the weapon the high queen and the Lēas had designed her to be. He was possessed by a malidaemon queen for a few hundred years before Syllē and Tarin freed him. As far as most people know, Falinor is Syllē's father.

Tēorg (Tay-org): Shara's last captain of the Guard and a loyal subject to Tarin, he and his sons, Varger and Birger, help Tarin rule Exulias and keep the kingdom safe. Syllē's ability to save his daughter-in-law, Bree, and granddaughter solidified his family's devotion to her as well.

Oran (Oar-on) and Eirik (Air-ick): two human brothers from the neighboring city of Helmfirth. They were on the trip that freed Syllē from her tomb and unfortunately were fooled by the treacherous merchants who tried to feed the dwarves to the Strygoi. Since that time, they have become friends of Exulias; but now Oran is lost to the dark somewhere in the Perdarus. Hopefully, they will find him before it is too late.

Thēorin (Thay-o-rin): the son of Lord Hadrin and Lady Sariel, the rulers of Helmfirth, and now Exulias's ally. He is an excellent archer and decent with a sword, but most importantly, he trusts and believes in Tarin and the dwarves of Exulias. He has a strong sense of right and wrong and a stubborn streak that could rival a dwarf's, which is how he ended up in the meadow with his militia after hearing the horns of Exulias reverberate across their valley.

Amarris (Ah-mar-ris): half elf and half human, this stunning redheaded archer from Helmfirth carries her own plan for revenge against her uncle, Therendē'al, the murderer of Amarris's mother.

Flarne, Carne, and Sarne: three dwarf brothers devoted to each other and their clan. These three are some of Tarin's best warriors and will fight by the side of their lord and his allies with everything they have.

Current Line of Asger

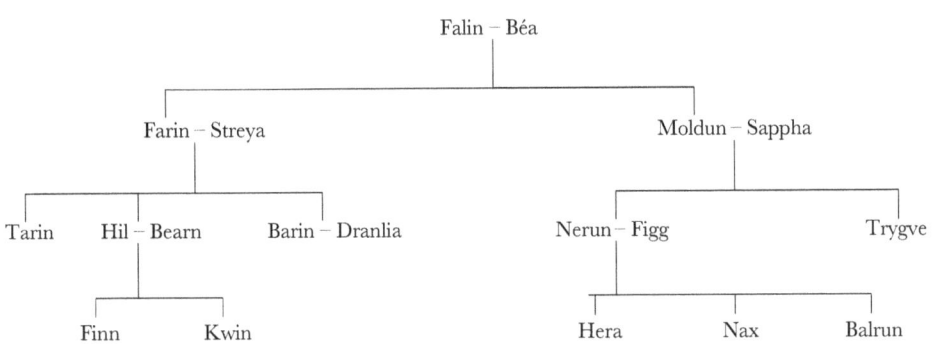

Background notes on Asger's line:
1. Farin is six generations from King Asger.
2. Asger was three generations from Drégon.
3. Asger received aid from Arterius to set up the kingdom of Shara.
4. Asger's wife was from Norolin and not 100% dwarf.

PROLOGUE

Syllē was jarred awake by the arrival of more orc and their prisoners. Her world was a nightmare of darkness and pain. She could taste the metallic signature of the poison in her blood. It was a dull fire searing through her veins that she knew would grow and consume her. *Funny,* Syllē thought to herself, pressing her forehead against the cold metal of her crow cage, *I didn't think I would end up here. Some weapon I turned out to be.*

Her musings were cut short as her eyes focused on two of the new arrivals—an elf and a dwarf. It was strange enough that the two appeared to be together, but they were totally oblivious to the chaos around them. Their total focus was on her. More than that, the dwarf felt strangely familiar, and as her eyes locked on his, Syllē was certain she knew him. Before Syllē could decipher how she knew the dwarf, she was struck by a sharp pain that erupted in her head before coursing through her body. She had not expected Therendē'al's poison to work so fast.

Suddenly, a voice seared through her brain. "It is time, Princess. High Queen Sedivar commands it."

Syllē felt the pain build, surging through her like a rogue wave, and as it grew, Syllē noticed every part of her body awakening. Catching a glimpse of K'tanna's face next to her, Syllē was startled to see a triumphant grin spreading across her friend's face. What was happening?

Syllē heard the voice again: "Don't fight it, Princess. Let it out. Awaken!"

With that last sharp command, Syllē felt the powerful wave within her grow to a point she could no longer hold back. Unconsciously grabbing the bars to her crow cage, she pulled herself to her feet and emitted a scream of pure fury fueled by her months of torture, pain, and loss that released the wave within her. The bright navy light exploded into the prison, knocking cages to the floor, wrenching prison doors open, and incinerating orc. When everything calmed, the only two still standing were the elf and the dwarf with the familiar eyes.

Smirking a bit at his companion, the elf, Falēon, commented wryly, "I stand corrected. That was impressive."

The dwarf, Tarkin, simply grunted as he watched Syllē swiftly help K'tanna out of her prison and follow the others escaping through a far door. Everyone seemed oblivious to the pair standing in the aftermath of Syllē's chaos. Everyone, that is, except K'tanna, who deftly caught the war hammer Tarkin threw her way. Tarkin's eyes grew sad as he watched them flee.

"Come on," Tarkin's voice was heavy with weariness, "this isn't something I wish to see."

Falēon nodded sadly as the two began to exit the prison. "There is no place for you in this memory, niece." Tarkin's voice startled Falēon, and he turned to look behind for his companion. Tarkin had stopped and was staring into the shadows of a tunnel opening. "Return to him."

1

"Uncle?" Kwin stood by Tarin on the road that was winding through Mosslight Forest, the path they needed to take to get to their rendezvous point in the Oloro Valley amid the Arcasian Wilds—a place, if Tarin was being honest, intimidated him. The race who lived there was rumored to be even more wild than the land and one of the most feared armies to ever take the field of battle. Tarin wasn't too sure they'd be welcome in the Drengas' domain, and if they weren't, he wasn't too sure they'd survive the encounter, even with Syllē on their side.

Now, Tarin, who'd been pushing his group hard and fast as though he was trying to make it to the Arcasian Wilds in record time, had suddenly stopped in the middle of the road and was intently peering off to their right. Finn had been about to make some smart comment about Tarin's head being cocked to the side like Syllē's customary trait, but after a good look at his uncle's face, Finn quickly swallowed the smart comment. Trygve gazed behind them, appearing worried as well.

Tarin finally spoke, looking forward and behind them as he spoke. His concern was evident in his voice. "Something feels wrong. I have travelled this road many times, but it feels off. Where is the light? Where are all the forest sounds? It's too quiet."

Amarris came forward, warily looking around as she did. "I agree, Lord Tarin." Turning in a cautious circle in the road, Amarris continued,

"I know this forest like the back of my hand. I have travelled its paths so often on my way to Vanguard to visit my father's family." Shaking her head, Amarris finished, "Something is off."

Hearing something, Tarin held up his hand for silence and then listened intently. At first, he heard nothing, but then, he caught the distinctive sound of soft padded footfalls. His eyes narrowed. "It would appear that we are being hunted," he warned.

"By what?" Finn asked, but before anyone could answer, the attack began.

* * *

Wargs are a domesticated species of wolf, but when we say domesticated, we simply mean that they are a specific breed bred by the Dark for their use and purpose. Wargs would turn on their Drēor, Vikari, or orc handlers just as quickly and ferociously as they would on elves, humans, dwarves, or any other species. They were also the advance guard for the Dark, going into places ahead of the Drēor to clear it of as many inhabitants as possible; thus, rendering the area an easier conquest. Obviously, at least one warg pack had invaded Mosslight Forest, which would explain the eerie feeling that the woods had begun to give Tarin and Amarris and support Tarin's assertion that their group was being hunted—because it was.

* * *

The first warg burst out of the forest onto the path to the right rear of the group, who luckily had clustered together in a defensive ring after Tarin's stop. This made them a more difficult target as they were quickly able to knit together and not be one-on-one against a warg. While a dwarf could kill a warg when on their own, they would have to be seriously lucky to do so, or exceptionally skilled. Usually, if a dwarf came up against a warg, the dwarf was soon dead. An entire pack, which averaged eight to twelve wargs—well, that was a totally different horror.

The first warg was felled by one of Amarris' arrows through its right eye. The rest of the pack was rapidly upon them from all sides of the road. In very short order, the group was surrounded by nine snarling, huge wargs, who appeared to be anticipating the kill.

"Amarris, your arrows are our greatest weapon here, so the rest of you circle around her and keep those beasts off her." Not taking his attention off the pack surrounding them, Tarin continued, "Watch each other's back and don't let anyone get dragged out of the circle."

That was going to be easier said than done. As the wargs cautiously advanced, Amarris felled two more with perfect shots through an eye, but there was no way for her to get all of them before they could launch on the group. There were still seven left.

"Wait for it," Tarin cautioned. "Don't jump out of the circle. Make them come to you."

Sensing the charge from behind, Amarris whirled and felled another warg with an arrow through the throat as it tried to launch at Tarin. She was noticing something. The wargs were less concerned with her or most of the dwarves. They seemed intent on Tarin.

Angry over the loss of four of their pack, the wargs decided to launch at once. Trygve and Tarin deftly handled the large male who would have landed on Tarin, except Tarin anticipated and dodged left and slightly forward under it, hitting its belly with his axe, knocking it off kilter. Trygve finished it off with a smashing blow to the warg's forehead.

Hil and Flarne took out a large female who tried to fight past them to the center of the circle and forward towards Tarin. Then, Hil spun and aided her sons in dispatching two more wargs who had tried in vain to break past the twins and Varger. One was successful in biting down on Amarris' side, but the bite was "merely a scratch. Don't worry about me."

Amarris maintained her focus on the warg trying to creep past them, intent on Tarin at the top of the circle. With a solid shot behind the shoulder and through its heart, she stopped that one dead.

"Tarin," Amarris called out, "they're hunting you, not us. Stay back behind Trygve."

Her warning came too late. Tarin sidestepped one warg, only to be grabbed from behind by another and slung down the road. Trygve and Flarne dispatched the one warg Tarin had avoided but were in no position to stop the other that was now heading full tilt at Tarin, who had had his bell rung when he hit the ground.

Amarris shot the warg as it headed for Tarin, but it wasn't a fatal shot as it went in the warg's rear. The animal didn't even stumble. Before Amarris could notch another arrow, the warg launched at Tarin, who was struggling to regain his feet.

Suddenly, the warg was grabbed by the throat by a huge black shape that launched itself from the trees on the right side of the road. Flipping through the air, the two creatures cleared Tarin. The black one landed on all fours right before the trees on the opposite side of the path and threw the warg against the nearest oak with such force the group could hear the warg's spine crack.

"Stop!" Amarris yelled at the dwarves as they started to charge. "That's not a warg."

"But, Tarin…" Trygve growled.

"If it were going to harm Tarin, it would have let that warg kill him," Amarris reasoned. "That's a wolf, not a warg."

Kwin, who had made it to Tarin, turned to find himself face to face with the largest wolf he had ever seen. His eyes widened as the huge canine slowly approached him. Squaring his stance and gripping his axe tighter, Kwin tried to remain calm and protect Tarin, who was still struggling to regain his feet.

"Kwin, trust me. Lower your axe," Amarris instructed as calmly as she could.

"But his fangs are as large as spears," Kwin stuttered, trying to sound brave, but failing. The wolf seemed to grin at that remark, which did nothing for Kwin's confidence since it just further showed the huge array of exceptionally large teeth in its mouth.

Swallowing hard, Kwin slowly lowered his axe, never taking his eyes off the approaching wolf. Kwin felt the hair on the back of his neck stand straight up. "I think there's another one behind me in the woods," Kwin called out. He noticed, as he did, the black wolf's yellow eyes narrow. Could it understand him? How was that possible?

Stopping only a foot from Kwin, the wolf suddenly rocked its head back and howled, sending chills through everyone in the group. A second wolf emerged from the trees behind Kwin and limped onto the road. It was only slightly smaller than its companion and Kwin could tell that its front right paw was injured. How badly, he couldn't decipher.

Keeping an eye on both wolves, Kwin reached behind himself for his uncle, who grabbed his nephew's arm to help himself rise. Shaking his head to clear the cobwebs, Tarin kept his hand on Kwin's shoulder while he tried to get his bearings.

"What happened to that warg?" Tarin finally managed to ask, his hand holding his head as he leaned on Kwin.

"Umm, that happened to the warg," Kwin explained, pointing at the first wolf.

Tarin's eyes grew wide as he focused on the huge black wolf in front of him. His eyes grew even bigger when his mind registered that the first wolf had a companion. Looking between the two wolves, Tarin suddenly realized what they were.

"What should we do?" Trygve asked, standing with the others on the road where they had stopped a few feet away.

"Put your weapons away," Tarin instructed. "I don't think either of these is out to harm us."

"They're the largest wolves I've ever seen," Finn commented, wonderingly.

"That's because they aren't just wolves. They're Lēasean wolves," Tarin explained, the awe apparent in his voice.

"Lēasean wolves?" Amarris breathed incredulously. "Never thought I'd see any of those. They haven't roamed these lands in at least an age."

Tarin suddenly squinted at the black wolf's chest, "More specifically, this one is a Hound of Sedivar."

"How do you know that?" Amarris asked curiously.

"He bears the High Queen's mark on his chest—the crescent," Tarin pointed at an almost indecipherable shape on the chest of the black wolf. Turning to study its partner, Tarin noticed the same markings. "They're both Hounds of Sedivar."

Squinting at the wolves, Amarris muttered without thinking, "I can't believe you can see that. I didn't think dwarves had such keen eyes." Mortified, Amarris tried to take it back. "I didn't mean—I just had always heard…" At a loss, Amarris remorsefully shut her mouth.

Tarin and Kwin simply scowled at her, while the wolves regarded her with what appeared to be disdain.

Trygve broke the awkward moment with his customary growl, "I don't think we should stay here in the road. We need to keep moving and put as much distance between us and this spot as we can." Trygve looked warily around them at the woods.

"I agree," Tarin nodded. Noticing the blood on Amarris, he asked, "Are you able to travel?"

She nodded. "I can make it. The bite's not bad, I promise."

Carefully, the rest of the group joined Tarin and Kwin, cautiously watching the two wolves as they approached. Neither wolf really seemed all that bothered by the group and just calmly watched them back. Kwin was taken aback when the wolves turned and walked on either side of Tarin as though they were his bodyguards. Looking at his brother's face and the faces of the others, Kwin could tell they were just as shocked as he.

2

"So, Hil, how bad is the bite?" Tarin had asked Hil to look at Amarris' wound as soon as they found a hidden clearing for the camp for the night.

"The tooth missed anything vital, I believe. Alas, I am looking with my dull dwarf eyes." Amarris cringed at Hil's obviously affronted jab. "I believe that I just need to clean it and stitch it," Hil calmly continued as she worked on Amarris. "Kwin, help me with this."

Tarin noticed Finn staring at the two wolves, which had decided to lie down on the outskirts of their camp. "What's wrong?"

Finn turned to look at his uncle, "I think the one's paw is really hurt, and I want to help it, but I don't want it to eat me."

"Why would it eat you?" Tarin asked curiously.

"Well, because it will probably hurt, and it probably won't understand that I'm trying to help it, not hurt it," Finn explained.

Tarin noticed that the pair of wolves was regarding them, almost as though they were listening to their conversation. As if in confirmation, the wolf with the injured paw stood up and limped over to Finn. Sitting down in front of Finn, it quietly offered its paw, which was almost half the size of Finn.

"Well, there you go, Finn. I believe she wants you to fix her paw." Tarin clapped Finn on the back. "Just don't make her mad," Tarin grinned at his nephew before heading to check on Varger by the fire, where he was cooking their dinner.

Swallowing hard, Finn looked at the humongous wolf in front of him. "Okay," he began, "I want you to know that I am only trying to help, and if I cause you pain, it would be really wrong of you to eat me."

At Finn's words, the wolf gave an exceptionally disconcerting grin, showing all its massively large teeth. "You find that funny—the fact that I find you terrifying." In response, the wolf's grin grew wider. "Fine," Finn continued, a little irritated, if he was being honest. "Place your injured paw on the ground so I can get a good look at it." The wolf obeyed and Finn got to work.

Once Amarris and the wolf had their wounds addressed, the group had their dinner and then settled in for the night. Tarin moved to the top of a large rock near the wolves and sat on it, staring into the night.

Finn, who was sitting near the wolves as well, having slightly conquered his fear of them by aiding the one with the injured paw, sat back on his hands and mused out loud, "I wonder if Syllē ran into any wargs."

With a sharp intake of breath, Hil quickly backhanded her son's head while glancing at her brother's back in concern. The rest of the group alternated between glaring at Finn and holding their breath as they stared at Tarin on the rock.

"If he tries to go off into the night in search of Syllē thanks to my stupid brother," Kwin quietly muttered to the two wolves, "we're going to need at least one of you to sit on him."

The black wolf rose and walked to the side of the rock and stared at Tarin, who turned and returned the stare. Worry permeating his voice, Tarin asked, "Do you think she did? She can't take on a whole pack of those things. What if she's out there hurt?"

"First of all," Hil responded, although she had the feeling Tarin was talking to that wolf, "Syllē is not alone. She has Halicyon, Falinor, Thēorin, and Eirik with her, and they could certainly take on a warg pack together."

"And secondly," Kwin finished for his mother, "you can easily find out how she is by simply doing that thing you two do that Halicyon taught you."

Tarin looked uncertainly at Kwin. "I think we're too far apart for that. I'm not exceptionally skilled at it, you know; and I think it's only worked in the past because Syllē was nearby."

"Well, you certainly won't know unless you try, cousin," Trygve responded with a shrug.

Tarin looked uncertain. Trygve was right, though. He certainly wouldn't know unless he tried, and if he didn't know how Syllē was, he'd spend the entire rest of their trip distracted and severely worried. Taking a deep breath and slowly letting it out to try and steady himself, Tarin closed his eyes and thought of Syllē. *Syllē?* His question was immediately greeted with the face of a massive, snarling orc. Horrified, Tarin jerked backwards, grabbing for his axe, and opened his eyes.

"What's wrong?" Hil asked.

"Orcs," Tarin answered, terrified for Syllē. "She was surrounded by orcs. She's in trouble," Tarin finished, as he jumped down from the rock. It was obvious that he was intending to head out into the night to find and rescue Syllē.

"Now, Tarin," Hil began, trying to calm her brother, "you can't just go running off into the night. You have no idea where she is or if there's another warg pack out there. It's too dangerous."

Before Tarin could reply, he heard Syllē's voice. *I'm a little busy right now, Tarin.* Tarin could hear the muffled sounds of growling orcs and battle behind Syllē's voice. *Don't worry. We're all going to be fine. I will see you soon, my lord.* And then she was gone, as were the battle sounds.

"Did anybody else notice what happened to Tarin's eyes just then?" Finn asked, a little awestruck.

Leaning back against the rock he'd been sitting on earlier, Tarin glanced curiously at his nephew. "What do you mean? What happened to my eyes?"

"They turned a solid ice blue," Hil answered. "Why?"

Tarin shrugged before answering, "Syllē was talking to me. She told me she'd be fine, and she'd talk to me when it was all over."

Amarris nodded, "Don't worry, Tarin. A bunch of orcs are no problem for Syllē, especially with everyone she has traveling with her. She'll be fine," she tried to reassure Tarin.

Tarin tried to smile, but he wasn't very successful. He knew he had to have faith, but it was hard when you knew that somewhere out there in the night was someone you cared a lot about, fighting for her life. "I'll take the first watch," Tarin offered. "Asger knows I won't sleep anyway." Climbing back up onto the rock, Tarin stared forlornly out into the night, trying desperately not to worry, but failing miserably.

* * *

Finn awakened with a start and immediately looked towards the rock where he'd last seen Tarin, but to his horror, his uncle wasn't there. The dwarf sitting on the rock was Kwin with Amarris next to him. Tarin must have left while everyone was asleep to go after Syllē. Erupting out of his bed roll, Finn almost fell into the fire which, thankfully, had died down a bit during the night, or he may have had a few bad burns to deal with.

"If you wake him up, I will make you regret it," Trygve growled quietly at Finn from the bedroll beside him.

Turning to Trygve, Finn whispered, "What do you mean? Didn't he go off to find Syllē?"

Without even sitting up, Trygve answered, "No, he didn't. He wakened me for my watch and then went and sat with the wolves," Trygve explained, nodding towards the two wolves. "Currently, he's leaning against the black one, sleeping, and he needs to stay that way for a little longer," Trygve finished with quiet steel in his voice.

"Has he heard from Syllē?" Finn asked curiously.

"Have no idea," Trygve responded as he rolled away from Finn. Shortly after, Finn could hear Trygve's quiet snoring.

Walking silently over to the rock, Finn climbed up and sat down next to his brother and Amarris. No one spoke as they looked out into the darkness, but they didn't need to speak. They all knew that they were as worried about Syllē as Tarin, and the twins couldn't imagine her fighting orc without them. They couldn't reach the rendezvous point soon enough.

3

Three more days' journey, and Tarin's group was almost on the other side of Vanguard and heading towards the Oloro Valley. If they didn't have any more issues and pushed hard, they would reach their rendezvous point with Syllē's group in two more days. As far as the dwarves were concerned, they couldn't reach Syllē too soon, which was why Tarin was slightly impatient with Hil's sudden caution. She was slowing down and watching the forest around them very intently.

Then, he saw it—a quick movement out of the corner of his eye, but when he focused on that spot, there was nothing. Something or someone was hunting them again. Tarin also suddenly noticed that both wolves were missing. They had been walking in the back with Finn, but as Tarin gazed intently around the group, he noticed that they had disappeared. They must have slipped into the woods without anyone noticing. Tarin allowed himself a slight smile. Whatever or whomever was hunting them was going to have a rude awakening when they realized what was now hunting them.

Speaking quietly to his group in dwarvish, Tarin instructed, "Stay close and keep an eye on the woods around us. We're being hunted again." Looking at his nephews and Flarne, he ordered, "Stick to Amarris like glue."

Picking up on the tension but unable to understand dwarvish, Amarris looked questioningly at Kwin as he circled closer to her. "Tarin said to stick to you like glue," he shrugged in a whisper. "It appears something is after us again."

Amarris nodded, watching the woods around them with caution. Suddenly, she felt herself pulled backwards off her feet. Before she had time to get angry with Kwin about the indignity, she felt the whoosh of an arrow fly lethally by her where her head had just been. When she looked up, she saw they were surrounded by a group of hooded and masked figures who looked very ready and very anxious to engage them in a fight.

"Who shot that arrow?" came a very angry voice from in front of them. "I said not to start anything and to simply secure them."

Moving to a more solid kneeling position by Kwin, Amarris recognized the voice as belonging to the son of the master of Vanguard. She had met him several times during her visits to her family in Vanguard and found him to be a slightly arrogant and unpleasant young man. Unfortunately, he was her cousin Firth's best friend.

A tentative voice spoke up from the left of the group, "Bull said you wanted me to take out their archer."

"Are you insane? That's my cousin." Amarris recognized that shout as belonging to Firth. Based off the stance and stature of two others in the group to their right, Amarris was pretty sure that her other cousins, Firth's two older brothers, were also in the group. It didn't make sense to her. Why would her cousins be in a group that was attacking them?

Surreptitiously touching Kwin's arm to gain his attention, Amarris whispered one of the only dwarf words she knew, "Smaryn,"[1] tapping her chest as she said it. Briefly taking his eyes off those surrounding them, Kwin nodded. Using hand signals, Amarris quietly conveyed her plan to the twins and Flarne.

"I never gave that order," the master's son, Garath, berated the archer. "Where is Bull?"

---

1   Trust

"Probably either running as far away as he can or setting up an ambush for us with his other Vikari pals," Tarin growled.

"Vikari?!" Garath spun on Tarin angrily. Tarin noticed how the others in the group also reacted to his use of that word. Most were obviously angry, but a few seemed to recede into themselves and start to slyly slink backwards into the cover of the forest with the Vanguard men remaining none the wiser. "There are no Vikari in Vanguard, Dwarf." Garath spat out Tarin's race like it was the filthiest word he'd ever said.

Controlling his anger, Tarin nonchalantly shrugged, "Well, recently I met a Bull, large man with bad teeth, and his four friends, one being an almost equally large man with a pock-scarred face, when they insulted Lady Syllē at Helmfirth's Fall Festival a short time back. They all stunk of rot like the other agents of Merilik we have unfortunately run into lately in Helmfirth and Kilead and the surrounding lands."

While Tarin was talking, Amarris put her plan into action. She had noticed the quiet retreat of several of the group surrounding them, as well as the stealthy entrance of two figures, who were sneaking up behind her two older cousins with knives drawn. Amarris notched the two arrows Finn had pulled from her quiver for her and used the combined strength of the twins and Flarne to vault herself into the air. Her higher vantage point gave her perfect shots at the two Vikari slowly approaching her cousins with the obvious intent of stabbing them both in the back.

Continuing her vault to the ground, Amarris landed right in front of Garath, who had begun to move menacingly towards Tarin, and did something she'd been wanting to do for a very long time—she knocked him to the ground with a solid left to his nose. Whirling, she notched another arrow and shot the Vikari advancing on Firth. Her cousin, obviously startled, spun to follow her arrow's path only to see it connect with a man intent on killing him—a man who had been with their militia group since Firth joined it three years ago.

"And that is why I told you to kill her," snarled a familiar nasty voice from the woods to Tarin's left. Bull emerged from the woods, lethally stabbing the young Vanguard archer as the Vikari made his way onto the road to confront Tarin.

Tarin noticed an eerie stillness growing in the woods surrounding them. Bull noticed Tarin glancing warily around at the woods and grinned maliciously. "Oh, don't worry. You're not dying today. I'm looking forward to watching you writhe and scream for a bit before you die," Bull finished, as he stepped up onto the road in front of Tarin.

"Overconfidence. It's always the Dark's downfall," came Syllē's voice from the woods behind Bull.

Bull started angrily at her voice and then charged at Tarin, obviously intent on killing the dwarf lord if it was the last thing he did. His charge was the last thing he ever did. From the bushes beside Tarin, the black wolf leapt out onto the road, grabbing Bull in his jaws as he did so. A rather pathetic yelp was the last sound Bull ever made as the wolf grabbed him and then slung Bull against a tree almost as hard as the wolf had slung the warg a few days prior.

With one leap, the black wolf made his way to Tarin's side where he stopped, turned, and glared menacingly at Garath and Firth. Garath was standing unsteadily—thanks to Amarris' wicked punch—leaning against Firth, who was petrified at the sight of the wolf. Trying to rally, the remnants of the Vanguard militia unit leapt onto the road around Garath, bringing the gray wolf to stand beside Tarin, leaping from the woods on the opposite side of the road as her mate to glare as lethally at the men as her mate was. Tarin had to admit to himself that he'd never felt so indomitable in his life, and it was awesome. He couldn't stop himself from grinning.

Really, Tarin? Did you not hear what I just said about overconfidence? Tarin's grin just grew wider, especially as he viewed Halicyon and Falinor emerging from the woods to his right and Thēorin and Eirik stepping onto the road in front of him and behind the Vanguard militia. Tarin also noticed several elves he didn't know emerging from the woods slightly behind him and to his left. If he'd turned around, Tarin would have noticed several more elves standing in the road behind them, bows drawn and ready.

Just give me this moment, Syllē. Tarin continued to grin. Her answering laugh swept joyfully through him.

4

"I thought I told you to stick to Amarris like glue. What was she do-ing vaulting out on her own?" Tarin scolded Finn when his nephew joined him.

Finn looked incredulously at his uncle before retorting, "We had about as much of a chance of ordering Amarris around as you do Mother or Syllē."

Tarin glared at his nephew's impudence for a moment before chuck-ling, "In the name of Asger, how did I end up surrounded by all these strong-willed, reckless females?"

"I wouldn't complain, Tarin. Those are the best kind," Halicyon laughed as he joined Tarin and Finn on the road.

As Tarin scowled happily at Halicyon, Syllē spoke from where she and Hil were trying to save the young Vanguard archer, "We need to get to a sanctuary now. There are too many orcs coming for us. Therendē'al has no intention of allowing us to make it through Mosslight alive."

"Will Flynn live?" Amarris called.

Syllē motioned a tall elf to her right towards her and instructed him to pick up the fallen archer. Turning to the group on the road, she tersely an-swered Amarris, "Probably not, but he's not dead yet. And I refuse to leave him here to die alone or be devoured by the orcs that will soon be here." Syllē grinned at the twins before turning to bow to Tarin, who returned the salute. "Let's move and fast. Our survival depends upon our ability to win this foot race."

Keeping Garath and his militia subdued in the center of their group, they plunged swiftly off the road and into the woods. Syllē led them deep into Mosslight, obviously heading somewhere she knew. Every now and then Halicyon or Falinor would drop behind the group for a moment, listening to the ground to see how far off their pursuers were. Syllē didn't need to do that. She could feel the darkness gaining and growing behind them.

Finally, Syllē shoved aside what looked like an impenetrable thicket of brambles and motioned everyone into a small clearing, replacing the brambles when the last elf came through. "Syllē, I don't think this is actually that safe a place," Tarin cautioned, looking around at the very small clearing that had very little maneuverability in it, especially if the orcs decided to set the surrounding trees and brambles on fire.

Syllē wasn't listening. She was looking for something and shortly found it—the door in the wall of moss-covered stone on the far left of the clearing. Quickly, the group entered the cave, and Syllē again shut the door behind them.

"Well, this is certainly a better place," Tarin nodded once everyone was inside.

Syllē shook her head, "This isn't the sanctuary, Tarin. The orcs know of this place and how to enter the clearing as well as how to find that door over there."

"That's impossible," Garath argued, finally finding his voice. "I don't know how you knew about this place, but it's a sanctuary of Vanguard. No orc has ever found its way into this place, and none ever will," he finished emphatically.

Not turning from her search of the walls of the room, Syllē tersely responded, "And Therendē'al is the leader of the orcs and Vikari in this area.

The orcs hunting us know this place, but hopefully they won't know of the actual sanctuary that exists here."

"Why would that matter? Who is Therendē'al?" Finn asked curiously.

"He is a friend and ally of Vanguard," Garath asserted stubbornly. "He would never work with the Dark."

Ignoring Garath, Syllē answered Finn, "He is the Drēor who sent the changeling to Helmfirth and tried to slaughter Tarin and Hadrin." Finally finding whatever it was she was looking for, Syllē pushed something on the wall and a door slid open. Turning to face Finn, she further explained, "He is also the advisor to Master Sigurd, the leader of Vanguard." Smiling a tad tensely at the group, she continued, "Now if you all would kindly and quickly make your way through this door, the orcs are almost to the brambles."

Once everyone was inside the actual sanctuary, Syllē swiftly removed all traces of them and shut the door, which, once closed, was invisible to all who might enter the outer room. Moving through a long hallway that seemed to lead almost straight down, the group made their way into a lower chamber that was large and filled with the light of crystals that reminded Tarin of Shara, not as pure and iridescent as Shara's crystal chambers, but a close second.

"I never knew this was here," Garath whispered in awe.

Tarin moved over to Syllē who was standing by the door to the hallway, her head cocked as she listened intently. He was about to speak when Syllē, without looking at him, shook her head while placing her fingers across his lips. A little angrily, Tarin started to step closer when he heard the orcs in the room they had just left, and they were furious at losing their prey. Their loud yells could be heard by the rest of the group in the lower cavern, causing everyone to almost stop breathing.

Without turning towards Tarin, Syllē instructed, *Make sure Hil keeps that archer as quiet as possible. Any sound from in here, and we're in trouble.*

Taking Syllē's hand off his lips, Tarin held it for a moment, unconsciously interlacing his fingers with hers, before heading towards Hil. *I am glad to see you, too, Tarin.* Syllē's warm voice in his head brought him to a halt. When he looked back towards her, he saw she had turned her head to watch him go. Syllē smiled warmly at him before returning to her vigil at the door.

* * *

It was obvious that the orcs had fully expected to find Tarin's group in the room above and were furious to find the room empty. It also became clear that the orcs weren't alone as an argument broke out between the orc leader and a man from Vanguard, who apparently had been taken prisoner along with his son.

"Where are they?" growled the massive orc, getting menacingly close to the man being held by two of his underlings.

"How would I know?" responded the man as bravely as he could. "You told me to show you how to find this place, and when I did, you would let my son and me go. Well, I did that, so let us go," the man finished, trying desperately not to give in to his fear.

Syllē could hear the malicious grin in the orc's next words, "Well, letting you go was dependent upon finding our dinner here; but since the only food around is you and your son…"

The boy's terror-filled screams for his father and the father's yells at the orcs to stop filled the room below, as did the sound of the orcs' horrific laughter. It was more than Syllē could bear, and she fell to her knees in the doorway, slamming her hands into her ears, trying desperately to block out the terrible screams coming from above. Seeing this, Tarin made his way to Syllē, frantically wading through the waves of terror slamming into him as the boy's screams from the room above grew louder the nearer he came to the door. Finally making it to Syllē, Tarin wrapped his arms around her, pulling her close against his chest, using her closeness to help him rise above the terror that filled him.

All in the room were sickened by what they knew was causing those screams and even more sickened by the fact that none of them could do anything to help the man and his son. All they could do was listen. Amarris, who had been standing with the twins, Trygve, and Flarne, also fell to her knees and pressed her hands against her ears, trying to drown out the sounds. Kwin stepped closer to her and put a hand on her shoulder protectively. Turning towards him, Amarris grabbed Kwin in a bear hug. Kwin wrapped his arms around her, laid his head against hers, closed his eyes, and desperately tried to block out the horror coming from above.

As the boy's screams rose in pitch and the father dissolved into sobbing, a new voice viciously cut through the noise, "What is going on here? You were to find those dwarves and their companions. Where are they? Why aren't you hunting them?"

The orc leader from before snarled, "We're hungry, and since our promised dinner wasn't here when we got here, we're using the resources we have."

Syllē felt the dark power growing as it filled the room above. Booming out in fury and deadly retribution, the Drēor yelled, "You were to find Tarin and those with him. You can eat the boy later. Now, move!"

Soon, the room above was clear of orc and Syllē could discern that they were leaving the clearing as well. But she couldn't bring herself to leave Tarin's arms just yet. They kept the nightmares at bay.

Sickened by what he had heard, Garath began furiously, "What is…"

Halicyon whirled and almost threw Garath to the ground as he put his hand over Garath's mouth. "If you make one more sound, I will have no problem slitting your throat to save the rest of us," Halicyon menacingly whispered to the young man, who simply nodded in response, eyes wide.

Soon, the presence of the Drēor was no longer apparent in the room above or the clearing. Halicyon and Syllē were fairly certain that he had left along with his orcs to continue the hunt for their group. Finally rising from her position against Tarin, Syllē smiled at the dwarf lord, placing her forehead against his momentarily before turning to survey the room. Nodding towards Falinor, who quickly joined her, Syllē headed to the back wall of the room. Sensing what they were doing, Tarin hurriedly joined them.

"No, my lord," Syllē shook her head when she noticed Tarin beside her. "You cannot join us on this journey."

"Syllē," Tarin growled in frustration. "There are too many orcs for just the two of you. You need me and I'm going."

Placing her hands on Tarin's shoulders, Syllē gazed steadily at him as she responded, "Tarin, I do not want you going because you would be a liability."

"Because I'm a dwarf?" Tarin growled.

"Yes." Syllē didn't know how else to answer Tarin other than simply and truthfully.

Tarin was startled by her directness. He could feel his anger starting to rise until he met her gaze. Tarin could see the affection in Syllē's eyes. Taking a deep breath, Tarin pressed, "How would I be a liability?"

Syllē sighed, gazing with fondness at Tarin. "Because Falinor and I are going to use the trees as our road." Noticing Tarin's silence and slightly averted face, Syllē leaned down, trying to get the dwarf lord to look at her. "Tarin? What are you doing?" Syllē finally asked.

"Counting to one hundred," Tarin responded tersely.

Laughing despite Tarin's scowl, Syllē pulled Tarin forward and pressed her forehead against his. "I will keep my promise, my lord, and I will see you soon."

Tarin returned the embrace before turning on his heel and returning to stand with the wolves who had bedded down near the dwarves. Tarin crossed his arms and somewhat glared at Syllē as she turned to head out a second entrance that no one had known was there. Striding forward, Halicyon started to follow Falinor and Syllē out of the sanctuary. Apparently, he planned on going with them as well, but Syllē turned around and placed a hand on his chest to stop him.

Quietly, Syllē instructed Halicyon, "No, my friend. Just Falinor and I are going. I need you to stay with Tarin and the rest. I don't trust the men from Vanguard, nor do I completely trust a few of your elves. But you I do trust. Please, Halicyon, keep my family safe," Syllē pleaded, looking up into her old friend's face.

Not at all happy, Halicyon responded, "I don't like this, Syllē. I don't like it at all."

Syllē smiled sadly at him and nodded before starting to turn to leave. Reaching out, Halicyon caught her arm and pulled her back into a tight hug. "You have just returned to my life. Don't go leaving it again. Promise me," Halicyon murmured against her hair.

Hugging him back, Syllē nodded against his chest before pushing back and joining Falinor to head out into the night after the orcs and the father and son. Halicyon stood where she had left him, watching the door for some time.

"I don't agree with Lady Sariel," Amarris noted to Hil and the twins. "I don't think they're a couple."

"Who?" Hil asked, while checking Amarris' wound. The archer's vaulting and running activities that day had pulled her stitches, and Hil was repairing the wound.

"Syllē and Halicyon," Amarris responded before continuing, "I just don't see it." She shrugged.

"Please refrain from moving your abdomen while I'm fixing your stitches," Hil instructed irritably.

"Sorry."

"Why don't you think they're a couple?" Kwin asked curiously.

Amarris started to shrug again but remembered in time. "Because that was more a hug between siblings or old friends than lovers, for one."

"Okay," Kwin agreed. "So, what's your other reason?"

"Because Syllē has *never* looked at Halicyon the way she looks at…" Amarris paused a moment, her gaze traveling to where Tarin was standing, arms crossed, still staring at the door through which Syllē had left. "…somebody else," she finished quietly, turning back to look at Kwin.

At this point, Halicyon stopped staring at the door and returned to the dwarves. Looking from the spot where Falinor and Syllē disappeared to the dwarves and their allies, Firth asked, "Where did they go?"

"To save the father and son," Halicyon tersely replied without even looking at the men of Vanguard.

"That's suicide," Garath exclaimed incredulously.

Tarin started out of his reverie at Garath's outburst and ferociously glared at the master of Vanguard's son. Placing a steadying hand on Tarin's shoulder, Halicyon snarled at Garath, "It would still be to your benefit to keep your mouth shut."

Looking slightly insulted, Garath started to open his mouth to say something; but upon catching a glimpse of Halicyon's face, he wisely shut it and moved over against the wall on the other corner of the room from the dwarves and their allies.

Firth and his brothers approached Amarris, "Come on, cousin. You can sleep over there with us."

Amarris gazed angrily at her cousins. "I'm sleeping between the twins. You can go over and stay with the other Vikari and leave me alone."

Firth was taken aback by Amarris' hostility. "But they're dwarves. We're your family, Amarris," Firth reminded her.

"No," Amarris' tone had taken on a steely edge as she rose and advanced menacingly on her cousins, "we are not. We stopped being family the moment you decided to choose the Dark and fight with the one who slaughtered my mother. Now leave me alone." Amarris turned and threw her bedroll down between the twins and sat down on it with her back against the wall. Crossing her arms, she turned to Kwin, "By the way, thank you for earlier."

Startled, Kwin falteringly nodded at her. "You're welcome." In his peripheral vision, Kwin could see Firth unsteadily turn and walk back to the Vanguard group with his brothers.

* * *

An uneasy silence broken occasionally by Flarne's or Trygve's quiet snoring settled over the group in the sanctuary. Halicyon rested near Tarin and the wolves—his back against the wall in a spot that gave him a complete view of everyone in the room. Syllē's comment about his elves disturbed him greatly. Like all elves, Halicyon loathed orcs; but Drēor were a special kind of filth. They were elves who had chosen to turn their back on the Light and walk in darkness; and the thought that he might have a few, or even one, within his own patrol made him seethe with anger.

Unable to sleep and deeply confused about everything that had happened, Firth rose from the Vanguard corner and approached Tarin and Halicyon. As the young man approached, Tarin noticed Halicyon surreptitiously draw both his knives and keep them hidden under the folds of his cloak. Both elf and dwarf cautiously watched the young man from Vanguard draw closer.

Sensing the tension, Firth stopped a reasonable distance from Tarin and Halicyon. Speaking tentatively, Firth addressed both elf and dwarf, "We have seen the Dark encroaching on our lands for months now and have sent emissaries to Helmfirth and Kilead for help, but none have ever returned save for one survivor who claimed her group had been attacked and slaughtered by dwarves from Exulias just outside of Kilead. Then, of course, Bull's group who returned saying that they never made it past the outer edge of Mosslight when they were attacked by orcs working with dwarves. Based on what happened today, I am guessing they were lying?"

Both elf and dwarf slowly nodded but said nothing. Swallowing hard, Firth continued, "So, those men who joined with Bull and would have killed us this afternoon on the road were Vikari?"

Again, both elf and dwarf nodded but did not speak. Stepping closer before sitting down in front of Tarin and Halicyon, Firth said forlornly, "And Therendē'al isn't a friend but is actually Drēor?"

Again, a joint nod was all Firth received. "So, Vanguard is inundated with the agents of the Dark, and we truly have no idea whom we can trust," Firth finished with a slightly plaintive whine to his voice.

"That's not completely true," Tarin finally spoke. At Firth's questioning glance, Tarin explained, "Bull and his pals, as well as several other Vikari I have come up against over these past months, all had a distinctive stench—eggs which had been left out in the sun for far too long. None of the men in your current group have that same stench attached to them." Catching Halicyon's look, Tarin chuckled slightly, "Not even their annoying leader, my friend. He's irritating and deserves a good spanking, but I don't believe he's Vikari… not yet anyway."

"So, my cousin was right," Firth sighed sadly. "I aligned with the Dark and chose the side that would have murdered her." Firth mournfully dropped his face into his hands.

"I wouldn't berate yourself too hard," Halicyon offered. "Dark Elves and Men excel at deception and misinformation. They, unfortunately, can be anyone, including members of your family or your best friend."

"You speak as though from experience," Firth noted, curiously.

"Yes," Halicyon tersely responded.

Sensing the conversation was over, Firth rose and started to head back to the rest of the Vanguard group. Stopping and turning back to face Halicyon and Tarin, Firth addressed them both sincerely, "For what it's worth, I am truly sorry for my part in everything today."

Tarin nodded at Firth and the young man rejoined his group. Amarris watched him go, a small smile playing across her face.

* * *

Several hours before sunrise, Hil was shaken gently awake. Opening her eyes, she was overjoyed to see Syllē bending over her. Reaching up, Hil pulled Syllē down into a major hug, slightly causing the Valaraii to lose her balance for a moment.

Smiling at Hil's affection, Syllē whispered, "I need two sleeping draughts quick, Hil. We need these two…" At that, Syllē nodded towards where Falinor was removing blindfolds from the eyes of the rescued father and son. "…to sleep nightmare free for the final hours of the night. Any night terrors from them, and we could be done for."

Hil rushed to comply, and shortly both father and son were sleeping soundly against each other and near Halicyon and his elves, whose job it would be to rapidly silence them if the events of the night turned into night terrors for the two.

Sliding between Halicyon and Tarin and resting against the black wolf Braxis' neck, Syllē pulled her hood down over her eyes and almost immediately fell asleep. Tarin's and Halicyon's eyes briefly met across her head. Quietly, Tarin slid closer to Syllē and gently pulled her towards him until her head was resting in his lap. If she was going to leave again or try to do anything else stupid, Tarin was determined that she wouldn't be leaving him behind. Without fully waking, Syllē left her head in Tarin's lap and turned onto her side. Reaching up, Syllē interlaced her fingers with Tarin's and pulled his arm further down around her before dropping back off into an exhausted sleep.

Halicyon smiled at the two, sighing with relief at Falinor and Syllē's safe return. Before the sigh was even complete, both dwarf and elf were sound asleep.

5

"I don't like this," Tarin growled quietly to Halicyon as the two surveyed the far walls of Vanguard. "Our friends are going in there," Tarin emphasized his displeasure with a disgruntled jab of the finger towards the darkened city, "totally alone and at the mercy of the Vikari and their Drēor leader."

"I don't like it much either, my friend," Halicyon agreed without taking his eyes off the city in front of them, "but Syllē knows what she's doing, and she has at least three with her whom she can trust. So, let's focus on that and our job in this attack."

Surveying the walls, Elēandil, one of the elves accompanying Halicyon from Kuaryll, thought he caught a glimpse of something. Taking a slight step forward, he peered intently at a spot on the lower outer wall of the city. About to give up, his eyes suddenly found their mark. Nodding knowingly, he turned towards Tarin and asked the dwarf lord, "Do you see anything interesting to the right of center of that lower outer wall of Vanguard?"

"Interesting, as in what?" Tarin snapped irritably in response. He was not in the mood for elven riddles. He'd much prefer if they were more like dwarves and just came out and said what they wanted. This guessing game just took up precious time and simply made his blood boil.

Elēandil's eyes flashed with anger at Tarin's perceived insolence, but Halicyon quickly explained, "Dwarves don't like riddles, Elēandil. Just simply ask Lord Tarin exactly what you want to know."

Swallowing his irritation at the dwarf lord, Elēandil tried again, "Vanguard reminds me of another ancient city, whose walls and defenses were designed and built by a team of elves and dwarves—mainly dwarves. The dwarves oversaw putting escape doors—which could also be used to enter the city—into the walls. So, I was wondering if you saw anything like that in the walls of Vanguard."

"A door in the outer defensive wall?" Tarin asked incredulously.

Elēandil simply nodded, so Tarin peered at the walls of Vanguard intently. His eyesight, however, wasn't an elf's; and he couldn't discern anything but a solid defensive wall. Even if there had been a dwarf door, unless he had built it or designed it, Tarin would have no idea how to spot it, since dwarf doors were invisible to all, even other dwarves. Halicyon, on the other hand, thought he saw what Elēandil was talking about. It wasn't a door, but it was the symbol of the Lēas, the Ancients—a spiral fern—etched so subtly into the wall that it was basically indiscernible.

Whistling quietly under his breath, Halicyon softly instructed Tarin, "New plan, Tarin. Head for that portion of the outer wall."

* * *

Garath looked incredulously at Vanguard as the group rounded the final curve in the main road before approaching the west gates of the city. He had never noticed how dark the city had become. How was he able to see it now? Had it been this dark when they left only two days ago? Looking around at his group, he could tell that the other members of his militia were as shocked as he was. Thēorin and the rest of the group from Helmfirth, however, didn't appear at all surprised by the darkness of Vanguard.

"Almost as bad as Kilead," Thēorin shrugged. Trying to help make

Garath and his militia feel better, he continued, "And we kicked the Dark out of that city."

"Sure, 'cause a city full of Vikari and orc led by a Drēor is no way near as bad as a city full of Vikari, orc, and a hive of malidaemons," Amarris muttered a little irritably as she pulled her mask down to cover her face and brought her hood up over her head.

Thēorin tensely grinned at her before following suit with his own mask and hood and then checking to make sure Eirik was properly disguised as well. Garath and his militia, as well as the rescued father, also pulled on masks and hoods.

Wondering out loud, Garath mused, "I can't believe I am only now questioning why Therendē'al ordered us to mask and hood ourselves while on patrol."

"Because it easily hides the Vikari in your midst," Amarris' tone was steely.

Garath gave her a sharp look, almost as if he wanted to argue that point, before nodding sadly. Looking at the walls of his home as the group tried to approach normally without generating any unwanted attention, Garath asked almost under his breath, "Where is she? Why isn't she coming in with us?"

"Because Therendē'al would sense her immediately, as would any other Drēor who might be within those walls," Amarris quietly responded. "And if that happened, we'd all be toast before we even got close to him."

"Speaking of avoiding detection," Thēorin whispered, "Amarris, get to the center of the group. You may be wearing a Vanguard militia uniform, but you stand out from the rest of us with the way you move." Thēorin could feel Amarris' angry glare through her mask and hood, but she complied and melded into the center of the returning group. Shaking his head, Thēorin suddenly had a deeper appreciation for the lord of Exulias. No wonder he was always on edge.

A slight movement on the far wall caught Thēorin's attention. "We need to move," he muttered, slightly pushing Garath forward towards the gates of Vanguard. "Or we'll be late for our meeting."

6

Garath was surprised by how easily they made it back into Vanguard. No one confronted them at the gates. No one seemed to take any notice of them as they journeyed through the city towards his father's citadel and the town square. He wasn't sure what he had expected, but either Therendē'al had no clue what was going on or he was simply drawing them into his lair. Garath was discomfited to realize he was suddenly afraid of Vanguard—the city, its people, and his father's house.

Squaring his shoulders, Garath did what he always did best—he bluffed his way through his fears and headed for Vanguard's square, which was framed by his father's house, the courthouse, and the market, and was where Therendē'al and his father spent their days, trying to combat the Dark encroaching on Vanguard… or at least, his father, Garath hoped, was trying to fight Merilik's forces. The alternative—that his father was Vikari—was an option Garath had no intention of entertaining at this point.

For his part, Thēorin had already considered it, and Amarris had already decided she had no problem whatsoever putting an arrow through Master Sigurd if he turned out to be in league with Therendē'al. In fact, she had already moved past that decision and was fully anticipating the showdown that awaited her in Vanguard's courtyard. Her quickened step belied her eagerness to begin the fight she had been anticipating ever since she understood it was her uncle who had slaughtered her mother.

Sensing Amarris' energy, Eirik reached over and placed a steadying hand on her arm. "Steady, Amarris. It won't help any of us if you charge in there without any kind of a cool head," he quietly cautioned.

Irritated for a moment, Amarris quickly realized her hatred of Therendē'al would be her downfall if she didn't get control of her emotions and soon. Taking a steadying breath, Amarris slowed her step and returned her heart to a calmer beat. To divert herself, she surreptitiously looked around at Vanguard as the group wound its way through the streets heading towards the courtyard.

Master Sigurd was a burly bear of a man who looked as though he was more at home on a battlefield fighting than behind a desk running a city. He was not a bureaucrat. He was also, thankfully, not Vikari, but because of his foolhardy belief in the good of all elves, he had been rather easily manipulated by Therendē'al. Unfortunately for Therendē'al, Sigurd had figured out he was being manipulated. Fortunately for Therendē'al, Sigurd just wasn't sure yet by whom.

Sigurd looked up from the most recent reports a patrol had brought to him about the extent of the Dark's encroachment and a rather detailed account of the treachery of the dwarves of Exulias. Sigurd was beginning to wonder about that information as well. Why were the dwarves suddenly attacking his city and his outlying villages? Why, when he visited some of the areas of attack, did he find no evidence whatsoever of dwarves? Yes, there were axe marks, and many victims had axe wounds, but they didn't gel with his knowledge of dwarves and the way they fought.

For instance, he had come across one corpse on a farm a few miles from the city that was just all wrong. Sigurd had known this man. He was well over six feet tall, a giant compared to a dwarf, and yet, his head had been cleanly cut off with an axe. Sigurd could easily see that for a dwarf to have done that, the dwarf would have had to have been standing on the back of a wagon or some other raised area; and there was no evidence of anything like that near the body, which meant that whoever had done the beheading had been close to the same height as the dead man. That ruled out a dwarf. Yet, disturbingly, Therendē'al had said the corpse was positive proof of the violence of the dwarves. Sigurd knew Therendē'al should know better, so why would the elf say such a thing?

Now, here was another report of dwarf treachery against his people that just didn't make sense. Rubbing his face in frustration, Sigurd caught a glimpse of another patrol coming into the square. By the way the leader walked, Sigurd knew it was his son's patrol, and he was startled to notice a rising tension in the square as others recognized the group that had returned. Sigurd suddenly wondered if someone had sent his son's militia out with the intention of none of them returning. Straightening to his full height and surreptitiously checking that his daggers were within quick and easy reach, Sigurd smiled at his son and moved around the table towards Garath. He had the feeling that his desire to know who was manipulating him was about to be met, and knowing what he did about the Dark, there was going to be a fight. So, if he was going to fight, it would be by his son's side.

"Garath," Sigurd began warmly, smiling at his son, and holding out his arms to draw his son into a welcoming embrace.

Garath startled his father by sharply and quickly interrupting him. There was no warmth in Garath's voice. There was, however, a great deal of anger. "Are you one of them, Father? Are you Vikari?"

Thēorin sucked in his breath in alarm. This was not the plan. What was Garath doing? Garath knew he'd made a mistake, but when he saw his father check his daggers before heading towards him, the question just spilled out of him. He had to know. Was his father Vikari?

For his part, Sigurd understood. Garath must have realized on his patrol that someone wanted him and his militia out of the way. Looking his son dead in the eyes, Sigurd simply shook his head no and then waited.

Swallowing hard over his emotions, Garath responded difficultly, "Well, we have an infestation in Vanguard, and…"

"Garath," Therendē'al spoke up, falsely welcoming in tone. He was quick to cut the young man off before Garath could say anything more. "We had expected your group back two nights ago." Therendē'al stealthily looked at the walls for his archers as he greeted the young man. Satisfied, Therendē'al slowly made his way to the right of the group and continued, "Your absence made us fear the worst. Where—"

Garath disgustedly cut Therendē'al off, "Oh, shut up."

Therendē'al's eyes flared with outrage. How dare this pup speak to him that way? Sigurd suddenly noticed the shadows growing and spreading through the square. Astonished, Sigurd realized they were emanating from Therendē'al. How was that possible? Was he the traitor? But he was an elf.

"Therendē'al?" Sigurd began, uncertainly.

Garath interrupted his father angrily, "So, do you see it now? Your precious advisor is a Drēor."

Now it was Sigurd's turn to be filled with outrage. Turning towards Therendē'al, Sigurd roared, "You? Drēor? You have been killing my people while claiming love for and allegiance to us! You filthy…"

With a condescending smile, Therendē'al stopped Sigurd in his tracks, "Me? Harm the people of Vanguard? You forget, Sigurd, that the real danger to Vanguard is Tarin and the dwarves of Exulias. I have only tried to help your city. The dwarves have killed…"

Now it was Sigurd's turn to interrupt. With a lethal smile, Sigurd responded, "Dwarves don't cut a man's head off without first taking off one or both of his legs, so cut the bogus dwarfish treachery story. No one in this square is buying that lie today."

Therendē'al's eyes narrowed again, but he knew he had the upper hand. His men were in place on the catwalks above, and most of the people in the city, while not in allegiance with the Dark, still believed in him, even more so than Sigurd. He didn't know how Garath's militia had survived the "mission" he had sent them on, but it didn't matter. They certainly wouldn't survive this square.

Feeling secure in his superiority, Therendē'al decided to play some more with the master of Vanguard and his son before having them slaughtered. Smiling just as lethally as Sigurd had at him, Therendē'al said, "Well, don't you remember what Bull said about having to fight his way through the dwarves to return to Vanguard? Where is Bull? Let him tell his story again and let the people decide about dwarfish treachery." Therendē'al looked expectantly at the militia group.

Sigurd noticed several of the council members behind Therendē'al smirk and look confidently at each other as the Drēor spoke. *So, his treachery has infiltrated my council,* Sigurd noted to himself. At least he knew three he would make sure to kill in the coming fight.

"Bull?" Garath asked. Cocking his head towards his militia, Garath asked, "Where did we leave Bull's body?"

The smile fled from Therendē'al's face. "What do you mean, Bull's body?" he asked furiously.

"Well," Garath began, enjoying Therendē'al's surprise, "he made a very large wolf angry, and it didn't end well for him."

Therendē'al was taken aback, "What do you mean, large wolf? You mean he was taken by one of the wargs that have started roaming these lands?"

"No," Garath shook his head. "It wasn't a warg. Plus, I have it on good authority that the warg pack, which has lately been terrorizing our woods, has been exterminated..." He emphasized his final comment with an insolent shrug of his shoulders and a snarl, "...by dwarves."

Therendē'al threw away all pretense at that and roared for his personal guard to destroy Garath. Amarris almost instantaneously felled three men as they rushed Sigurd. Thēorin took out two who came from the shadows to their left. Therendē'al waited for his archers to unleash, but nothing happened. Roaring with anger at the archers on the catwalks to do their jobs, he was deeply disturbed when one of them slowly fell and landed at his feet. He noticed for just a moment that the man's throat had been slit.

With absolute and deadly fury, Therendē'al started to launch himself at Sigurd, who, along with Garath and the militia, was fighting Vikari that had flooded into the square in answer to their leader's call. Therendē'al had every intention of killing the master of Vanguard but was brought up short by an arrow, drawn and ready just inches from his face.

"Hello, uncle," Amarris snarled. "Tell your Vikari to stop, or it will be my absolute pleasure to kill you."

Therendē'al could tell she meant it. Things may have ended right there for Therendē'al, but unfortunately, the Dark always seems to get a second chance. Before Amarris could react, she was attacked from behind by three Vikari, giving Therendē'al a breather.

Before his men could kill her, though, the Drēor stepped in. "Leave her alive," he snarled, "and bring her with us. If that boy can't tell us which Lēas has left Lumenas to help Tarin, then she can." Whirling, the Drēor headed towards a secret door in the wall as an escape. His men followed, dragging Amarris, who was not going willingly and giving the men an extremely difficult time.

As the group neared the wall where Therendē'al's escape door was, Amarris managed to incapacitate one of the men dragging her with a solid elbow to the nose and almost made it out of the others' grasps; but the remaining two men were able to regain control of her and continue to drag her after the Drēor.

So engrossed in escaping and not losing Amarris, both Therendē'al and his two Vikari were shocked when a voice from the shadows in front of them yelled furiously, "Get your hands off her!" The two Vikari were even more shocked when those words were punctuated with an axe blow to each of their chests.

Before Therendē'al could even react, he felt himself being flung backwards into the square. He had just enough time to see the two dwarves who had killed his Vikari joined by several more dwarves and elves, coming out of a passage he had never known was there. Once he finished skipping across the ground and regained his feet, Therendē'al could see who had thrown him. He quickly recognized Halicyon, an elf who he had once tried to turn, but no matter what he did, including orchestrating the murder of Halicyon's wife, Halicyon never relinquished his light. It was one of Therendē'al's few failures.

With Halicyon were several other elves from Kuaryll, several dwarves, and an elf that gave Therendē'al's heart a turn—Falinor. How in the world did he escape the malidaemon queen alive? Gathering himself, Therendē'al looked for another route of escape. Before he could even begin his new plan, though, he heard a battle cry that sounded extremely familiar and sent chills down his spine. It must have done the same for his Vikari because several hesitated in their fighting and looked around the square warily.

It was when the war cry ended that Therendē'al was hit solidly in the head from behind by a punch of such force, he was almost knocked unconscious and was sent to the ground. Looking up from where he had faceplanted, he could see Tarin running towards him, obviously to engage him in a fight. Not far behind him were Amarris and the two younger dwarves who had killed his Vikari dragging his niece earlier.

Still fuzzy-headed, Therendē'al heard a voice slightly behind him and to his right say, "He's mine, Tarin. Today I get some payback. Take your group and help the others cleanse this place of the remaining Vikari." As he watched Tarin's group change course, Therendē'al heard the voice again, "Get up, Drēor." The tone with which those words were said made it clear that the speaker viewed him as somewhat lower than excrement.

Turning slowly towards the voice, Therendē'al was confronted by a figure wearing the Vanguard militia uniform, hooded and masked. He didn't recognize the form but could feel the power. "You must be the she-elf who has been slumming it in Exulias," Therendē'al purred maliciously, trying to regain his feet and bearings.

Syllē's laugh was savage. Removing her mask and hood, Syllē continued, "Don't you recognize me, Therendē'al? You took such pleasure in tormenting me in your master's prison. How could you forget me? I even sent you my regards recently. Didn't Marielle tell you?" Syllē's voice was ferociously harsh. As she spoke, she moved slowly and menacingly towards Therendē'al, her long knives drawn and deadly ready.

"Sylēmar, Granulas' irritating wife," Therendē'al breathed incredulously. "But that's impossible. You cannot have survived all this time with that blade in your leg. You should be dead."

"The dwarves of Exulias saved me," Syllē shrugged, almost happily, "and I am not Granulas' wife—not anymore. Now, let's see how well you fight against an opponent who can fight back."

Syllē launched her attack, and it became clear to Therendē'al rather quickly that this was not the same woman he had tortured in prison all those years ago. It also became clear that if she had had half her current strength back then, he would have died in that prison by her hand. Desperately searching for an out, Therendē'al kept trying, in vain, to draw their fight towards the walls where he knew several escape routes; but he had no chance. Syllē kept him in the center of the square.

Noticing Therendē'al continuing to look up at the catwalks as if expecting aid, Syllē taunted him, "Looking for someone, Therendē'al? Another Drēor or two or four, accompanied by a large orc pack, perhaps?"

Startled, Therendē'al looked quickly at Syllē. What did she know about the Drēor and orcs he had here? Noticing his look, Syllē smiled with relish,

"You won't find any help from them today. One is rotting in Mosslight with an arrow through the head—thanks to Falinor—and your orc pack has fled back into their lair in the Perdarus." Therendē'al thought Sylēmar's smile rivaled a Drēor's in its viciousness. "The other three? Well, they are dead." Syllē pointed above at the catwalk as she spoke, "Dead, and..." Turning to her right, she started to say, "De...," when they both saw Marielle rise unsteadily from where she had fallen on the catwalk, only to fall forward and down to the square below. "Dead," Syllē finished, satisfied.

Appalled, Therendē'al realized she was playing with him. It was also at this point that Therendē'al noticed he was being surrounded by the combined group of dwarves, elves, Vanguard militia, and Vanguard citizens as his Vikari were either dead or had fled. He realized there was no escape unless he could overpower Sylēmar and use her as a bargaining chip to get out of the city. He quickly realized that was not an option; however, Amarris wasn't too far away. If he could steer the fight in her direction, he could grab her and use his niece as a hostage.

"I thought you told Syllē it wasn't appropriate to play with her opponent," Finn muttered quietly to Falinor from the sidelines.

Without taking his eyes off the fight in the middle of the square, Falinor replied curtly, "In this instance, it is justified."

As Therendē'al tried to surreptitiously draw closer to Amarris, he noticed something crawling slowly out of the shadows on the catwalk slightly above and to the right of them. Smiling gleefully to himself, he spun back towards Syllē, trying to divert her and everyone else's attention away from what was above them.

Therendē'al purred malevolently, "You may have escaped the dungeon and the fate of the blade, but you cannot escape me and your death today."

Syllē simply scoffed. "After today, Therendē'al, you will *never* bring harm to anyone I love again. Or anyone else, for that matter."

His eyes narrowing at Syllē's obvious show of disdain for him, he relished the image of her dying at his feet. With that in mind, Therendē'al silkily continued, "It's too bad about you and Granulas. How is it possible that you two, who were so deeply in love, are no longer married?"

"Wow," Syllē breathed, "you really are desperate. Fine, I'll give you a slight breather." Shrugging uncaringly, she slightly lowered her long knives and answered, "Granulas asked to be released, and I granted his request. End of story."

"That must have hurt," Therendē'al returned sarcastically. Inside he could barely contain his glee at Syllē's guard drop.

Shrugging just as nonchalantly as before, Syllē responded, "Not really. Nowhere near as painful as this is going to be." As Syllē said that last sentence, she whirled slightly to the right of Therendē'al before shoving him forward and into the path of the arrow from his dying Vikari archer on the catwalk.

Therendē'al would have been shocked if he hadn't had the wind completely knocked out of him as the barbed arrow found its mark. He felt darkness start to close in as his strength fled his body and he slid to his knees in the square. Staring disgustedly at the dying Drēor, Syllē knew what type of arrow was embedded in Therendē'al's chest. She had seen them used before and knew that the barbs were so designed that when pulled out of a body, they expanded and made a gaping, devastating hole in their victim. Knowing the trauma that would cause him, Syllē decided, for her salvation and for the love K'tanna had once felt for this Drēor, mercy was better.

Not taking her eyes from the dying Therendē'al, Syllē sheathed her long knives and then said harshly to Sigurd, "He's all yours, Master Sigurd. I have had my payback." Turning away, Syllē headed towards Tarin and their group.

Sigurd walked towards Therendē'al with his sword drawn. "In Vanguard, traitors are beheaded," he snarled.

"But let me die, Sylēmar, and you will never find him," Therendē'al spoke, using almost the last of his strength.

Sigurd stopped beside the Drēor and looked expectantly at Syllē, who had stopped dead a few feet in front of Tarin and the twins. Spinning slowly back around to face the Drēor, Syllē stood a little unsteadily for a moment, as if making up her mind. Suddenly, she lunged forward, grasped the shaft of the arrow sticking out of Therendē'al's chest, and pulled, whirling so her back was to him as he fell. Unable to even utter a death scream, Therendē'al fell forward and lay still.

Sigurd looked down at his fallen former advisor. "Beheading was too good for him," he observed with satisfaction. Turning to his men, he ordered harshly, "Get this trash out of my square and burn it with the rest of the filth."

"Why would he think Syllē would believe we need him to find Oran?" Finn asked, confused.

Looking with concern at Syllē, who hadn't moved since pulling the arrow from Therendē'al's chest, Falinor responded, "He wasn't talking about Oran."

Even more confused, Finn asked, "Then, who was he talking about?"

Tarin answered for Falinor, "Farin."

With a start, Finn looked incredulously at Falinor, but the elf only nodded and placed a compassionate hand on Tarin's shoulder. Tarin watched Syllē take a deep breath, straighten, and start walking towards them. Realizing what she carried in her right hand, Syllē disgustedly flung the bloody arrow to the ground and kept moving. Tarin could see pain and fury written all over Syllē's face.

Syllē stopped in front of Tarin and the twins. Her eyes caught Falinor's first, almost as if she couldn't bear to look at the dwarves. Tarin grabbed her hand and looked up into her face, trying to will her to look at him. *Syllē?*

Reluctantly, Syllē met his gaze, and her face clouded for a moment before she squeezed his hand tightly. "I'm sorry, Tarin."

He could feel the pain in her voice. "For what? Ending a Drēor?"

"No," Syllē shook her head slightly. She was still having a hard time meeting Tarin's and the twins' gazes. "For Farin."

Tarin squeezed her hand reassuringly and stepped closer to her, looking up into her face. "He was Drēor, Syllē. He would have said anything to get you to save his life."

Syllē briefly met his gaze before dropping her eyes again. After a moment, she sighed deeply, "I miss my friend, Tarin."

Taking another step forward, Tarin did something he rarely ever did—give a real hug. As he wrapped his arms around her and pulled her close, Tarin felt Syllē grab on tightly to him and bury her face against the top of his head. The twins and Hil joined the hug as well. The five stood together in the square, holding tightly to each other, and saying nothing.

Syllē finally broke the silence with a sadness-laden sigh, "I really miss my friend." Tarin knew exactly how she felt.

7

They stayed in Vanguard for the next few weeks helping Sigurd root out Vikari and cleanse his city as best as possible. It had been difficult to start, as Therendē'al had done an excellent job of poisoning many in the city's population against dwarves. The Drēor had played on the citizens' predisposed dislike and distrust of dwarves to further his goal of creating a massive wedge between the citizens of Vanguard and the dwarves of Exulias. However, stories of Therendē'al's true treachery, including the terror-filled depiction of the father and son's recent ordeal with the Drēor's orc pack—an ordeal directly orchestrated by the Drēor himself—circulated Vanguard. Soon, more stories filled with neighbors betraying neighbors, orc attacks hidden as dwarf raids, and Therendē'al "errands" that turned into life and usually death situations filtered in from the outlying areas from people who had been driven into hiding by Therendē'al and his Vikari, causing the sentiments towards Tarin and the other dwarves to shift.

One relationship, though, that had taken a definite turn for the worse worried Syllē. She couldn't have two of their team on the outs, especially since, in a few days, they were going to have to continue their journey into the Perdarus in search of the orc's lair and, possibly, Oran and the missing Helmfirth children. Syllē thought perhaps if she left it alone, the two would work out their differences, but as the days passed, Kwin worked extra hard at avoiding Amarris, borrowing one of his uncle's old standbys: leaving every area in which the object of his anger was and absolutely refusing to be near her or work with her on any of their patrols. The rift between the pair grew, so Syllē decided to intervene.

Finding Kwin sitting sullenly in the town square where he was watching Sigurd and his remaining council discuss with Tarin and Falinor their search of the city's extensive dungeon complex that had been expanded and changed under Therendē'al, Syllē approached Kwin and tapped his shoulder lightly. "Come with me, Kwin. Let's take a walk around the city."

Begrudgingly, Kwin got up off his stool and almost skulked along with Syllē. His scowl rivaled Tarin's in its ferocity.

Looking with concern at Kwin, Syllē asked, "Have I done something to make you angry with me, Kwin?"

Startled, Kwin stopped scowling for a moment and shook his head emphatically at Syllē. "No," he growled.

Soon, however, Kwin began to squirm under Syllē's quiet stare. It was obvious she wanted an explanation for his mood, but he didn't know how to tell her. He would much prefer they toured the city in silence, so Kwin tried to ignore her stare and survey the city around them as they walked. He looked everywhere but at her. Syllē, for her part, did not stop her disconcerting, steady stare. Even when Kwin felt her turn her head back to look in the direction of where they were walking, he could still feel her eyes on him.

Syllē remained quietly studying Kwin as they walked. Deftly, Syllē steered their walk up onto the city walls until she found a vacant corner looking towards the Perdarus. Syllē caught Kwin's arm and quickly sat down and hung her legs over the wall like she did on Exulias' rooftop. It was obvious Syllē wanted them to sit, but Kwin refused. This would be worse than walking. They'd have to make small talk, and Kwin did not want to talk.

Scowling at Syllē, Kwin refused to sit and instead stood with his arms crossed, and barked at her, "I thought we were going on a patrol of the city. We have no time to goof off. Let's go." Kwin turned on his heel and tried to head farther down the wall and away from Syllē, but the Valaraii refused to release his arm, and she wasn't budging from her seat.

"Sit down, little brother." Syllē's tone could be incredibly steely and even slightly more frightening, Kwin decided. "We have something very important to discuss, unless you would prefer to return to Exulias, instead of continuing on our journey."

Shocked that Syllē was considering sending him back to Exulias, Kwin plopped onto the wall next to her; but he still refused to speak. He simply crossed his arms and stared scowling off towards the Perdarus.

Cocking her head to the side, Syllē gazed quizzically at Kwin for a moment as if she was waiting for him to begin, but Kwin refused to even look at her, let alone talk. Finally, Syllē sighed heavily before addressing Kwin, "Well, I guess you actually would prefer to return to Exulias over continuing this journey with me." Turning her gaze from Kwin, Syllē gazed out towards the darkened Perdarus Range before quietly continuing, "I will inform Tarin of your decision."

Kwin glared angrily at Syllē now. "I do not wish to return to Exulias," he growled.

"Then start talking, little brother, because I cannot have this friction dividing our group when we leave Vanguard. It's not even very safe here in the city, but out there," Syllē stabbed her hand at the Perdarus, "it'd be deadly. For all of us," she emphasized sharply, staring hard at Kwin as she spoke.

Kwin withered slightly under her stare but still refused to talk. Well, *refused* wasn't the right word. Kwin didn't know how to explain it to Syllē. He wasn't exactly sure why Amarris' actions had caused such anger and hurt in him as they did, and that made him even angrier.

Softening her gaze, Syllē leaned back against the stone parapet and kindly asked, "What is it, Kwin? Why are you suddenly so angry with Amarris?" Kwin looked down at his hands, still at a loss for words. Leaning slightly towards him, but still speaking softly and kindly, Syllē asked again, "Why, Kwin? I thought you and Amarris were friends. What happened, little brother? Talk to me, please."

Still looking down at his hands, Kwin responded bitterly, "She kissed me."

Syllē's eyebrow raised at that. Waiting for more and not receiving any further information, she eventually prodded, "And this made you uncomfortable because you don't see Amarris in a romantic light?"

"No," Kwin looked sharply at Syllē. "I'm not uncomfortable. I'm angry. She shouldn't have done that to me. She shouldn't have used me that way."

"Now you've lost me, Kwin," Syllē said, confused. "How was she using you?"

"Because she only did it to hurt her fiancé," Kwin practically spat out.

"Kwin," Syllē's tone was equally sharp at this point, "Amarris isn't engaged to anyone. So, what are you talking about?"

Looking back at the Perdarus, Kwin continued in a voice strained by betrayal, "She and Garath were arguing in the hall. Garath wanted her to stay in Vanguard so they could marry. She told him she had no intention of staying, and that her interests lay elsewhere. That's about when I entered Sigurd's Hall, and when she saw me, she grabbed me by the front of my shirt, pulled me towards her, and then kissed me hard. When she let go, I could see the absolute disgust on Garath's face and the laughter on the faces of Sigurd and Firth. Kissing me was just a joke to her. A way of hurting Garath by kissing a gross dwarf."

Kwin finally looked Syllē squarely in the eye. She could see the anger, pain, and confusion that the situation had generated in him, and her heart truly hurt for him. Smiling gently at Kwin, Syllē tried to be gentler in her questioning, "Did Amarris tell you that she kissed you simply to hurt Garath? That the kiss was a joke, meaningless?"

Shaking his head, Kwin answered, "No. She didn't say anything. She just stepped back and smiled at me."

"And what did you do?" Syllē prodded.

"I just stood there. I couldn't move." Catching Syllē's questioning glance, Kwin continued, "Then Garath stomped out of the hall in a huff, and Amarris walked out of the hall another way, humming." Kwin's bitterness deepened with the memory. "That's when Firth and his brothers and Sigurd all started laughing, and somebody—I think Firth—said, 'Well, I guess she showed him.'"

"And you've been avoiding Amarris and treating her abominably ever since?" Syllē's sharp tone brought Kwin out of his reverie. "Have you even given her a chance to explain?"

"She only did it because there's nothing worse than kissing a dwarf," Kwin responded stubbornly.

Syllē's eyes began to spark navy as she forcefully answered him, "Dwarves are some of the most stubborn, frustrating—I thought you were different, but you are much more like your uncle than I realized! Did it ever occur to you that Amarris kissed you to show Garath where her interests lie—with you?"

"That's impossible."

Kwin's stubbornness was causing Syllē to seethe with frustration. "Why?"

Looking back down at his hands, Kwin's response was sad. "Because I am a dwarf, and she could never truly love a dwarf."

Leaning forward, Syllē reached out and put her hand under Kwin's chin, raising his head so he had to look at her. "Why not?" she asked gently.

"Because she is not a dwarf," Kwin began haltingly. At Syllē's quizzical raised eyebrow, Kwin blustered, "She's Therendē'al's niece, which makes her at least half-elf, and elves don't fall in love with dwarves." Syllē said nothing, but Kwin could hear the "why not" in her eyes. Stubbornly, he persisted, "She could never truly love me."

Syllē tried another tactic. "Could you ever love her?"

Kwin's eyes grew wide at Syllē's question. Trying to deflect, he blusteringly answered, "She's not a dwarf. It would never work."

"That's not what I asked you, little brother." Syllē was gentle, but firm. "Answer my question, please. Could you ever love Amarris? Truth, Kwin."

Swallowing hard, Kwin's pain and uncertainty swirled in his eyes. "I think I already do." Stopping Syllē before she could get the words out, he continued, "But she could never love a dwarf."

"Why not?"

"Because women like her—they just don't fall in love with dwarves," Kwin's voice was heartbreaking.

"What kind of women are you talking about, Kwin?"

"Strong, independent, beautiful women," Kwin's answer was wistful.

"You know, your mother falls into that category." Syllē smiled lovingly at Kwin.

Slightly irritated, Kwin curtly changed his previous answer, "Fine. Strong, independent, beautiful, non-dwarf women. Women like you." Suddenly, a thought occurred to Kwin. Looking directly at Syllē, he asked, almost hopefully, "Truth, Syllē. Could you ever love a dwarf?"

Syllē smiled warmly at Kwin in response. "Yes."

Kwin's eyes widened in surprise. Before he could respond, though, he noticed Syllē's attention was caught by something or someone on the ground. Turning to see where she was looking, he caught a glimpse of Sigurd and Falinor walking out of the main gates of Vanguard. As they journeyed farther down the road away from the city, Kwin was able to see his uncle walking in between the two.

Remembering what Amarris had said about Syllē not being in love with Halicyon but someone else, he asked almost incredulously, "Truth, Syllē. Are you in love with Tarin?"

The question brought Syllē's eyes back to Kwin's face. He noticed they were almost gray at this point. He'd have to ask Finn what that color meant. Syllē smiled sadly at Kwin before turning to gaze back down at the trio on the road. As she did, the three turned back towards Vanguard, obviously searching the walls for something. Tarin noticed Syllē and Kwin sitting high up on the parapets and smiled and waved at them. They returned the greeting.

Sighing heavily, Syllē quietly answered Kwin, "Yes, I am, but I am not free to follow my heart just yet, Kwin."

Searching her face, Kwin pressed, "Okay, but if you were, what would you do?"

"Kwin…" Syllē's voice was slightly broken.

"This is important, Syllē. I need to know. If you were free to follow your heart, what would you do?" Kwin looked earnestly into Syllē's face.

It was Syllē's turn to swallow hard. Breaking Kwin's gaze, Syllē looked down at Tarin below them on the road. "I would walk down there, grab your uncle by his shirt, and kiss him hard." Laughing slightly, she continued, "Of course, he'd push me away and yell at me that I'm not a dwarf so I shouldn't be making passes at him." Syllē turned her eyes back to meet Kwin's. "Go talk to Amarris, Kwin. She deserves better than suspicion and prejudice."

"You really think she likes me?" Kwin still couldn't wrap his head around the idea.

"I don't think, Kwin. I know," Syllē informed him. "She asked me if we were a couple. She asked me if you had anyone special. She asked me if you had a type. On top of that, she spent the entire Harvest Festival Dance trying to dance with you. Why do you think I kept dancing off with Finn? I was trying to help her get a dance with you." Syllē playfully jabbed Kwin in the chest.

Kwin opened his mouth to respond but was at a total loss. Finally, he managed, "Did I screw it up completely or do you think she'll forgive me?"

Syllē shrugged carelessly and grinned at Kwin, "You'll have to talk to her to find out, Kwin. I would start with the words 'I'm sorry.' Those are always a good choice." Laughing, Syllē returned to watching the trio on the road.

Getting up and standing beside Syllē so he could have a better view of the trio as well, Kwin placed a hand on Syllē's shoulder. "He loves you, Syllē. He doesn't care that you're not a dwarf."

Smiling sadly, Syllē covered Kwin's hand with her own. "I know he cares and thinks of me as family, Kwin; but that is it. He is not in love with me. He has told me so. He can only love another dwarf like that, and that is something I will never be," Syllē finished with a sigh.

Kwin started to argue but was cut short by yells coming from the woods east of the road. It was Finn accompanied by Halicyon, Thēorin, and Trygve. They had found something. Something dark—really dark. Swiftly, Syllē and Kwin headed toward the group below the walls of Vanguard. Syllē had to admit that the snatches of information she had caught before starting off the wall had her heart in her throat.

8

Syllē was in a waking nightmare full of Therendē'al's dead. Once they found a receptive audience for their sorrow, the dead would refuse to let go and usually drove the poor soul on whom they had latched mad with their grief. The dead had found Syllē, and they weren't about to let go.

"Kwin," Syllē could barely whisper. "Help...me."

That was all she could get out before she sank to the ground under the crushing weight of the dead's pain. Their screams inundated her mind, and their fear pressed on her body. Everywhere she looked, Syllē saw horrific scenes of death and torture and felt the dead's final moments. The horror was bone-crushing, and Syllē desperately tried to fight through it and regain control, but there were too many of them and more coming, and they wouldn't leave her alone for even a second.

"Tarin!" Kwin's frantic call brought everyone up short. Kwin had been walking cautiously beside Syllē in the back of the group heading to investigate whatever Finn's and Trygve's noses had found not far into the woods east of Vanguard. He hadn't noticed her slowly falling behind because he was so intent on what might launch itself at him from the woods. It was her whisper that Kwin wasn't even sure he had heard that made him turn around, and what he saw when he did got him running full tilt back to her.

Syllē was on her knees, holding her head between her hands and swaying back and forth. She kept repeating in a deeply broken voice, "Stop.

Please, stop. I cannot help you all. Stop." She didn't even notice Kwin in front of her franticly trying to get her to focus on him. She couldn't hear his words or feel his hands shaking her shoulders. The dead had found an outlet and weren't about to stop.

"Elēandil!" Halicyon yelled at the nearest elf to Syllē when he registered what was happening. "Grab her and run for the river!"

It was Sigurd who got to Syllē first. He had been walking only slightly in front of Kwin, so when the young dwarf yelled, he whirled around and saw exactly what was happening. Sigurd roared at Garath to take some of the group and head back to the road to keep anyone else from entering this area of woods. "And whatever you do, do *not* leave anyone behind!" Garath quickly followed orders, taking several elves and militia with him.

Sigurd launched himself at Syllē, grabbing her without even checking his stride. He threw her over his shoulder and started bulldozing his way through Mosslight towards the river because, as he remembered from an incident in his childhood, the dead could not cross water. But the dead were not about to give up. Sigurd could feel invisible hands grabbing his clothing and tearing at his hair, almost pulling him backwards. He could also feel the dead try to wrestle Syllē from his grasp. Holding her all the tighter to him, Sigurd tried desperately to get to the river. Sigurd was strong, but the dead were stronger. He felt as though he were wading through quicksand. Just as Sigurd began to think he couldn't make it any farther, he was slammed into from behind and felt two arms link behind his back and help shove him forward. It was Halicyon and Elēandil. Their momentum helped drive Sigurd forward and briefly out of the reach of the dead.

Calling behind him as he helped Sigurd, Halicyon instructed the men and elves remaining with them, "When we get to the river, grab a dwarf and plunge in. Get over to the other side quickly."

Tarin and the rest of his clan weren't that keen on being carried by anyone, especially an elf, but there was no mistaking Halicyon's urgency.

They were going to have to swallow their pride and rely on others to help them. Tarin really didn't know why they couldn't stay on the shore. He didn't understand what the difficulty was or the danger; but he trusted Halicyon. So, if the elf said to get to the other side of the river, then that's where they needed to get. The fact that Tarin couldn't see or feel the presence of the dead wasn't unthinkable. The dead couldn't affect dwarves, really; however, as Syllē and Halicyon knew, the dead could kill dwarves if they focused their energy on them.

Rounding the last turn, Sigurd saw the river only a few yards in front of him. With a last-ditch effort, he plunged forward, wading chest deep into the center of the flow, pushing onwards towards the far bank. Halicyon and Elēandil and another elf with them stopped long enough on the riverbank to grab a dwarf and plunge into the current, making their way to the center of the river and heading for the other side. Thēorin, Amarris, Eirik, and Falinor did the same. Tarin was at least mollified by the fact that Falinor had grabbed him, but he could tell by the expression on Trygve's face that his cousin was mortified to be carried, even by Halicyon.

When he reached the far bank, Falinor helped Tarin down off his back before heading swiftly towards where Sigurd was kneeling holding Syllē in his arms, trying to get her to respond. Moving just as quickly to Syllē, Tarin was taken aback at how Sigurd looked. The master of Vanguard's clothes were torn, his hair horribly disheveled, and his arms and back covered in scratches, some exceedingly deep. Obviously, something had attacked the man, but Tarin had never seen anything near him. What had attacked Sigurd? And Syllē? Why wasn't she waking up?

Falinor quietly reached out his hand and touched Syllē's head lightly. Closing his eyes, Falinor whispered something in elvish that Tarin couldn't decipher, but it must have worked because Syllē's eyes started to flutter before opening fully.

After a moment of disorientation, Syllē suddenly sat up and urgently instructed, "Get out of here, now. We aren't safe." She rose quickly but had to grab hold of Sigurd's arm for support. Syllē rubbed the side of her head as though she could disperse the cobwebs that way.

"What do you mean?" Sigurd asked, confused, rising and looking with concern at the river. "I thought the dead couldn't cross water. At least, that's what I'd always been told."

Finally regaining her bearings, Syllē looked out across the water and ominously replied, "Unless there are elves among the dead."

As if on cue, Tarin saw a mist rolling out of the woods and starting to slowly creep across the opposite shore and onto the water. Tarin could have sworn that the tendrils of mist leading the way were shaped like long, thin, skeletal fingers.

Walking over to Kwin, Syllē quietly spoke while not taking her eyes off the mist slowly wending its way across the river towards them, "I need you to make sure Tarin leaves with you, Kwin. Don't let him come back. Make him go."

Kwin's eyes widened. "What are you going to do?"

"Try and release the dead."

"Uncle won't leave you behind, Syllē," Kwin warned her.

Briefly taking her eyes off the encroaching mist, Syllē looked almost pleadingly at Kwin, "The dead will use him to get what they want: me. Please, Kwin. Make sure your uncle leaves."

Kwin nodded reluctantly before launching at Syllē. Releasing her after a moment, Kwin reminded Syllē, "You're family, Syllē, and dwarves always make sure to return to their family. So, I expect to see you in Vanguard soon."

Squeezing his shoulder affectionately, Syllē nodded. Turning towards the riverbank, she took a deep breath and slowly released it as she took a step back towards the river.

Halicyon joined her, sword drawn and ready. "Don't even think about telling me I can't help you. Not this time, Syllē," he responded tersely to her questioning head tilt.

"It's time to leave," Syllē called urgently over her shoulder without taking her eyes off the creeping mist. "Go. Get back to Vanguard." Then she and Halicyon stepped back into the river.

Tarin started to head back to the riverbank after her when he heard Trygve's voice behind him say, "I'm sorry, cousin." That was the last thing he heard as he was struck on the back of the head and dropped to the ground, unconscious. Elēandil grabbed him and gently slung Tarin over his shoulder for their run back to Vanguard.

9

For the third time in a matter of minutes, Syllē said the release prayer for the dead: "O Hiril Sedivar, Vanwadil â Cálëdil, Patha tâlnta, sívë fëanta, â gresta tai an sérëlta."[2] Syllē's words were punctuated by a ring of bright light that radiated out of her and into the mass of dead surrounding them. Then, there was a third great sigh, as many souls found the relief of freedom. Soon the mist on the river was gone. Syllē sank slightly into the water, exhausted from her efforts.

Sheathing his sword as there were no more dead on the river for him to keep off Syllē while she worked on releasing them, Halicyon waded towards her, wrapping his arm around her waist as soon as he reached her. Syllē gratefully sank against him for support. She was breathing hard and close to exhaustion. Releasing the dead, especially elven dead, was exceptionally draining.

"If there had been any more, my friend, we would have been lost," Syllē breathed against Halicyon's shoulder.

Looking worriedly around them, Halicyon answered, "There are more. I can feel them coming. They are on both banks now."

Syllē looked up at the far bank, straining to see through the trees. Her heart dropped and she sank a little further into Halicyon as she viewed

2   "O High Queen Sedivar, Friend of the Dead and the Light, guide their feet, calm their souls, and help them to their rest."

more dead heading for the river. Thankfully, she didn't see any elven dead yet, so she and Halicyon were safe where they were for the moment, but that might not last. Plus, this river was mountain fed, which meant it was icy cold.

"We could float with the current downstream," Syllē mentioned hopefully.

Tightening his grip on her, Halicyon responded morosely, "They would simply follow us. They could certainly move faster on land than the current would take us."

Slowly, Syllē raised her head off Halicyon's chest and gazed downriver—a sliver of hope started to grow. "Allies are coming. We just have to hold on a little longer."

Halicyon turned slightly to look in the direction Syllē was gazing, but he couldn't see anything. He could feel a slight charge in the water, which indicated something he was pretty sure he wouldn't be too thrilled about. Resigning himself to who was coming, Halicyon wrapped his arms around Syllē tighter and helped her keep her head from slipping below the current.

* * *

"When he wakens, we're all going to be in serious trouble," Hil said.

They had made it back to Vanguard and were currently in Sigurd's version of a Great Hall. Falinor had positioned the majority of the elves on the four corners of the city walls to keep an eye out for not only Therendē'al's dead but also Syllē and Halicyon's return. The rest were drying at one of the opposing fires in the large stone fireplaces located in the center of each long wall in the room. Elēandil had gently laid Tarin on a chaise Sigurd had pulled near one of the fires, and Hil was tending the dwarf's head wound. Trygve had hit him hard enough that the wound needed a few stitches.

"Was it necessary to hit your cousin so hard?" Hil glared furiously at Trygve.

"I heard what she said to Kwin. I also knew Tarin would never willingly leave her behind, so I did what I thought was right for all of us, including him and Syllē," Trygve growled.

Falinor dropped a hand on Trygve's shoulder for a moment as he headed to check on Tarin, "You did the right thing, Trygve. If Tarin or any of you had stayed, the dead would have leveraged you to get to her. Leaving her was her only chance." Falinor's voice was sad and slightly worried.

"So, again, my being a dwarf is a liability to Syllē." Tarin's frustrated growl caught everyone's attention.

Elēandil and Thēorin moved to guard the door in case the dwarf lord decided to make a run for it. Everyone took some sought of position in the room that would impede Tarin's possible exit from it. If Tarin was going to try and go after Syllē, he would have an almost insurmountable gauntlet of allies to pass through—a fact not lost on him, which caused his mood to sour even more. Kwin and Finn reached for his arms to help him sit up better on the chaise, but he angrily shoved their hands away, glaring menacingly at the twins and his sister.

"Don't even think about giving me that look, brother," Hil admonished Tarin, hands on her hips and feet planted squarely in front of her brother.

"You left her behind, sister," Tarin spat.

"To give her a chance to survive," Hil returned, equally ferocious in her tone to her brother. "If the dead had gotten to any of us, they would have used us to hurt Syllē." Throwing her hands in the air in frustration, Hil continued, "What? You think Syllē would have allowed the dead to drown any of us? She would have given herself to them before allowing that to happen and you know it."

"We could have fought beside her," Tarin insisted.

"Fought what?" Hil answered back. "Other than that mist, could you see anything to fight?" Hil, her hands squarely back on her hips, looked pointedly at her brother, "Because I couldn't."

Rising from the chaise so he could look down on Hil, Tarin simply scowled at his sister in answer. He knew she was right. He couldn't see anything but that mist. He wouldn't have been any help to Syllē, but he refused to relinquish his foul mood. It was helping him ignore the terror he felt for Syllē and Halicyon, lost in the night and possibly surrounded by vengeful dead.

Without really considering his words, Tarin spat, "This is what I get for associating with elves—menotho."[3]

"Cousin!" Trygve's voice, surprisingly, admonished Tarin. Stepping forward, Trygve glared just as furiously at his cousin.

Tarin glowered even more furiously at Trygve's stance. "We left them. We ran away and saved ourselves, instead of standing with them. That is what elves do. You used to know that." Tarin's words were biting and cruel, causing Trygve's face to blanch with anger.

Looking almost with pity at Tarin, Falinor quietly said, "And sometimes elves disobey their king and ride into battle to fight beside a friend, even though they know it is suicide."

Tarin's eyes widened as he met Falinor's kind gaze. Swallowing hard over the self-revulsion Tarin was now feeling, the dwarf sat back down heavily and put his head in his hands. "I am sorry, Falinor."

Before Falinor could respond, a runner from the walls came into the room. Finding Sigurd, he caught his breath a moment before saying, "The elf on the east wall says that the dead are amassing outside the city; but they can't seem to come near our walls. It's as if there is an invisible barrier keeping them at bay. The elf says to tell Falinor he thinks they are unable to pass into the city based on a hahta spell."

Falinor nodded, "Makes sense. Therendē'al wouldn't want the dead,

---

3   one of the dishonored; untrustworthy

especially as they increased in number, infiltrating the city. Too much chaos, and it would have put his forces in jeopardy and possibly even himself."

Tarin glanced up with concern, "But if the city is surrounded by the dead, how will Halicyon and Syllē get through?"

Falinor gazed quietly at Tarin for a moment before tersely answering, "They won't."

Tarin lowered his head back into his hands. He had failed Syllē. He had failed Halicyon. He had left them both to the dead. He *was* menotho.

10

Syllē and Halicyon were reaching the end of their strength. The fight with and release of the dead coupled with the extreme deep cold of the river was taking its toll. Halicyon struggled to maintain his grip on Syllē as his limbs were starting to refuse to work and he could almost barely hold himself above the water, let alone help Syllē. On top of that, he could see and feel the dead who had amassed on the banks, so even if he did get them to shore, they'd never survive what waited for them there.

"They're here, Halicyon," Syllē whispered through frozen lips. Taking a small step forward, she wrapped her own shaking arms around Halicyon and pulled him closer against her. He couldn't imagine where she got the strength. Before he could respond to her, he felt the water surge around them and haul them deep within the river's current. Their allies had come, but Halicyon wasn't too sure they weren't too late.

* * *

Staring out into the darkness surrounding Vanguard, Hil tried in vain to see what the elves were talking about. Leaning towards Amarris, she whispered, "Can you see them? It just looks dark out there to me. Maybe a little mist, but nothing else."

"I can see faint shapes, but not enough to really discern elf from human or who they were," Amarris responded. She noticed Kwin heading her way and quickly switched to Hil's other side, putting his mother between them. "Can you see anything, Thēorin?"

Without turning away from the territory outside the walls, Thēorin shook his head, "Not really. I just see a creeping mist along most of the ground, but not really any shapes."

"What about when we were running for the river earlier today?" Hil questioned. "Could either of you see anything other than the mist then?"

Amarris nodded, "I could. It was easier in daylight to discern the dead, especially as they ravaged Sigurd trying to get him to relinquish Syllē." Thēorin also acknowledged a better view during the day.

Hil shook her head with wonder, "No wonder we would have been a liability to Syllē. We wouldn't have been able to evade any of them because we wouldn't have seen them coming for us."

Kwin, who had noticed Amarris' avoidance, walked around his mother and planted himself directly in front of Amarris and asked, "Why are the dead here and what do they want with Syllē?"

Elēandil, however, spoke first over his shoulder in answer to Kwin's question, "Those dead killed by a Drēor can become trapped within this realm, unable to leave, which makes them desperate and angry. Drēor like to keep the dead they have tortured and killed around because they, especially elven dead, enhance a Drēor's power; but once the Drēor is dead or has too many dead to control, the dead will wander, looking for someone—anyone—who can release them from this world. Once they find someone who can hear them, they will all latch on hoping to get that poor soul to help them access the afterlife. Now, a powerful elf or wizard could free them from this realm; but not when so many are attacking them at once. It's just too much, and that's what happened to Syllē today. She was overwhelmed with the dead trying to get her to free them and there were just too many for her to handle."

"Can you hear them?" Kwin asked.

Elēandil shook his head, "I can see them—who they once were—but I can't hear them; so, I am useless to them."

"But Syllē could hear them?"

"Obviously," Elēandil nodded.

Finn quickly spoke up, walking towards his brother and Elēandil, "Do you think Syllē and Halicyon survived the dead at the river?"

Elēandil hesitated, glancing quickly at Tarin's back. Even though Tarin appeared fixed on staring out at the plain that surrounded the city and into Mosslight beyond from his seat on the wall, they all knew he was listening intently to their conversation. Deciding honesty was best, Elēandil answered simply, "I hope so."

A gloomy silence settled over the group on the walls. The elves could tell that no dead would be jeopardizing the city and its occupants that night, so it was safe to leave the normal guard on duty and go to bed. However, no one left. No one could sleep, and Tarin continued to stare into the night, looking and hoping for a miracle.

* * *

Syllē felt the forward rush through the water change to an upward trajectory. Keeping her eyes closed against the rush of water and still clutching tightly to Halicyon, Syllē felt the Limnades lift them upright and set them gently down in the shallows very near the river's shore. Opening her eyes, she caught a quick glimpse of the Limnades who had come to their aid and gave them a nod of thanks before starting to push Halicyon towards shore. Arm in arm the two reached the bank and climbed exhausted out of the water, falling with relief onto the ground.

The Limnades had carried them far upriver away from the dead and did so without the dead being able to see or perceive them in any way. Most likely, for the time being, they were still wandering the bank near where Syllē and Halicyon had once been, looking in vain for the one who could release them from their imprisonment. Syllē was relieved, even if she did feel a little sorry for them. What Thcrcndē'al had done to them was truly a fate worse than death.

Suddenly, Syllē's and Halicyon's attention was caught by rustling in the forest behind them. Soft footfalls of padded feet were rapidly heading their way. Halicyon tried to stand and draw his sword, readying himself for the attack he knew was coming, but his body just wasn't working right. Syllē, meanwhile, remained lying on the ground gathering her strength. Strangely, Halicyon noticed she was smiling. As the footfalls came closer, Halicyon tried to stand over Syllē and protect her, but thanks to the loss of coordination caused by the day's activities and extreme cold, he actually fell on top of her—his knee landing squarely in her chest. The smile left Syllē's face, as did most of the air from her lungs.

"What are you doing?" Syllē finally managed to gasp painfully.

"Protecting you," Halicyon could barely speak. He looked out towards where he had heard the footfalls approaching. "Wargs."

Syllē reached up and feebly but angrily shoved Halicyon off her. "Not wargs. Braxis and Pyrrha, you idiot," she managed, testily.

At that moment, Braxis and his mate Pyrrha bounded through the final line of brush and stopped next to Halicyon and Syllē. They both looked with concern downriver and then back at the two lying at their feet. The message was clear. *The dead are coming. Get a move on.* Syllē shakily stood and wearily mounted Pyrrha while Halicyon climbed onto Braxis. The two held on tightly to the scruff of their mounts as the wolves whirled and headed through Mosslight towards Vanguard, hoping to beat the dead to the city gates.

* * *

Shortly before midnight, Tarin thought he saw movement—a tall dark figure moving quickly through the trees and onto the plain to the east of the main road into Vanguard. "Falinor!" Tarin called urgently. "I think I saw a figure moving to the right of the main road!"

"I see nothing but the dead," Falinor replied after a moment.

"Look!" One of Halicyon's elves pointed into the night. "The dead are moving toward the road."

"Why would they do that?" Kwin asked, worried.

"Because something is there that interests them," Falinor answered ominously, still staring intently in the direction the dead were moving.

"They are moving from all sides," the same elf continued.

"I wonder," Falinor muttered, staring intently down the road.

"Is it Syllē and Halicyon?" Tarin asked.

"Not that I can see," Falinor responded, peering intensely where Tarin had pointed earlier.

Suddenly, a deep voice shouted from the road in front of the main gates, "Lacho calad! Drégo morn!"[4] As the shout rang out, it was punctuated with a great wave of light that swept the entire road to the main gates and outward onto the plain and then into Mosslight. Following the light wave, Elēandil made out the forms of two Lēasean wolves, one black and one gray, with riders.

"Open the gates," Sigurd shouted as the wolves and their riders bore down upon Vanguard.

Turning to Finn, Elēandil grinned, "It would appear that they did survive, Master Dwarf!" He found he was talking to himself as Finn and the rest of his family were already running full tilt down the steps behind Sigurd heading for the group who had just entered the front gates.

Braxis and Pyrrha took their riders directly to Master Sigurd's home. Syllē was grateful, as was Halicyon. Syllē really didn't think she could make

---

4   "Flame light! Flee night!"

the brief walk through the city, so a ride directly to their lodging was awesome as far as she was concerned. Tarin, on the other hand, was a tad put out that when he reached the gates, he only caught a glimpse of the wolves' tails as they ran down the street. By the time Tarin reached Sigurd's home, he was ready to kill the two whom, only moments before, he had been praying to Asger would make it back to him alive.

* * *

"You two!" Tarin growled as he ferociously entered Sigurd's Hall, slightly behind Falinor.

Braxis and Pyrrha curiously turned their heads to gaze at the dwarf lord as he aggressively headed towards Halicyon and Syllē, who were warming themselves by the fire. The wolves were lying next to the opposing fireplace, greatly enjoying the warmth after a cold night wading the river and eluding the dead. Braxis grinned at Tarin's entrance, possibly happy to see the dwarf lord or just amused by his bluster. Who could tell?

Sigurd, upon entering the room and catching a glimpse of the wolves, whistled softly and observed to his son with a twinge of awe, "Those are big wolves."

"Now you understand why Bull didn't stand a chance against that black one when he attacked Lord Tarin," Garath nodded back.

"Should I be worried?" Sigurd was still cautiously eyeing the wolves by his fire, staying towards the opposite wall.

"Not unless you make them angry or irritate them," Thēorin gleefully informed Sigurd as he headed towards Syllē and Halicyon.

At a loss for words, Falinor, who reached Syllē and Halicyon first, simply enveloped his daughter in a hug and refused to release her. Tarin tapped his foot impatiently behind them, waiting for his turn at the two.

Pulling back from Falinor, Syllē smiled warmly at the elf before turning her attention to Tarin. Seeing his bandaged head, Syllē asked with concern, "Tarin, what happened to your head?"

In his usual growl, Tarin responded irritably, "Trygve struck me at the river. Hil stitched me up once we got back here. Now…"

Looking confusedly between Tarin and Trygve, Syllē interrupted, "Wait! Why did Trygve strike you?"

"Because I knew he wasn't about to leave you behind, and since he's extremely thick-skulled, if I didn't knock him out with the first blow, he'd kill us all trying to stay with you," Trygve irritably answered Syllē.

At that, Halicyon tried in vain to hide his laughter behind a fit of coughing. Syllē glared a tad testily at the elf, who just shrugged his shoulders and sat down amused on Tarin's chaise lounge by the fire.

"You seem to have coughing fits quite a bit at my expense," Tarin glowered at the elf.

Seeing Tarin's apparent sour expression, Syllē sighed wearily and sank down on the chaise lounge next to Halicyon. Leaning her head against her friend's shoulder, she looked up at Tarin and wearily spoke, "Tarin, I am cold, hungry, and exhausted; so just let us have it so we can move on."

Startled, Tarin opened his mouth but quickly shut it. He wasn't sure where to begin. Really what he wanted desperately to do was launch himself at the two on the couch and, by Asger, just hug them with relief. So, he did, barely missing head-butting Syllē in the process. Taken completely by surprise, both Syllē and Halicyon took a moment before returning Tarin's embrace.

His voice muffled against both their heads, Tarin muttered thickly, "I need you two to promise me that you will stay alive, because thanks to these past months, my world no longer works without you two in it." Tarin blustered on, pulling back and looking forcefully at the two on the chaise, "And if anything were to happen to either of you when I had abandoned you, I—"

Tarin didn't finish because Syllē stood up and wrapped her arms around him in a fierce hug, while a smiling Halicyon looked on. Wriggling, Tarin tried to extricate himself, but Syllē held on tight.

"I like proper hugs, Tarin," Syllē whispered a tad hoarsely into his hair, "so just deal with it." Tarin contritely did just that. Finally pulling back, Syllē looked directly at Tarin as she firmly told him, "You did not abandon us, my lord. You," Syllē emphasized that pronoun, "helped to save us by leaving, even unwillingly," she finished with a slight smile.

"Well, then," Tarin sputtered, "you are wet and cold, so go with Hil and Amarris and get some dry clothes on. We'll have some hot food ready for you when you get back."

Syllē shook her head. Looking over Tarin's head at Kwin and Amarris, she said sternly, "Not Amarris. She and Kwin have something to figure out. Hil can help me."

Amarris looked stunned while Kwin resembled one of the condemned on the way to the gallows. Finn's grin didn't make the situation any better for his brother.

11

Tarin tossed and turned in his bed. He didn't know why he was so restless. After the horrid nightmare the day and the beginning of the night had been, it had ended well with both Halicyon and Syllē's safe return to Vanguard. He was pretty sure that Kwin and Amarris had used the trek to rustle up something hot in Sigurd's kitchen to figure out whatever it was Syllē was talking about, but he wasn't confident. Kwin was a dwarf, and dwarves were known to be an exceptionally stubborn race and extremely good at holding grudges. Plus, Kwin was his nephew, and Tarin knew he, personally, took holding grudges to a whole new level. Thankfully, Amarris and Kwin were now actually speaking to each other again, which was a definite improvement, so some fixing must have happened.

If that situation wasn't what was keeping him up, then what was? Irritated, Tarin forcefully punched his pillow to "fix" it and lay back down on his side. Determined, he shut his eyes tight and willed himself to sleep. No dice. Rolling onto his back, Tarin listened to Flarne and Trygve snore almost in unison and felt his irritation rising. How was it that everybody else could sleep and yet, he, who was exhausted after his day of worry and stress and a major head wound thanks to his cousin, couldn't shake this feeling of something being off.

Sitting up in bed, Tarin looked around the room. Nothing appeared amiss with anyone. Kwin was restfully sleeping in the bed next to him.

Looking at Finn, Tarin mused to himself that his poor nephew's future mate would have a hard time sleeping as Finn was sprawled across the full width of his bed. Anyone sharing with him would have been shoved out and onto the floor by now. Varger was out like a light, too. So, if nothing was amiss here, why couldn't he sleep?

Closing his eyes, Tarin found his mind journeying to Syllē. *Syllē?* As he was calling her, he thought better of it. What was he thinking? She was probably sound asleep after her ordeal, and here he was waking her just because he couldn't sleep.

Tarin? Syllē's voice was tired. He had awakened her, but the vision that came with her voice wasn't a bedroom. He saw Sigurd's Hall and Braxis' fur, as if Syllē were leaning against the wolf. He could also see Pyrrha clearly, and she had a very concerned look on her face.

Are you in the Great Hall? Why aren't you in bed? You should be sleeping! Tarin scolded, forgetting totally that he had called her and may have just awakened her.

I can't sleep, Tarin. Tarin could hear Syllē's exhaustion in her voice. *Too many night terrors from dealing with Therendē'al's dead.*

Jumping out of his bed, Tarin started grabbing his blankets and pillows. *Hang on. I'm coming.*

Tarin, you don't have to—

Remember, what I said about me being stubborn? Tarin felt Syllē smile.

"Uncle?" Kwin's voice startled him. "What's wrong?"

"Your sister is having nightmares. I'm going to keep her company," Tarin replied tersely as he headed for the door.

Shortly, a bone weary and slightly gray Syllē looked up to see Tarin, Kwin, and Trygve, their arms laden with bedding, walk into the Great Hall. Tarin was struck by how haggard she looked. Syllē, her voice choked with emotions, barely managed, "I adore you all."

Trygve, obviously embarrassed, muttered as he moved towards Syllē and the wolves, "Well, there is no need to get all sappy on us."

Laughing, Syllē leaned towards the dwarf as he drew near her and kissed Trygve on the cheek. Turning beet red, Trygve stopped dead in his tracks and looked everywhere but at Syllē. "Well, that certainly wasn't called for," he finally blustered, dropping his bedding at his feet.

Standing up, Syllē gently turned Trygve's face so he was looking at her and said with a smile, "Oh, my dear, dear, Trygve, it was more than called for."

"Let us get a spot here with the wolves ready for you, Syllē," Tarin butted in, slightly amused by Trygve's embarrassment and slightly perturbed that his cousin had gotten a kiss from Syllē.

"Oh, Tarin, you don't need to…" Syllē began.

"Syllē, you need rest, and we're here to help you get just that. So, go sit on that sofa with your brother, and Trygve and I will get this area near Braxis and Pyrrha ready," Tarin ordered Syllē sternly.

Syllē cocked her head to the side as she briefly regarded Tarin standing knee deep in bedding with his hands on his hips, trying to authoritatively glare at her. Smiling fondly at him, she leaned slightly down and planted a kiss on his cheek before stepping back and saying, "Yes, my lord." With a joyful smile playing around her lips, Syllē took Kwin's hand and walked with him to the chaise lounge by the other fire and happily sat down.

Tarin shook his head for a moment as if to clear the fog and muttered irritably, "I wish she wouldn't do that."

"I don't know," Trygve shrugged. "I kind of liked it." And he grinned broadly at his cousin.

Scowling back, Tarin testily ordered, "Help me get some soft rugs over here by the wolves."

Once Trygve and Tarin had the stone floor covered with soft rugs and pillows, Tarin took a seat leaning up against Braxis, who was gazing extra fondly at the dwarf lord. Turning to look at her, he ordered Syllē, "Come back over here and lie down against Braxis or Pyrrha. Kwin and Trygve, come here as well. You'll be safe from your nightmares with us and then we can all sleep or, at least, rest."

Syllē slid down beside Tarin against Braxis and placed her hand on Pyrrha's head as the she-wolf had snuggled up against Syllē's leg as soon as the Valaraii sat down. Kwin slid down against Braxis' front paw and used it as a rather comfortable pillow and Trygve leaned up against Pyrrha's side. He caught Syllē grinning at him as he settled into place, so Trygve quickly crossed his arms and closed his eyes to simulate sleep. It really wouldn't do for others to start realizing how fond he had become of that female.

Still grinning over Trygve, Syllē turned her head to her right and caught Tarin's eye. He was grinning at his cousin as well. Her smile softening, Syllē leaned towards him, and gently pressed her forehead to his. "Thank you, Tarin," she whispered softly before leaning slightly against his shoulder and rapidly falling asleep. Tarin found himself wishing Syllē would kiss him again. Tarin was right about one thing: the presence of the dwarves did keep the night terrors at bay.

When Sigurd entered his Great Hall early in the morning, he found the group curled up together, all sound asleep, including Braxis and Pyrrha. Smiling at the sight, he backed quietly out of the room and ordered the doors shut and no entrance into the room until its occupants had awakened. The group slept deeply and nightmare free, well into the morning. When Syllē finally woke, she couldn't remember feeling that rested in a long time. Opening her eyes, Syllē found Tarin already awake and watching over her. Interlacing her fingers with his for a moment, Syllē smiled happily at the dwarf lord, briefly forgetting the horrors of the day before and the darkness still to come.

12

Syllē's happy mood lasted for only a short while after she awoke. She'd had a pleasant enough late breakfast with everyone, including Amarris' cousins and Elēandil, who, despite his elvish prejudices, had grown slightly fond of the dwarves. Syllē had moved to Tarin's chaise and was happily leaning against its back with her feet crossed under her, just watching the group laugh and harass each other. Elēandil was taking the brunt of the twins' mischief but didn't appear upset by it. In fact, the elf seemed to be enjoying himself, returning as much mischief on the twins as they were doling out to him.

Laughing heartily himself, Tarin was caught by a shift in Syllē's energy. Turning his attention to her curiously, he saw her sitting upright with her head cocked, staring intently towards the door that led to the main hall into the square. Soon, Tarin watched the happy grin slide off Syllē's face to be replaced by tired resignation.

Sighing, Syllē swung her legs to the floor, stretched a moment as if trying to forestall the inevitable, and then reluctantly rose from her seat. Catching Tarin watching her, Syllē explained, "Well, it would appear it is time to get back to the battle at hand, Tarin. I should probably go and put on something more appropriate for our day ahead and then meet you all and our visitor in Vanguard's square." Turning, she left Sigurd's Hall, heading towards the room she was sharing with Hil and Amarris.

Watching her go, Tarin called over his shoulder, "Halicyon? Is she going to be facing more dead?"

Getting up from where he had been previously watching the merriment between the twins and Elēandil, Halicyon came to stand by Tarin's side. "Yes," he responded, placing a hand gently on Tarin's shoulder.

Sighing heavily, Tarin lowered his head slightly, as if contemplating something distasteful. After a moment, he turned his head towards Halicyon and looked the elf straight in the face, "I don't do well watching those I love go into battle while I stay safe on the sidelines. It does not feel right to me."

Falinor, who had been listening, spoke up, "Tarin, there is a difference between turning your back on someone and giving them the best shot at survival you can."

Hil finally understood her brother. Stepping forward, she caught Tarin's arm and turned him towards her. Speaking just as forcefully as her brother had, she asserted, "Tarin, you didn't abandon Da. He ordered you and Bearn and Trygve to get his family to safety."

"But I left him to fight the Dark alone," Tarin's voice was harsh with pain, "and now I may have to watch that happen again to more people I love."

"Tarin," Hil continued, a little more gently now, "if you hadn't obeyed Da, Mother never would have made it out. Nor would I, and the twins would never have been born." Pulling her brother into a dwarf embrace, Hil finished, "Because of you, our people are safe and thriving in Exulias and my sons have grown into men." Stepping back and looking at Finn with a slight smirk, Hil continued, "Or at least one of them has. The other? Who knows when he'll grow up!" Hil finished, throwing her hands in the air in mock frustration.

"Hey!" Finn blustered, insulted as the group, including his uncle, laughed.

Turning back to Halicyon, Tarin asked, hope twinging his voice, "Is there nothing I can do? Am I truly just a liability?"

Halicyon placed his hand on Tarin's shoulder and looked fondly and seriously down at the dwarf. "I would much rather have you in battle beside me than leave you behind, Tarin. But if you can't see what you are fighting, I don't..." Shaking his head at the look on Tarin's face, Halicyon promised, "I will think on it, Tarin, I promise. But I really don't know what to tell you."

Tarin nodded. Taking a deep breath and slowly letting it out, he walked with Halicyon and the rest to the city square to meet their visitor.

13

The visitor turned out to be the voice behind the light wave at the gates the night before—a wizard named Gydion, although he didn't look like much to Finn. Whenever Finn had thought of a wizard, he'd imagined a tall, terrifying, ancient man with a great beard and a pointy hat obviously capable of immense destruction. This wizard wasn't that large or imposing at all. In fact, he wasn't much taller than Syllē. He did have a great beard, but it was gray and tangled and full of stuff that it seemed to have collected during the wizard's travels, like twigs and leaves and mud. Plus, this wizard didn't look very powerful. Really nothing to get excited about, which was a massive let down for Finn, who had dreamed of meeting an all-powerful wizard of lore someday. *Obviously,* Finn mused, *this isn't a great wizard. More like a wannabe wizard,* Finn smirked to himself.

Syllē wasn't smirking. She wasn't even smiling, and Finn noticed, neither was his uncle, who had taken a place standing beside where Syllē was seated. It was obvious Tarin wasn't letting Syllē get too far away from him just yet. Finn noticed that the wizard seemed intrigued by Tarin and Syllē and was trying, and failing, to stealthily study the two from under his very bushy eyebrows.

Sigurd finally broke the silence with a brusque and distrustful comment, "We haven't had many dealings with wizards in Vanguard."

"No, I should say not," the wizard answered, turning to Sigurd.

"Wizards aren't welcome where Drēors live," he finished forcefully, raising a bushy eyebrow at the master of Vanguard.

Finn finally realized what the wizard's eyebrows looked like—two large, gray, instead of brown and black, woolly worms. The realization made him smirk even more, which did not go unnoticed by the wizard.

Turning his attention to Finn, Gydion growled, "You know, wizards are known for turning impish dwarves who annoy them into all manner of unnatural things."

Tarin heard metal embedding in wood and was startled to see one of Syllē's throwing darts sunk into the table directly in front of the wizard. From the expression on the wizard's face, so was he. Neither had even seen Syllē move.

Without changing her stony expression, Syllē said tersely, "Threatening my brother is never a smart move, old man."

Glaring at Syllē, Gydion responded, slightly miffed and definitely exasperated, "This is not the reception I was expecting."

Smiling grimly, Syllē asked, "Well, what did you expect?"

"Certainly not all this disrespect!" he returned angrily. "And definitely not you," he continued a tad bitterly. "Besides, I thought you were more reasonable and smarter than most."

Tarin saw Syllē's eyes start to grow navy, which was never a good sign. Syllē spoke slowly and with forcefulness, "Yes, I was, but you taught me the truth about wizards many years ago when you got my friends slaughtered." The raw harshness of Syllē's tone broke Tarin's heart.

It must have affected the wizard adversely as well, as his eyes grew very sad. The wizard's response was full of regret, "Those deaths will forever haunt me, but they were not my fault."

"You sent us on that quest," Syllē's eyes were solid navy now. "A quest that was unnecessary and simply for your own gain, and my friends paid for it with their lives." Tarin noticed Syllē had still not moved from her seat, but her anger seemed to be growing and filling the square.

Before the wizard could respond, Falinor calmly broke into the confrontation, "Daughter, what is done is done. Learn from it and move on. Getting stuck in your memories never helps."

Tarin felt Syllē's anger slowly abate. Her eyes were still sparking navy, but she seemed calmer. Without turning her gaze from Gydion's, Syllē said, almost too calmly, "You are right, Father." Cocking her head, Syllē curtly addressed Gydion, "What has brought you to Vanguard, wizard?"

Eyeing the throwing dart still embedded in the table in front of him, Gydion took a deep breath and began, "I have noticed the encroachment of Merilik's forces into the Perdarus and beyond for some time and have sought ways to counteract him, but in vain. The rest of my order refuse to help. They say we are not wanted in this realm and, therefore, this battle is not ours to fight. I feel differently."

"Why?" Syllē asked. Tarin noticed her tone was still hard and unyielding. She must really dislike this wizard. Tarin wished he knew the reason.

"Because I love this world and all its races," Gydion answered passionately. "Plus, I took an oath to protect this realm, and standing back and hiding in my stronghold while Merilik lays claim to it is not something I can do. I cannot turn my back on my oath or this realm." Gydion stared hard at Syllē, who seemed unmoved by his speech.

"A wizard with a conscience," she responded sarcastically. "How very refreshing."

Unnerved by Syllē's viciousness, Tarin took a step towards her and touched her shoulder. He found it unsettling that this time, he was going to have to be the calm one. *Syllē, you are beginning to sound just like a dwarf.* Looking directly at her, he added with a slight grin, *Actually, you sound just like me.*

Syllē's eyes grew wide for a moment. Tarin held his breath, readying himself for her fury, but it didn't come. Instead, she suddenly smiled before laughing outright at Tarin. "Well, we can't have that, my lord, can we?"

Turning back to Gydion, Syllē asked, "So, Vanguard?" Tarin noticed that her tone was less harsh.

"I journeyed here slightly over a year ago," Gydion explained. "No sooner had I entered the gates than I was accosted by Marielle and another I did not recognize. I barely escaped the city. If it hadn't been for friends, who grabbed me and threw me into a secret passage in the market square wall over there, I never would have made it out of here alive." Gydion paused a moment before finishing, "So, I have carefully watched from afar and tried to help where I could, but sadly, I haven't been that successful. So many have died at the hands of Therendē'al and his darkness."

The look of intense sorrow on Gydion's face helped Syllē to release her last vestige of anger towards the wizard. She could tell Gydion truly felt the pain of fighting a losing battle against such a powerful enemy these past months and losing so many friends in the process. Still, she kept silent, waiting for the rest of the wizard's tale.

After a brief pause, Gydion continued. The sadness in his voice was obvious. "So, I did what I could and helped hide as many friends as I could. We would strike in small groups from a sanctuary in the mountains that hadn't been compromised and bring more friends to safety. It was during one of our raids that I found Mosslight felt less oppressed and came across a few spirits of Therendē'al's dead. I realized they had been released from his grasp, which meant Therendē'al was possibly dead, so I headed for Vanguard and saw the city surrounded by dead and the wolves and their riders trapped outside. You know the rest."

"So, you know there are more dead that must be released and a prison that must be cleansed." Syllē eyes were locked with Gydion's as she spoke.

Gydion nodded. "And I know where the prison is. It is in the old tombs of the Indili."

"Makes sense," Halicyon spoke up now. "Therendē'al would want to draw power from such a place of Light as those ancient tombs are, especially since they are the resting place of the humans of the First Age."

Tarin noticed Syllē's eyes were sparking navy again, but he didn't think it was at the wizard this time. "I consider several, who rest there, as friends. We need to return their sanctuary to them." Placing her hands on the table with a deep sigh, Syllē pushed herself up from her chair and looked at Gydion, "Well, old man, are you ready?"

Gydion rose as well and nodded at Syllē. Tarin read wariness and relief in the wizard's face.

"I should probably tell you that Halicyon and I were able to release quite a lot of the dead while trapped in the river, but there might be some elven dead left. I do not know." Syllē's voice was tired suddenly.

Gydion nodded again, "And I should tell you that I know what Therendē'al kept in those tombs. Its presence helped him control the dead." At Syllē's questioning head cock, Gydion continued ominously, "His changeling."

"Yes," Syllē nodded, not at all surprised. "We've met. The changeling is dead."

Gydion stared sternly at Syllē. "You may have killed the one he sent to Helmfirth, but I believe there may have been more."

"Which means," Syllē responded tersely, "if there were and they are in the tombs, they are exceptionally hungry right now."

"More changelings? Well, those I can see," Tarin said, obviously grasping at any reason to go with them into the tombs, "so those I can fight."

"No!" was simultaneously and forcefully shouted by the entire group.

"Well, there was no need for all of you to yell at me," Tarin muttered a tad sulkily.

14

Two days later, Tarin stood on the walls of Vanguard with Kwin, stonily watching as the group led by Syllē and Gydion disappeared into Mosslight. He had contributed a vital piece of the group's weaponry for their trek into the Indili tombs—two sets of changeling shackles like those they had made for the one Therendē'al had sent to Helmfirth. Tarin may have been the ruler of Exulias, but his father had demanded that he learn every aspect of the clan, including metal work. So, while Tarin wasn't Haldor, the master, he was a very close second because whenever Tarin did something, he did it with all that he had.

The fact that Tarin had made such an important contribution to the hopeful success of Syllē's quest into the tombs did not stifle his angst at being left behind. Tarin did not like being left when others would be facing danger. None of the dwarves were too keen on being left in Vanguard. As Kwin watched Amarris, who was walking next to Syllē, disappear into the shadows of Mosslight, Kwin could still feel the touch of her hand on his shoulder. She would be facing any number of possible changelings with Syllē, not to mention the rest of the dead, an idea that filled Kwin with a terror and dread he found very difficult to handle.

About an hour after the group had headed for the tombs, Firth found all the dwarves still standing on the wall watching the spot where their friends had disappeared. Tentatively, he addressed Tarin, "Lord Tarin?

We've found a hidden trapdoor in Therendē'al's old chambers, and Garath requested that I ask you if you would accompany us to investigate it."

Tarin turned almost gratefully from his vigil. He knew that a trapdoor in Therendē'al's chambers could house its own set of horrors; however, he was happy about the distraction from his worry over Syllē and the rest of his friends facing the dead and Asger knew what else in those tombs. Nodding his assent, Tarin swiftly followed Firth to the dead Drēor's former rooms.

* * *

Standing in Therendē'al's chamber staring at the trapdoor in the floor, Tarin hesitated. He really didn't like the smell of that door. It smelled like terror. He didn't want to even think about what had happened to the poor souls who had been forced through it. He found himself wishing that one of the elves were here or Syllē to tell him if his concerns were grounded in anything.

Swallowing hard, Tarin turned to Thēorin and said, "I want everyone to back up towards that door. If anything horrific comes out of this hole, get out and bar that door. You are to keep whatever it is from escaping into Vanguard." Staring sternly at Thēorin with more confidence than he felt, Tarin asked, "Am I clear?"

Thēorin didn't like the idea of leaving Tarin inside a room with whatever horror might come out of that trap in the floor and said so, but Tarin was adamant. Nothing was to escape into Vanguard regardless of whether he was to be left in this room with it. Thēorin argued that like Tarin, he had no desire to leave a friend behind to save himself; Trygve and Tarin's nephews seconded Thēorin's comments.

The stalemate might have continued had it not been for the master of Vanguard. Stepping forward, Sigurd sternly interjected, "Lord Tarin is right. The rest of you get behind us and follow through with his orders if necessary." Catching Tarin's eye, Sigurd continued, "This city is my responsibility, Lord Tarin, and I have failed it miserably for months now. I will not leave you to face whatever comes out of this hole alone." It was obvious by Sigurd's tone that he would broker no arguments with his decision.

Tarin nodded. Taking a deep breath to steady his own nerves, Tarin waited for the rest of the group to step reluctantly back towards the door and then purposefully and assertively pulled the latch on the trapdoor and swung it open.

15

For her part, Syllē was facing her own dark hole as she stared at the desecrated entrance to the Indili tombs. She and Gydion had made short work of the remaining dead. Thankfully, no elves remained to be released; so, the effort for them had not been as intense. Now, though, facing the tombs and feeling the darkness within, Syllē found herself wishing Tarin and the twins were by her side.

Talking to the group while still staring at the entrance to the tombs, Syllē sternly instructed, "Split into your groups and stay close to each other, because if there are changelings within, I do not want anyone to try to face one alone. That's just suicide. Use the chains and then let Gydion or I finish it."

Halicyon and Falinor moved forward to join Amarris and Syllē while Elēandil and the remaining elves joined Gydion. Taking a steadying breath, Syllē moved forward and entered the tombs while the rest followed. The sight that greeted them once inside was devastating. The final resting place of the Indili had been turned into a tomb of horror. The opening antechamber was obviously where Therendē'al had tortured his victims, as the walls were lined with chains and cuffs and stained with blood, as were the floors.

Syllē and the others could feel the terror and pain of the Drēor's victims and Syllē could taste their blood in her mouth with every breath.

Realizing she was breathing heavily, Syllē closed her mouth and slowly steadied her heartbeat, releasing her anger at what Therendē'al had not only done to the tombs of her friends but also the horrors he had inflicted on so many innocents. It helped her to know that she had ended his reign of terror, but she only wished she had somehow been sooner.

Moving through the front antechamber, Syllē's group entered the tomb's maze. She could see how Therendē'al had turned the various inner rooms into prison cells and thrown out the former occupants. Their bones lined the walls of the maze and littered the floors under their feet. Anger started to swell in Syllē again. Even once she had cleansed the tombs of Therendē'al's evil, there would be no way for her to put the Indili dead back in their proper resting places.

"Gydion," Syllē's voice was harsh from her outrage, "take your group and clear the west side. We will go east." Catching the wizard's eye as he nodded his assent, Syllē continued sternly, "Remember, changelings can't be harmed by conventional weapons. Stay together and watch each other's backs!"

For the next few hours, the groups trekked through the maze that connected the various parts of the Indili tombs. Therendē'al's evil was on full display, and it was apparent that at one time, this complex had been full of prisoners, orc, and at least one changeling. It was also apparent that someone had emptied the tombs of their prisoners shortly after Therendē'al's death and, thankfully, left no changeling behind.

Amarris found the trail they had taken out of the tombs. A back exit had been blasted into the bottom east wall of the final tomb and had a solid iron grate placed in the opening that had been left open as the orc fled the tombs with any prisoners left. Cautiously following the trail, they found it dead-ended at a river landing. Peering across the river, Syllē could just make out another landing on the opposite shore, which was shrouded in darkness. The orc and their prisoners had fled further into the Perdarus away from Vanguard and its rescuers. The darkness of the far shore gave Amarris a chill, and she wasn't the only one.

Returning to the tombs, Syllē closed and secured the grate. Sigurd and his workmen would have to safeguard the tombs with a more solid door, but until then, the grate would have to do. As Syllē turned back into the tombs, she heard a slight noise. Cocking her head, she listened intently for the sound to recur, but there was silence. Relaxing slightly, Syllē rejoined her group and started to head back towards the front of the tombs; but after only a few steps, Syllē heard the sound again.

Stopping almost in unison, Syllē, Halicyon, Amarris, and Falinor simultaneously turned back towards the final tomb with the grate in the wall. Striding purposefully to an innocuous spot on the far wall, Syllē reached into a camouflaged hole and pulled a small lever. When the door slid open, Syllē cautiously entered the hidden grave of an old friend, Dol'kah. Adjusting to the darkness of the room, Syllē was startled to find several pairs of eyes staring back at her from the recesses of the grave.

* * *

The descent into Therendē'al's private dungeon was worse than the actual dungeon. The anticipation of horror made it more terrifying than the actual room they found. It wasn't even much of a room—simply a widening of the hallway that followed. Tarin and Sigurd explored the short, twisting passage until it ended abruptly at a solid wall—or what seemed at first glance to be a solid wall—about twenty feet from where it started. Examining it closer, Tarin deciphered a portion of the wall that had been overused, so to speak. Pressing it caused a door in the wall to slide open and he and Sigurd found themselves within Vanguard's actual dungeons and, thankfully, a portion that had already been cleared.

Returning to the widened portion of the hall, Tarin studied the wall again, looking for any possible hidden doors. In one of the dark corners, he found what he was searching for. Motioning to Sigurd, Tarin opened the hidden door. The room they found was tiny—even a dwarf would not have been able to sit against the far wall and stretch their legs out fully before reaching the door. Someone had been chained to the far wall, but it wasn't the chains attached to the wall that caught Tarin's attention as he studied the small room.

Without taking his eyes off the walls, Tarin tersely informed Thēorin, who was standing by the ladder attached to the trapdoor, "Oran was in Vanguard."

* * *

"Light them," Syllē instructed Amarris and the elves as they stood in the central hub of the tomb's maze.

Quickly, six of the seven passages were aflame, cleansing the tombs of the stench and evil of the Dark. They could never put them back the way they were, but they could at least rid them of the stain of Therendē'al's reign, giving the Indili their peace back. Turning, they ran swiftly down the seventh passage back to the front room, barely ahead of the roar of the fire. It was almost as if the Indili were fanning its cleansing flames. As they passed into the final room before reaching the outside, Syllē turned and fired one last naphtha arrow. It met the flames coming from the rest of the tombs and exploded in the room, burning every trace of the Dark from the walls and floors and sending Syllē flying out the door with a searing blast of heat.

"You will live dangerously," Halicyon muttered irritably as he helped Syllē regain her feet.

Grinning at him, Syllē just shrugged, before walking beside him back to Vanguard. With them, they brought the eighteen children from Helmfirth that they had found in the hidden room in Dol'kah's tomb. It wasn't all the missing children, but it was a start.

* * *

Tarin stood with Halicyon in the small passageway under Therendē'al's old rooms looking at the wall of the hidden room. Halicyon was trying to decipher how Tarin knew that it had been Oran who had been imprisoned here. That multiple someones had been there was obvious from the scratchings in the stone wall, but Halicyon couldn't decipher anything that indicated Oran had been one of the prisoners chained to that wall.

At a total loss, Halicyon shrugged his shoulders, "Okay, Tarin. I don't see how you know Oran was chained to this wall. What am I missing?"

Tarin walked forward to a specific part of the wall where a series of letters was carved into it. Halicyon sounded it out, but he still had no idea how they indicated Oran's presence: "Thah yol ee nak eeron Xulias?" Shrugging at Tarin again, he said, "Except for that last word, it makes no sense. How does that tell us Oran was here?"

Before Tarin could respond, Syllē spoke from where she had stopped on the ladder leading into the passage, "What did you say?"

Halicyon looked at her over his shoulder. "Just some gibberish carved into the wall."

"Read it again," Syllē ordered.

Shrugging, Halicyon reread the wall, "Thah yol ee nak eeron Xulias."

Syllē's eyes met Tarin's. "Did you teach Oran that?"

Tarin nodded. Looking from Syllē to Tarin, Halicyon asked, "Okay, obviously I am missing something. How does that nonsense indicate that Oran was here?"

"It's dwarvish for, 'I am a friend of Exulias.'" It was Tarin's turn to shrug.

Halicyon pointed at the wall incredulously and asked, "That is dwarvish?" Tarin nodded. "I thought dwarves only wrote in runes."

Tarin nodded again, "We do, which is how I know this was definitely written by Oran." At Halicyon's raised eyebrow, Tarin continued to explain, "A dwarf would write this in runes, but a man, who had only been taught how to pronounce the words, would write it in sounds. I didn't teach Oran to write the runes. I taught him how to say the words."

"Ah." Halicyon understood now. "So, Oran was in Vanguard."

"Yes," Syllē answered, "which means he might still be alive."

16

Four days had passed since leaving Vanguard to continue the trek to the Perdarus. The children were on their way home to Helmfirth, escorted by Halicyon's elves, as well as Braxis and Pyrrha, whom Tarin had offered a safe place for a den in the twin mountains. Tarin had allowed himself a slight wicked grin at the thought of Tēorg's face when those two showed up at the gates. The original thirteen had grown by two as Gydion and Firth both insisted on joining them. Syllē had shrugged her shoulders and left Tarin the decision of allowing the wizard and Amarris' cousin to join their expedition, and Tarin, who believed having a wizard along who could help with any more dead they might come across was a good thing, readily agreed.

Now, at four days out from Vanguard, the world was getting darker. They had left Mosslight behind almost two days prior and were now in the Arcasian Wilds. Tarin had thought that Mosslight had been unsettling, but here in the Wilds, Tarin found himself constantly on edge. The atmosphere was eerie—devoid of sound—devoid of life. He noticed they all seemed to speak in hushed tones—afraid to let their voices carry.

Although they had started by following the orcs' trail, Syllē now had them heading directly into the Oloro Valley. Tarin wasn't sure how she knew, but Syllē said it would be the last stronghold of the light before they headed into the Perdarus, and they could hopefully glean some solid intelligence about what they might be facing. Tarin trusted Syllē but he couldn't see how they could have any allies anywhere in this desolate, lifeless territory. Tarin was exceptionally glad he was not traveling through this alone. Somehow Halicyon, Falinor, or Syllē had found them safe places to rest each night, but they were short rests each time. There was an urgency to their travel that hadn't been there before. Syllē seemed determined to get them into the safety of the Oloro Valley as quickly as possible.

As they paused once again for a rest, Tarin noticed Syllē intently studying the edges of Pangdon Forest to their right—her head familiarly cocked. Wanting to be close to her, Tarin skirted around the group causing himself to walk closer to the dark forest. Syllē's warning cry came too late. Before Tarin could react, he found himself lassoed and dragged forcefully into the air and through the trees deep into the darkness of Pangdon.

Flarne reacted quickly, throwing himself at Tarin, but he was only able to grab Tarin's foot. Syllē tried to reach them in time, deftly dodging goblin lassoes meant for her, but she was slammed into and knocked to the ground by Amarris, who was lassoed as well and heading for the depths of Pangdon. Masterfully, Thēorin shot the rope, causing it to fray as Kwin launched himself at Amarris, wrapping his arms around her legs and yanking down hard. The rope broke and the two tumbled to the ground. Syllē looked up desperately for Tarin, but he and Flarne had disappeared into the darkness of the forest.

"Stay close!" Syllē yelled behind her as she plunged into Pangdon, trying to follow the path of Tarin and his captors.

* * *

As Tarin and Flarne were dragged through the trees, Flarne valiantly increased his hold on Tarin. With no small degree of effort, Flarne had crawled upward to now grasp Tarin's waist. He had a dagger in his hand, which he obviously meant to use to cut the rope encircling Tarin's chest and pinning his arms, but that was no easy task as the pair continued to slam into tree trunks and bounce off branches. Flarne ran the risk of fatally skewering Tarin even if he was exceptionally careful.

Finally finding his balance during one particularly long ricochet arc, Flarne sliced the rope from around Tarin, causing them both to plummet quite a distance to the forest floor, bouncing off branches and tree trunks as they fell. Flarne took one truly wicked bounce, ricocheting off to the left a way before Tarin lost sight of him as he disappeared into a mulberry thicket. Then the ground rushed up to greet Tarin and he felt all the air flee his lungs. Trying to regain his footing and his senses, Tarin became horribly aware of a stench that was getting stronger—the foul stench of orc.

* * *

Syllē tracked Tarin and Flarne relatively well by simply following broken branches, and she soon reached the landing spot with the rest of the group not far behind her. There was no sign of Tarin, but plenty of sign of orc. A slight groan from the mulberry patch clued the group into Flarne's presence as hitting the ground had knocked him unconscious, which probably kept the orc off him—that and they were much more interested in Tarin.

As soon as Flarne could stand, the group was off again now following a rather blatant orc trail. Almost thirty minutes later, Syllē brought them up short. No one could really see why they had stopped, but they could all smell something in front of them. That smell of blood and rot combined. The smell of orc and goblins. Syllē could see the shapes of five men hanging by their wrists from goblin poles over low-banked fires. Something wasn't right. The fires should have been higher, and the goblins should have been dancing and jeering as the men writhed and cooked. Yet, this was not the case. It was as if something had interrupted their cooking.

Then Syllē heard it: the sound of orcs and goblins fighting. Quickly, she motioned for Falinor, Thēorin, Eirik, and Firth to cut the men down. The rest followed her carefully and stealthily towards the sounds of growling orcs and shrieking goblins.

* * *

Tarin awoke face down on the ground. No one had bothered to tie him up. He guessed they must have thought that blow to the head their leader gave him would keep him out for a while. The orcs had been interrupted by the goblins shortly after getting back to their camp. Surreptitiously, Tarin ventured a look around. Next to him were several men: two he recognized from Helmfirth, but the rest he did not know. All had their hands bound behind their backs and the two from Helmfirth also had a rope wrapped around their necks and tied to a stake behind them. Tarin heard the orcs and goblins arguing and had a horrified jolt when he realized they were arguing over him.

"He's ours," growled a particularly ugly orc, glaring at the horde of goblins menacingly advancing towards him. "We found him, and everyone knows that rule."

"Finders keepers," laughed a slightly smaller but equally ugly orc in a mockingly sing-song manner.

"We captured him," shrieked what appeared to be the goblin leader as he angrily jabbed his blade towards the orc. "We are taking him to Master! We get the reward, not pond scum like you." The goblin punctuated his final words by spitting something which reeked into the face of the first orc.

The orc disgustedly wiped his face, flinging the remnants of the foul substance onto the ground at his feet as the goblins grinned and cackled at him. Then with one swift and deadly swing of his own blade, the orc deftly decapitated the goblins' leader.

Now the battle was on, and Tarin adeptly used the fight to his advantage. As his captors were distracted, he pulled out two of his daggers and swiftly cut the ropes of the three men closest to him. Moving to the two whose necks were also tied to the stakes, Tarin deftly sliced through their bonds and was in the process of slicing the last man's hands free when he felt himself grabbed from above and again rocketed upwards into the trees. *Not again*, briefly passed through his mind before his head smashed into a tree branch, knocking him out cold.

Syllē entered the clearing just in time to see Tarin ascending swiftly back into the trees. She also noticed that the orcs and goblins had done much of her work for her, but there were still plenty to give her a slight challenge. Syllē wasn't the only one to notice Tarin's dramatic flight. The orc leader also noticed and roared his frustration at losing his prize. The goblins remaining—and there were very few—headed into the trees after Tarin, but they were quickly cut down by a barrage of arrows from both the trees and the fighters on the ground. The only captives the orc had left were the two men from Helmfirth. One was so badly injured his friend had refused to leave him behind to save himself and was desperately fighting off orcs while standing over his downed friend.

As the orc surrounded the two men, the lone fighter prepared himself for one last fight, until he caught a glimpse of someone behind the orc leader and strangely began to chuckle. "You all are so dead," said Syllē's former opponent from the Helmfirth Fall Festival, almost gleefully.

* * *

Tarin awoke yet again to the sound of arguing. And again, it was about him. He closed his eyes and tried to call Syllē, but the pain in his head exploded into thousands of pinpricks of light, causing him to grab his head in his hands. When he could focus again, Tarin opened his eyes and found himself confronted with the back of someone's right leg. It appeared the leg's owner was standing over him in a rather protective manner while arguing with another large group of legs facing them. Turning his head slightly, Tarin caught a glimpse through the foliage that made his vision blur and his stomach swirl. He had forgotten the stories of how tall the trees of Pangdon were known to grow.

Turning his attention back to the legs in front of him, Tarin heard his protector assert, "I will not take part in abandoning to orcs someone who refused to abandon us."

"Merilik has placed a huge bounty on that dwarf's head," argued a tall and lithe man in the front of the group.

"Spoken like a true Vikari," came a familiar voice as a pair of legs deftly landed to Tarin's left and joined his protector. *What is Elēandil doing here?* Tarin wondered. *He should be home in Kuaryll, not here in the Wilds.*

Elēandil's words caused quite an angry stir among the group in front of them. Their furious advance was stopped by the lethal promise of Elēandil's next words, "I have no problem killing every last one of you if you dare come any closer."

"But we can trade him for our people the orcs have stolen," the same speaker as before, obviously a leader of the group, asserted, frustrated at the resistance he was facing. "That huge bounty on his head means he's valuable to them. Valuable enough they will give us back our friends and family they have stolen."

"They will give you a place in their fires," was Elēandil's quiet and steely reply.

"You're wrong!" shouted a shorter and younger member of the group. "The orcs will trade! They told Akin so!"

The startled and upset muttering in the group alerted the young man that he had said too much. Clamping his mouth shut, he slid slightly behind Akin, who it turned out was the tall, lithe man leading the group, while the rest slowly moved away. Tarin didn't have to see Eléandil's face to see that the elf had done the customary elven eyebrow lift. Tarin could hear it in Eléandil's voice, "So, Akin has dealings with orc."

At this point, a trio arrived from the west. "Where are the rest of our people from the orc camp?" Akin questioned them, choosing to ignore the effect his young cousin's words had had on the group or possibly trying to divert everyone's attention from it.

"The she-elf and her group have them, and we tried," said Mya, a young woman with almost dwarflike runes tattooed across her neck and down her left arm. She shrugged her shoulders, "But Sparrow thinks she knew we were there because she gave us no opportunity to get to them."

"Sounds as though you're going to have to negotiate with the she-elf," Tarin's original protector snarled at Akin. "But you're obviously used to dealing with orc, so dealing with her should be much safer."

Akin's anger erupted at those comments, but his forward charge was halted by a calm, steely voice that Tarin knew well, cutting through the air just above Akin's head: "Oh, I don't know. When provoked, I am infinitely more dangerous than orc." So saying, Syllé flipped down onto the tree branch just in front of Akin, her Scylarian long knives deadly ready. Tarin didn't have to see that her eyes were solid navy. He could just tell from her voice.

17

Tarin knew he was in trouble. His head was splitting. His balance was completely off, and he was stumbling way too much. Traveling through the trees wasn't helping, since it was not a truly smooth road; but he refused to give in to the pain and nausea. So, like any dwarf, Tarin sucked it up and forced one foot in front of the other, falsely assuming no one could tell; but Tarin wasn't fooling anyone. Everyone was aware of his condition and would have assisted him if they thought the dwarf lord would accept the aid, but they knew better.

When they reached a clearing in the forest and dropped down to the ground, Tarin noticed a sheer cliff, whose top disappeared into the clouds. Looking up made him dizzy, and the horn blast from Mya's horn made him grab his head, wincing significantly. He turned at the sound of Syllē's voice to see her holding a rope that ascended into the oblivion above them. The thought of where that rope might end made Tarin's nausea go into overdrive.

As she spoke, Syllē held out her hand to Tarin and placed her right foot securely into a loop in the rope, "Take my hand, Tarin. You and I can ride up together."

Syllē released the rope when she noticed Tarin swaying slightly, trying to get his balance to walk over to her. Before she could reach him, though, Tarin heard Halicyon mutter angrily, "This is ridiculous," just before strong arms grabbed him from behind and lifted him off the ground, propelling him towards Syllē.

"I'm fine. Put me down," Tarin snarled, unconvincingly.

"No, you're not!" Halicyon shouted almost in Tarin's ear, making Tarin's head spin as pinpricks of light stabbed through his vision.

"Halicyon, don't shout at him," Syllē scolded her friend quietly. Reaching out her hand to Tarin, she caught his arm and pulled him to her.

"I did not spend the last 105 years of my life making sure Merilik never had to pay on that bounty he placed on this dwarf's head just to have him kill himself now through his own stubbornness," Halicyon firmly ranted. Leaning down so that his head was next to Tarin's, Halicyon tersely, yet more quietly, instructed the dwarf lord, "Now, Tarin, do exactly what she tells you to do, when she tells you to, or I will kill you myself." Turning on his heel, Halicyon strode angrily over to the rope that he, Trygve, and Hil were going to use to ascend into the Drengas kingdom.

Tarin's eyes began to focus again, but he avoided Syllē's gaze. He didn't want her to truly see how badly hurt he was. In fact, he was pretty sure that all those massive blows to his head had done more damage than just a concussion. He was positive that they had fractured his skull.

Syllē wouldn't be deterred. "Tarin," she said firmly, as she leaned her head down to his eye level, "let me see your eyes. Let me see how bad the damage is."

Tarin refused to turn his head, "No. I'm fine. Let's just go." Tarin made a grab for the rope and tried to figure out which of the four loops he saw floating in front of his eyes was a foothold and which were from his blurred vision, but Syllē grabbed his hands, pulling him closer to her.

Firmly, Syllē instructed Tarin, "Look at me, Tarin, now."

Keeping his head turned away from her, Tarin snarled, "You're not leaving me behind."

Syllē's eyes widened in surprise. Obviously, Tarin thought he was hurt badly enough that he would be left behind in the Drengas' kingdom. "No, Tarin, I will not leave you behind," Syllē softly assured Tarin. "I simply need to know how badly you are hurt so I know how to help…" Syllē's voice trailed off as her eyes met Tarin's. Smiling at him, Syllē murmured, "The strength of dwarves never ceases to amaze me."

Sighing heavily, Tarin pleaded, "You won't leave me behind?"

Shaking her head, Syllē responded, "No, I promise, but I need you to be honest with me. Do you need me to hold you on this rope all the way to the top, or do you have the strength to anchor us both onto this rope once we reach the cloud bank?" Syllē returned to the rope, still holding onto Tarin's arm to help steady him as she spoke.

"Why?" Tarin asked a tad testily, not happy about Syllē thinking she'd have to "carry" him in any way. Trying to appear stronger than he felt, Tarin stepped into a loop that was a level higher on the rope than the one Syllē was using. This made him an inch or two taller than Syllē. She smiled to herself when she noticed.

Tugging the rope to let the pullers know they were ready to move, Syllē deftly placed her left arm around Tarin's back and grabbed the rope, effectively locking Tarin against her—a fact that irritated him a bit, especially as they began to rise and the motion sent Tarin's nausea into overdrive, causing him to almost lose his balance. "Because I need both my hands free to effectively heal you once we reach the cover of that cloud bank." Looking steadily at Tarin, Syllē asked, "So, can you hold us both on this rope as I am holding us now?"

Tarin locked eyes with Syllē and nodded. "I won't let you fall," he promised.

Smiling, Syllē tightened her grip on Tarin and the rope with her left hand and used her right hand to reach into the small medicinal pouch hanging around her neck. Pulling out a few leaves, she held them to Tarin's mouth. "Here, chew this, but don't swallow it. When it's basically a pulp, roll it under your tongue. And I'm sorry. It's going to be bitter," Syllē admitted.

"It feels furry," Tarin complained before starting to chew. He grimaced. Syllē hadn't been lying. Whatever it was was bitter, but Tarin noticed as he chewed the leaves that his headache and nausea began to lessen. Feeling his strength returning, Tarin gripped the rope with his left hand and then threaded his right arm around Syllē's back and grasped the rope, effectively locking her against him.

He felt Syllē's arm leave his back as they began to ascend into the cloud bank. As soon as they were both hidden in the clouds, Tarin heard Syllē begin to sing quietly and saw he was being enveloped in her beautiful blue flame. As her voice filled his mind, he felt warmth flowing through his body. With each wave of warmth, the severe pain in his head abated more and more, and he heard a cracking sound like the bones of his skull being knit back together. Soon his nausea was gone. His head was clear, and he was totally rejuvenated.

Syllē's healing hymn ended and Tarin felt her slump slightly against him, resting her head on his shoulder. Before he could react to her closeness, Syllē instructed, "Spit that herb out now, Tarin. I'm just going to rest here a moment."

Tarin noticed that they were rising out of the cloud bank. He could see the others on the various ropes around them ascending the sheer cliff face. Soon, he realized the cliff face wasn't so sheer. There appeared to be homes and roads and other buildings cut into it. The thought of living in such a precarious place gave him pause.

Shortly, Tarin became aware that the others had noticed he and Syllē rise out of the cloud bank, and he became acutely aware that her head was still on his shoulder. Worried about what everyone, especially the elves, might say, Tarin muttered, "We're out of the cloud bank. Don't you want to stand up and hold yourself on now?"

"Why?" Syllē's voice was muffled against his neck. "I rather like where I am."

Irritated, Tarin tried to shrug back away from her. "We should not be this close together. It isn't appropriate. You're not…"

Syllē raised her head. Her eyes sparking navy. "A dwarf? I know. You make sure I never forget that." Looking slightly up at Tarin, Syllē tersely ordered, "Stay with me when we get off this rope. I mean it, Tarin. Don't leave my side."

It was Tarin's eyes' turn to spark with anger. Surly and irritated, he snapped, "I am not a child. I don't need you holding my hand. I can take care of myself."

Grasping the rope firmly in her right hand, Syllē tried to push back from Tarin, but his arm still held her firmly locked in. "Fine then," she testily responded. "Just move your arm and I will remove myself as far as I can from your space."

Startled by Syllē's anger, Tarin started to move his arm but then boldly grasped the rope even tighter and looked straight at Syllē. "No." Syllē cocked her head in surprise. "I rather like where you are," Tarin boldly finished, looking authoritatively down at Syllē.

Syllē's eyes widened for a moment, and then she erupted with laughter before leaning back up against Tarin. As they approached the top of the wall, Tarin contritely asked, "So, why must I stay close to you? What's the problem?"

"I don't know who is involved in the idea of betraying you to the orc other than those in this group. I can't believe I am saying this about the Drengas, but we can't trust that more aren't in league with Merilik," Syllē explained while quietly pulling her hood onto her head far enough to effectively hide her face.

Tarin noticed that her voice sounded weary, but at that point, he found they were at the end of the ascent. As he dismounted from the rope and stood beside Syllē, Tarin found himself confronted with some of the fiercest people he'd ever encountered. He really hoped they weren't in league with Merilik, because if these Drengas were, his little group was in serious trouble.

18

The Oloro Valley in the middle of the Arcasian Wilds had long been the center of the realm of the Drengas, a fierce and diverse people of formidable warriors who valued clan honor above all else. For the Drengas, battling the forces of Merilik was a duty and responsibility not to be shirked nor forgotten. It was a source of great pride for them that no Drengas had ever betrayed that duty.

The origins of the Drengas were almost as mysterious as those of the dwarves. Their royal family, now headed by King Herald, could trace their roots to the Indili and the elves of the Second Age. Thanks to this elven and Indili ancestry, the Drengas were known for having a long lifespan—easily tripling and quadrupling a normal human's. How much elf and how much Indili was in their blood was not known. Nor was known what else ran in their veins, for the Drengas were known for accepting all proven warriors, irregardless of origin race, into the Clan. Nevertheless, rumors and legends ran rampant about them—a fact that gave the Drengas a lot of amusement.

The Drengas of the Arcasian Wilds were an integrated group of three clans: the Efo, the Ursu, and the Lupan. In other words, the Boar Clan, the Bear Clan, and the Wolf Clan. The royal line drew ancestry from all three clans, binding them tightly together. Each clan had their own distinctive traits that melded well in battle. The Efo were known for their killer spear skills. They were deadly and brutally accurate from 150 yards easy. The Ursu were known for their ferocious and intense hand-to-hand combat skills. They had martial arts moves that were terrifying and deadly to opponents in battle. The Lupan were known for their endurance, strength in battle, and wicked intelligence. Independently, each clan was a fearsome opponent. Together, they were close to indomitable.

Currently, in King Herald's throne room, the Drengas' pride in their honor was shaken, and none more so than King Herald, as Akin was his adopted son. Tarin's protector, an Efo named Lothar, had explained the altercation in the trees and the subsequent admission of Akin's youngest cousin, Petr, that Akin had been negotiating with orc. Petr admitted that he had never actually seen Akin meeting with orc, but that he had been told of his cousin's attempts to find and return their people to them.

For his part, Akin remained totally silent, simply staring stoically forward, ignoring all around him. Tarin could tell that under her hood, Syllē was staring intently at Akin, studying him; and Tarin got the feeling that she didn't like what she was seeing. In reality, Syllē was studying the room more so now than Akin. She was looking for his puppet master, and when she had a pretty good idea who it was, she slowly stood.

Without looking away from the drama in the center of the room, Syllē quietly instructed the group, "Tarin, Halicyon, stay here and keep each other and everyone else safe." Turning to gaze solemnly at Tarin and Halicyon for a moment, Syllē insisted, "Watch each other's back." Halicyon and Tarin nodded slowly.

Halicyon asked softly, concerned, "What are you thinking?"

Syllē briefly met Halicyon's eyes for a moment before answering, "Wraith." Then, Syllē returned her attention to Akin before tersely saying, "Father, Gydion. With me."

Syllē quietly walked to a spot a few feet in front of Akin. Gydion and Falinor unobtrusively moved to either side of the Drengas, watching him intently. Tarin noticed the room had grown silent as the other Drengas watched and waited. He suddenly realized he was holding his breath.

Tarin was familiar with wraiths as one had infiltrated the mines of Shara somehow when he was only twenty. The encounter still gave him nightmares as the creature had killed many dwarves before his father and Guard were finally able to dispatch it. Tarin himself had almost died. If his father hadn't shown up when he did—well, the thought still made Tarin shudder.

Syllē wasn't shaking. She was steadily staring at Akin from within her hood. It was almost as if she was waiting for something. Finally, Syllē addressed Akin, "Where did you get that necklace?"

Her question confused Tarin. He didn't understand her focus on Akin's jewelry. Her question must have startled Akin as well since he jerked awkwardly, and his hand unconsciously rose towards his neck. Tarin noticed, however, that Akin never actually touched the necklace.

"My mother gave it to me." Akin's answer was hesitant and thick as though it was being forcibly pulled from him.

Syllē's tone never altered. "You mean Queen Anya?"

"No, my true mother." Akin's voice still sounded hesitant and forced. "She left it with me so I would always know who I truly am."

Before Syllē could respond, King Herald spoke, confused, "That's not possible. You weren't wearing any necklace when I found you."

"Yes, he was," Petr almost shouted from where he had been standing with his mother and older brother. Tarin noticed Petr's older brother place an apparently quieting hand on Petr's arm, but the young man shrugged it off. It was obvious he believed in his cousin Akin and was determined to defend him. Stepping forward, Petr continued, "You kept it from him, uncle, because you were afraid he would leave you to go find his true people."

Before King Herald could respond to his nephew's accusations, Syllē spoke again. Her tone was rife with that quiet steel that Tarin knew so well. "Werelings don't wear jewelry, especially not a necklace with a Drēor bloodstone as its centerpiece."

Petr's horrified look and sharp intake of breath was all the evidence of his innocence Syllē needed. He had been an unwitting pawn in another's scheme. For his part, Akin reached for the necklace. Grasping the cord, Akin ripped the necklace off his neck and held it out towards Syllē, carefully avoiding touching the bloodstone. He looked at the necklace with revulsion.

His voice soft with the betrayal he felt, Akin spoke, still not taking his eyes off the bloodstone, "I can hear her voice. She was in my dreams and my waking moments. Even now, she is telling me that I can save her." Raising his eyes to Syllē, Akin continued, "It's not her, though, is it? So, what was actually talking to me?"

"Crush the stone," Syllē instructed as she finally removed her hood and cloak and slowly unsheathed her labrys.

Tarin noticed King Herald suck in his breath when Syllē removed her hood. It was obvious that he recognized Syllē. Grabbing his sword and motioning to his guard, King Herald made ready to back Syllē up in the battle that obviously was about to erupt within his throne room.

Akin slung the necklace onto the stone floor of the chamber, but it didn't even crack. Raising his foot high off the ground, Akin brought his heel down with all his strength onto the bloodstone, pulverizing it. There was a moment of eerie silence as if the mountain itself was holding its breath, and then Akin was thrown backwards with such force he was airborne. The wereling Drengas landed hard on the stone floor, skipping slightly and coming to rest at Tarin's feet. Reaching down to grasp Akin's shoulder and pull him farther out of the battle area, Tarin's attention was caught by a bone-chilling shriek that filled the room. For just a moment, the shriek transported him back to that day in the mines of Shara; he realized he had broken out in a terrified cold sweat.

Swallowing his terror, Tarin grabbed Akin and pulled him backwards towards Halicyon. Turning, he saw the wraith attacking Syllē, and it was as terrifying as that day in the Shara mines. The wraith dwarfed Syllē and its frigid darkness seemed to fill the room. Tarin watched as the eerie blue light of Syllē's labrys cut through the creature's darkness, sending it back into the center of the room. Looking for easier prey, the wraith advanced on Petr, but Falinor blocked its progress.

Wraiths had many weapons, but their greatest weapon was that bone-chilling shriek, as that shriek could cause the wraith's enemies to falter and stall, giving the fiend a chance to dispatch its opponent. This wraith's shrieks, however, did not deter the Drengas or Syllē. Seeing this, the wraith's darkness started to build and spread through the room as the wraith slung its attackers against walls and pillars.

Falinor was slammed into one of the stone pillars holding up the throne room's roof, rattling him a bit. The wraith was following up its attack, intending to kill the elf, when Petr stepped in its way. The wraith forcefully slung the young man into the air and across the room. Before Eleandil rejoined the battle by Farinor's side, the elf deftly grabbed Petr and placed his limp body next to Akin, who had regained consciousness and was shaking his head trying to clear it.

Casting his mind back, Tarin recalled how Farin had dispatched the wraith that invaded Shara. Quickly, he grabbed a handful of naphtha from Amarris' bag and then grabbed a Drengas spear from off the nearest pillar and rubbed the naphtha along the whole shaft of the weapon as he began to walk swiftly towards Akin.

Halicyon grabbed Tarin's arm. "Tarin…" the elf began, the warning evident in his tone.

Undeterred, Tarin tersely cut Halicyon's warning short. "Just follow her orders and watch my back." Responding to Halicyon's raised eyebrow, Tarin asserted, "You have to trust me." Halicyon studied him a moment before nodding.

Tarin and Halicyon approached Akin. Without taking his eyes off the battle raging in the center of the room, Tarin asked the wereling, "You're a wereling, so can you use your animal form to force the wraith towards this room's central fire?"

Halicyon resignedly shook his head as he realized Tarin's plan. It was bold with a high probability of failure, but Halicyon noted that seemed to work for the dwarf. Sighing, the elf drew his sword and prepared to follow his friend into battle. At least a wraith wasn't a Malrauk.

Akin's eyes grew wide for a moment at Tarin's question. He'd only changed once in his entire life when he'd grown angry at his father for some punishment. He'd been twelve at the time and had awakened to find himself chained to a wall. When he'd seen his father, the man had been covered in deep scratches and some nasty bites. Akin had made sure that he never changed again. Now this dwarf was asking him to do just that. Looking at his father and guard being slung around the room by the wraith and his cousin out cold next to him, Akin made a decision.

The answer to Tarin's question came in the form of one of the most terrifying growls he'd ever heard. Then, a huge white shape bolted past him towards the wraith. Grabbing the demon in his mouth, Akin slung it away from Syllē and towards the fire pit. Regaining its feet, the wraith flung itself at Akin, but the wereling hit it with his paw, slinging the wraith back. In short order, Akin had the wraith right up against the fire pit, and Tarin acted quickly. His hands burning from handling the naphtha bare-handed, Tarin surged forward and drove the spear through the wraith and into the fire. The wraith hit Tarin hard, slinging him backwards towards Syllē, who had started to run forward to Tarin's aid as soon as she'd seen him enter the battle. The hit to Tarin was the wraith's last as the fire ignited the naphtha on the spear, rapidly incinerating the demon. King Herald threw a robe over his son as soon as Akin returned to human form and hugged him tightly. Syllē smiled at the exchange before turning her attention back to Tarin, who was being helped to his feet by Halicyon.

Angrily, she scolded both the dwarf lord and elf, leaning forward so that only they could hear, "I swear if you two just undid all my work from earlier…"

Without missing a beat, Tarin retorted, "Like we would ever allow you to fight one of those things without us. You should know better than that by now," Tarin finished, rising to his full height and glaring defiantly back at Syllē, who was irritably scowling at Halicyon's gleeful grin.

Before she could respond, Lothar stepped forward and slapped Tarin admiringly on the back, "Well, that settles it. You are definitely Efo."

Mya moved forward, grinning, "No, he's definitely Ursu. To push through injuries that would have sidelined many a Drengas and still find the strength to take that thing out is proof enough for me."

Smiling, Queen Anya spoke, "Based on his quick thinking in this battle, I would say that the dwarf is actually Lupan."

"Well, while I have been called an 'insufferable boar' before," Tarin laughingly responded, winking at Syllē, "I am Tarin, son of Farin, a dwarf of the line of Asger."

King Herald stood next to his son and smiled admiringly at Tarin. "So, you are the dwarf who has so terrified Merilik that he has placed a monstrous bounty on your head." Nodding firmly, King Herald walked towards Tarin and continued, "Whatever else you might be, one thing is certain—you are definitely Drengas." Then the king of the Drengas reached out and firmly grasped Tarin's arm with both his hands, bowing slightly to the dwarf as he did.

Tarin's eyes grew wide for a moment at the praise before he returned the Drengas king's salute. Out of the corner of his eye, Tarin could see a broad grin spreading across Syllē's face.

19

The atmosphere in King Herald's throne room after the battle with the wraith was considerably tense. The fact that someone had dared to use a Drēor bloodstone to manipulate and mislead Akin and allow a wraith into the Drengas stronghold—a place where no fiend of Merilik's had ever set foot inside until now—had the clans out for blood. If it hadn't been for King Herald ordering his guard to protect his nephew, the still unconscious Petr would have been strung up and lynched by many of the irate warriors. Tarin wasn't sure that might not happen anyway. There weren't too many in the King's guard who appeared very happy about their assigned task.

Now, everyone was waiting. Uneasiness, anger, and vengeance permeated the room, filling Tarin with trepidation. It was obvious they were waiting for someone to begin rooting out the traitor, and not a single Drengas in that room felt safe with their neighbor—something that'd never happened before. Their uncertainty tainted the mood in the room even more, causing the air to tighten with friction and Tarin to wonder about the safety of his little group.

"What's a bloodstone?"

Tarin started at his nephew's voice. It seemed to shriek into the tense atmosphere of the room—grating against already fiercely raw nerves. Finn, as usual, was oblivious to the tension around him or perhaps he just chose to ignore it. Tarin scowled at his nephew and would have scolded Finn for his idiocy; but Syllē spoke up first.

Looking up briefly from Tarin's hands, which had been burned from handling the naphtha barehanded, Syllē smiled grimly at Finn, "It's a gemstone a Drēor has corrupted with the blood of elves or men to his or her purposes. In this case, it was the prison of a wraith meant to manipulate Akin."

Syllē returned her attention to Tarin's hands, carefully and gently rubbing Hil's proffered salve over the burns. Tarin could hear her voice chanting quietly in his head as she rubbed. Soon, he noticed a faint blue flame mixing with the salve. As Syllē's chant ended, she turned to Hil. Nodding at the healer, Syllē left the bandaging of Tarin's hands to his sister.

Turning back towards the room, Syllē almost too nonchalantly took a seat next to Tarin, draping her arm carelessly across one raised knee. Her closeness and the tension in the room caused Tarin to straighten, unconsciously standing as tall as he could, glaring almost ferociously at the rest of the room, daring the traitor to even think about harming Syllē. Soon, Syllē felt their entire group take protective positions around her, causing her customary grin to spread across her face.

Addressing Akin, who was standing between his father and mother, Syllē asked, "So, I take it Petr gave you that bloodstone, saying it was from your wereling mother?" Akin nodded. Turning her attention to Petr, who was awake and now being kept between Falinor and Elēandil—more for Petr's protection than anything else—Syllē asked the young Drengas, "Who gave you that bloodstone?"

Petr shook his head. "No one. I took it from Uncle's jewel box in his rooms."

Syllē tried another tact. "But who told you about it? Who told you the false tale of the bloodstone and where to find it?"

Petr hesitated, his eyes betraying his uncertainty. Before Syllē could push Petr any further, she heard Halicyon whisper worriedly, "Tarin?"

Turning her head towards Tarin, Syllē noticed Halicyon's eyes grow wide. At almost the same time, the elf grasped his sword hilt tightly while stepping towards Tarin. "Are you sure?"

"Is he sure about what?" Syllē's concern and slight irritation at being left out of the conversation was evident in her voice.

Tarin simply nodded. Halicyon whirled towards Falinor. "Shackles," he instructed tersely, holding out his free hand.

Quickly, Falinor threw one of the pairs of Tarin's changeling shackles towards Halicyon, but Halicyon was slammed into from behind by a Drengas—Petr's older brother, Athos—the same Drengas who had tried to keep his little brother quiet earlier. It didn't take long for Halicyon to sling the young man off himself and towards King Herald and his guard, who were still protectively close to Petr. Athos regained his feet quickly and lunged towards his brother with his dagger drawn, but he wasn't quick enough. Before he could stab his brother, Athos was tackled and roughly dragged into the center of the room by Lothar, who adeptly and easily held the would-be assassin still.

Halicyon, meanwhile, had regained his feet and retrieved the shackles. "Where?" he asked Tarin, without taking his eyes off the dark recesses of the room behind him.

"I don't smell it now," Tarin hissed, surveying the whole room.

Syllē stayed close, understanding now what the two were talking about. Surveying the room, Tarin noticed that Syllē was also searching and not finding what she seemed to know was there. The tension in the room had grown as the Drengas understood that there was yet another grave danger hiding amongst them. Stepping forward, Tarin strained to catch another whiff of the changeling he had smelled as Syllē was interrogating Petr, but to no avail. He knew that thing couldn't just disappear, but where had it gone?

Kwin, who was standing towards the back of the group near Amarris, suddenly got a whiff of something truly foul. Turning to look at Amarris, Kwin saw what he thought was a Drengas woman slinking towards Amarris. *She can't be the source of that smell.* Kwin started to scan elsewhere when the woman caught his eye again. He was startled to notice that her eyes were solid black—no pupils, no color, no white, just solid black. As he studied her more closely, he realized that the foul smell was only getting stronger the closer she came to them. It was what Kwin noticed next, however, that spurred him into action. The woman began to reach for Amarris, and as she did, her hand seemed to transform into a black claw and her face dissolved into liquid black with an open mouth of fangs and a long, slithery tongue.

"Amarris, look out!" Kwin shouted as he grabbed her wrist and slung Amarris behind him.

Before he could draw his axe or sword, Kwin's chest encountered the black claw of the changeling. He felt a searing pain that almost brought him to his knees as the changeling ripped open his chest, but like his uncle, he refused to fall and allow the changeling access to its target. Thankfully, Halicyon surged past him and threw the shackles onto the changeling's neck. The changeling then proceeded to drag the elf closer to the center of the room as it looked for an escape. Thēorin grabbed Halicyon, helping the elf to his feet before grasping one of the chains attached to the shackles. They were quickly aided by nearby Drengas, and soon the changeling was sort of subdued in the middle of the room.

Tarin wasn't sure where to go—to his nephew or to help take on the changeling. He was surprised that Syllē didn't seem to be doing anything. She was simply standing frozen. Tarin caught a look at her face and instantly understood why. She was staring at Kwin, who Hil, Queen Anya, and Amarris were desperately working on to stop the blood and shut up his severe wound. But Tarin could tell it wasn't Kwin Syllē was seeing lying on that floor.

Grabbing her hand, Tarin roughly turned Syllē towards him. *Syllē. We need you.* As Syllē's eyes suddenly focused on his face, her hand reached up and gently cradled his cheek before she suddenly reached out and fiercely hugged Tarin to her. Shortly, Tarin felt Syllē's breathing calm and her heart steady. Stepping back, Syllē smiled grimly at him before she walked past him towards the changeling. Joining Gydion, Syllē had the wizard fire the blade of her labrys. Using the wizard's fire, she deftly chopped the head off the changeling before ordering the Drengas to burn the body in the same fire that had consumed the wraith.

20

Kwin awoke to a tightness in his chest and an almost fiery warmth spreading throughout his torso. He tried to take a breath, but it hurt too much, and he started coughing. Keeping his breaths shallow, Kwin opened his eyes and looked around. He was lying on a rather comfy bed within a spacious room carved out of the stone of the mountain. There were intricate carvings of stylized animals and battle scenes decorating the walls, which were also hung with thick, colorful tapestries that depicted what Kwin thought must be scenes from Drengas legend.

Looking more closely around the room, Kwin saw instruments and herbs like what his mother had in her healing room. Kwin also noticed that his wasn't the only bed in this room. Nor was his bed the only one occupied. Several of the survivors of the group from Helmfirth, who had been rescued from the orcs and goblins, were also resting in beds. Among them, Oran and Thēorin's good friend, Hern, who, thinking that everyone else had forgotten Oran, joined the ill-fated group on a rescue mission. They were betrayed by the cousin of Syllē's Helmfirth Festival opponent— a man named Borax. Only five of the twelve who had left Helmfirth were still alive. The rest had fallen victim to the traitor and his orc and goblin allies.

Carefully turning his head since it hurt his chest a bit to move, Kwin slowly focused in on Syllē, who was stretched out beside him in the bed.

Raising his head slightly to look up at her, Kwin's eyes met hers.

Searching his eyes deeply, Syllē allowed herself a relieved grin at the strength she saw there, "Well, brother. Just like your uncle, I see? Taking on changelings without a second thought." Syllē shook her head amusedly. "So, how do you feel?"

Kwin started to shrug his shoulders but stopped at the sharp pain that stabbed through his chest. Coughing slightly, he finally answered honestly, "My chest hurts and I can't breathe very deeply."

"No headache? No fever?" Syllē asked, placing her hand lightly against Kwin's forehead.

Kwin carefully shook his head in response. "Just the chest pain."

"How bad is the pain?" Looking sternly at Kwin, Syllē continued, "Truth, Kwin."

"It's sharp but not searing, if that makes sense," Kwin responded.

Leaning forward, Syllē gently kissed Kwin's forehead before getting up from the bed and stretching a moment. "I swear, Kwin, you and your uncle are going to be the death of me," Syllē sighed. Kwin was surprised to hear a twinge of sadness in her voice. Syllē pulled a chair close to Kwin's bed and sat down. Propping her feet on the bed, Syllē folded her hands across her lap and stared affectionately at Kwin. "So, little brother, what were you thinking?"

Her question startled a truly honest answer out of Kwin, "That Amarris was in danger." Syllē quickly leaned forward to help Kwin as he struggled slightly to sit up.

Once Kwin was comfortably installed against the headboard of the bed, Syllē sat back again in her chair and smiled fondly at him, "So, what did you two decide? Did you tell her how you feel about her?"

Kwin shook his head, "You were wrong. She isn't interested in me."

Syllē's eyes sparked navy. "So, she was just using you?"

"No," Kwin quickly defended Amarris. "She just realized after kissing me that we're better as friends, and that's what she wants from me," Kwin finished sadly.

Syllē looked kindly at Kwin, speaking softly but firmly, "You treated her abominably for days after she showed you—actually, showed everyone—how she truly felt about you. You," Syllē emphasized by pointing directly at her brother, "rejected her rather publicly. No wonder she responded as she did."

"Well," Kwin rather stubbornly responded, "she said she just wanted to be friends, so that's all we are."

"Coward," Syllē affectionately chided Kwin. "Do you know why I am the one sitting here with you right now?" She cocked her head at Kwin as she spoke.

Kwin shook his head. "I assume she wasn't all that worried about me," he responded sadly, looking down at his hands.

"Wrong," Syllē smugly informed Kwin. "I am the only one here because it took your mother, Firth, Thēorin, and Eirik to remove Amarris from your bedside to take a bath, eat some food, and rest. She only agreed to leave when she was promised that she could come back and rest here in that bed beside you, and even then, she went extremely reluctantly. That, my dear brother, is more than a mere feeling of friendship." As if to punctuate her beliefs, Syllē crossed her arms and stared Kwin down.

Kwin glared at Syllē. Why was she raising his hopes when Amarris had already dashed them? He'd told Syllē on the walls of Vanguard that women like Amarris didn't fall in love with dwarves and he'd been right. Why did she seem bent on rehashing his pain?

Syllē read Kwin's anger and pain in his look. Smiling fondly at him, she asked, "Do you love Amarris? Truth, Kwin."

"I already told you that I did. I also told you that women like her don't fall in love with dwarves," Kwin spat, frustrated.

"And what kind of woman would that be?" came an equally angry and frustrated voice from the door.

Kwin froze. His discomfort and surprise written all over his face. Syllē, however, grinned. Standing up, she leaned down until her face was level with Kwin's. Her amusement with her brother evident in her face and voice, Syllē quietly instructed Kwin, "Well, brother, I would answer her question honestly, and I would also tell her exactly how you feel about her this time." Syllē kissed Kwin on the temple before straightening up and turning to leave him. She grinned at Amarris, who was now standing at the foot of Kwin's bed, hands firmly on hips, glaring at the dwarf, who was refusing to look up from his hands in his lap.

"So, Kwin," Amarris began, anger evident in her tone, "what kind of woman am I?"

Syllē made it to the group at the door and forcefully shooed them out it. Finn, however, was having too much fun with his brother's discomfort to willingly leave, so Syllē grabbed him by his collar and slung him rather forcefully into the hall. As she turned to shut the doors of the healing room behind her, Syllē was pleased to see that Kwin must have answered Amarris' question correctly.

"Remember, healing rooms are public places!" Syllē called good-naturedly to the pair as she shut the doors.

21

"How's Kwin?" Tarin asked Hil as she entered the Drengas banquet hall where he had been sitting with Halicyon and Falinor and his new friend, Lothar, eating and swapping stories.

"Oh, he's awake and being tenderly cared for by Amarris," Hil amusedly informed her brother as she sat down across from him at the table.

"I bet he is," Trygve laughed outright.

Hil glared at Trygve, but Tarin cut off any angry retort she might have made. "So, they finally got together, did they? Good. It's about time." Catching Finn's incredulous look, Tarin asked almost irritably, "What? I see nothing wrong with those two having a relationship. She's not a dwarf, but..." Tarin shrugged carelessly and grinned. "...to borrow a phrase from you, 'we can't all be perfect.'"

Halicyon's laughter exploded into the room, causing the rest of the group to chuckle or grin as well. Tarin's irritation began to rise. "What is so funny?"

"Seriously, brother?" Hil answered. "You, the eternal dwarves-must-stick-with-dwarves spouter, is asking why your comments are amusing to the rest of us?"

Tarin grinned sheepishly in response. "I can learn like everyone else." Trygve harrumphed before covering his amusement by taking a long draught of the Drengas brew.

Finn, who was also enjoying a pint of the Drengas beer, which is possibly what made him so careless, grinned mischievously at his uncle, "Actually, I am not surprised that you are for Kwin and Amarris. I was more surprised you noticed there was a relationship between the two. You are a tad oblivious to the feelings of others, especially those of the romantic bent," Finn finished with an insolent shrug and another big gulp of his drink.

Tarin looked sharply at his nephew, but before he could respond, Hil slapped the back of her son's head hard. "If you're not careful, my son," she warned Finn, "you'll find yourself being slung across this room, instead of just out a doorway, and it would be warranted."

Rubbing his head, Finn retorted irritably, "Uncle wouldn't sling me anywhere."

"I wasn't referring to your uncle," Hil ominously answered while staring pointedly at her son.

Finn started to respond, but movement behind Tarin caught his eye. Syllē was standing there glaring at Finn, looking more than ready and quite capable of slinging him again. Catching her eye, Finn wisely shut his mouth, covering his discomfort with yet another gulp of Drengas beer.

"I'd watch how much I was drinking if I were you, little brother." Syllē's voice was twinged with anger and warning. "You know how potent Drengas beer is. Let's not have a repeat of two nights ago, because you might end up missing a few parts if you attempt to crawl in bed with me again."

Finn, who was raising his mug to his lips, immediately thought better of finishing his beer. Placing the mug back on the table in front of him, Finn looked across at Syllē, trying to appear contrite. Unable to contain himself, though, he grinned rather impishly at her.

"A very wise decision, Finn, but I'd lose that ridiculous grin," Halicyon advised the young dwarf.

Focusing in on Halicyon, Finn asked, "Did you know there was a bounty on my uncle's head?"

Before Halicyon could respond, Tarin spoke up, "I meant to ask you before but forgot. What did you mean by you've spent the last 105 years of your life keeping Merilik from collecting on the bounty? I only just met you a few months ago."

Halicyon laughed almost to himself before responding, "I've been patrolling your twin mountains for the last 105 years keeping Merilik's bounty hunters at bay. Over the years, Elēandil has been on my patrols several times as well." Halicyon shrugged.

To say Tarin was surprised would be an understatement. He was speechless. It was Finn who further questioned Halicyon, "But I thought you hated dwarves. Why would you risk your life to keep my uncle safe?"

"Because my king and queen requested I do so when they found out about the bounty on Tarin's head," Halicyon answered. "But if I am being truthful, I really did it for myself."

The dwarves looked wonderingly at Halicyon. "What do you mean? How could keeping my brother alive help you?" Hil questioned.

Halicyon's face darkened slightly as he said, "I lost everything and everyone—my wife, my son, and then Syllē—and was in danger of turning Drēor, if I'm being honest. Keeping Tarin alive became my crusade. I would keep him alive and out of Merilik's hands because Syllē had loved Farin and his people so much. So, I protected him for her, and ultimately, that saved me." Syllē, who was still standing behind Halicyon and Tarin, stared at him, her love for the elf apparent on her face.

Stepping forward, Syllē hugged Halicyon tightly from behind, leaning her forehead against his temple. "I am so sorry that I was not there to help you with that battle," Syllē murmured softly, her forehead still pressed against Halicyon's temple.

Standing and turning to her, Halicyon placed his hands gently on Syllē's shoulders, leaned his forehead against hers, and said softly, "But you were with me. You and Dol'kah."

Tears slid silently down Syllē's face as she leaned against her friend. They had both lost so much. Everyone had. She was determined that from now on, they were going to start having some wins.

"So that's why we kept seeing tons of sign of elf near and around the mountains," Trygve breathed incredulously. "You were protecting us, not spying on us." He gazed at Halicyon with wonder, but also—Trygve shook his head almost violently. This was getting absurd. It was bad enough he liked the Valaraii. He couldn't start liking elves, too.

At this point, King Herald approached them. "Speaking of that bounty," he began, "it appears that Merilik has changed what he wants. He no longer wants Tarin's head. He wants the dwarf alive."

"How do you know that?" Falinor asked.

"Athos refused to tell us how long it's been since the changeling took his mother, so we searched their quarters for answers and found this," King Herald said and handed Falinor a hide with what Tarin thought looked like random black slashes across it. Tarin quickly realized that they were more than slashes as he watched Falinor's face drain of color before it became flushed by sheer rage. Halicyon reached for the hide, and Tarin watched his face become transformed by fury as well. He caught a glimpse of Syllē's face as she read the bounty. Her laughter at what she read wasn't joyful, though. It was short and sharp.

Finn, his curiosity piqued by the elves' reactions and the rather ominous tone of King Herald's speech, asked, "So, is anyone going to tell us what that says?"

Halicyon tried, but he couldn't speak past his fury. Falinor, as well, was unable to answer Finn. Tarin grew concerned at the elves' anger. Their cold fury seemed to be filling the room and filling him with trepidation.

King Herald finally answered Finn, "It still promises payment for Tarin's head, but it offers an even bigger prize if Tarin is delivered alive, along with someone else."

"Who?" Tarin asked.

"The person is only described as your 'she-elf lover,'" King Herald answered with a slight shrug.

"But I don't have…" Tarin stopped and looked up with horror as he suddenly realized who the bounty meant. "Why does he want us alive?" Tarin harshly spit out his question. His own fury was rising.

"So that you must watch them torture her before you die, most likely," Halicyon savagely answered. His wrath, while finally under his control, was still apparent in every part of him.

Finn started to ask who the she-elf was, but Tarin stood and firmly gazed at Syllē. Speaking deliberately, Tarin reminded Syllē, "I made you a promise many months ago, Syllē, when you lay in Hil's healing room with that blade in your leg. I will keep it before I ever let Merilik's underlings harm you in any way."

Syllē's eyes widened a moment before she smiled sadly but affectionately at the dwarf lord.

22

Nearing day's end, Tarin sat on one of the fortification walls, looking out across the Wilds. The group was waiting for Kwin to heal a little more from his chest wound before continuing their journey. While waiting, Syllē had taken him along with the elves and Trygve on a few Drengas patrols through the mountains. It was good reconnaissance and Syllē had pinpointed their destination—the old kingdom of the werelings.

Tarin had just come from a meeting with King Herald after yet another patrol and learned quite a bit about the wereling kingdom. They had been a great ally of the Drengas for many ages, helping to keep Merilik and his forces bottled into his small domain in the far north and stopping any encroachment into the Perdarus and beyond. However, they suddenly disappeared from their kingdom—almost overnight—long before King Herald assumed the throne of the Drengas.

Herald had led a group of Drengas into the mountains to the wereling kingdom, but they were ambushed by an army of the Dark led by a Drēor, who sounded a lot like Therendē'al, before they could reach the wereling kingdom's entrance. It was almost a total loss for the Drengas, but Herald was able to rally his warriors with the help of one of his best—Anya, the woman he eventually made his queen—and they valiantly fought their way home. It was during the battle that he heard something in a crevice that turned out to be a skillfully hidden child, Akin. Obviously, the werelings were gone, but the Drengas never found out to where or if they had been exterminated.

Tarin had also learned at the previous night's dinner why Elēandil was with them. Elēandil had made sure that the children were delivered to Helmfirth and Braxis and Pyrrha made it to Exulias safely. (A slight, mischievous grin had passed across the elf's face when he described Tēorg's first response to the wolves, which had given Tarin and the rest a lot of amusement, too.) Then, Elēandil and the other elves headed home to Kuaryll; however, when he reached the elven kingdom, Elēandil found himself continuing. He walked in the front gate and all the way through to the rear gate without even thinking why and just kept going. In fact, he didn't really seem to realize what he was doing until he was past Vanguard and fully in the Pangdon Forest.

Now, Tarin sat on the wall mulling over everything he had learned as well as really wondering if he would be able to keep his promise to Syllē. When he'd made her that promise, he'd barely known her. She was just an old friend of his father. Now…Tarin paused in his musings. What was she to him now?

Before he could answer that question, he was startled by Halicyon joining him on the wall. "I have never understood the fascination with high places," Halicyon mused as he sat down next to Tarin and looked out across the Wilds, too.

Tarin laughed slightly to himself before answering, "I like it because it reminds me that I am part of something immense. Something much bigger than me and Exulias, and I find that oddly comforting," Tarin finished with a slight shrug.

Without taking his eyes off the vastness in front of him, Halicyon smiled. Yet again, Tarin was finding a way to surprise him. The pair sat quietly together for quite a long time, each lost in their own thoughts. Just as Tarin was about to speak, his attention was drawn by movement in a far valley. Something—or a lot of somethings—was coming down from the mountains and heading their way. Tarin started to alert Halicyon to what he was seeing, but the elf grabbed him by the arm and pulled him back off the wall and onto the platform before he could utter a word. Before either could alert the Drengas of the encroaching darkness, Tarin heard the Drengas' battle horns. He was impressed by how quickly the warriors responded to the wall.

Suddenly, Halicyon leaned quickly forward, staring intently at the army approaching the Drengas' stronghold. Tarin noticed the elf's eyes widen with alarm. "What? What is it?" Tarin asked, concerned. He stared towards the enemy advancing towards them, but other than their vast numbers, he really couldn't discern anything alarming.

"Basilisks," Halicyon replied ominously, as King Herald and his warriors began to prepare for the invasion.

"Order the Telimactar to the walls!" King Herald yelled as Syllē, Amarris, and Kwin arrived.

Stepping forward and pulling out her labrys, Syllē prepared to be hooked into the rope system for the Telimactar. Tarin watched as her navy light enveloped her and then disappeared into her just like on the boat to Kilead. He reasoned that the light wave must have something to do with her emotions, especially before battle. Shrugging his shoulders, Tarin was about to get hooked into the ropes as well, but like everyone else on the wall, was stopped by Halicyon's voice.

"You cannot use the Telimactar. It would just be suicide—their suicide," Halicyon announced. "There are at least two basilisks heading towards the walls."

The news seemed to suck all the air out of the Drengas, but Halicyon noted that Tarin was chuckling, which the elf found a tad irritating. Turning to the dwarf lord, Halicyon demanded, "What is so funny about basilisks, Tarin?"

Grinning at the elf, Tarin happily responded, "For once, my being a dwarf is actually an asset, instead of a liability."

At Halicyon's arched eyebrow inquiry, Tarin continued with a slight shrug, "Dwarves are immune to the poison of the basilisk's stare." Turning to the rest of the dwarves, Tarin ordered, "All of you strap in and, except Kwin and Hil, get ready to go over the walls." Looking at his nephew and sister, Tarin instructed, "Hil, Kwin, command the archers. Stand on the wall and call out locations of the enemy to the elves and the Drengas. Be aware of their archers as well. Don't get shot."

Smiling broadly at Tarin, Syllē continued his instructions, "Kwin, Hil, warn of troop movements, but also, keep your eye on the snakes. A properly placed naphtha arrow can ignite their venom sack in the back of their mouths. Tarin, Trygve, with me. We have some snakes to slay."

"Wait, where are you going?" Halicyon demanded, barring Syllē's access to the wall.

"To fight beside Tarin and Trygve," Syllē answered, slightly perturbed at Halicyon's actions.

"But the basilisks——"

"Don't affect me either."

Halicyon growled slightly with frustration as he pulled Syllē towards him into a brief embrace before releasing her and getting out of her way. "Make sure you return," Halicyon murmured quietly as Syllē started past him towards the wall. Stopping briefly, she caught the elf's hand, interlacing her fingers with his for a moment before continuing towards the wall.

Battle axe in hand, Tarin took a deep breath and slowly released it. Turning to Trygve, who was harnessed and ready on his right, Tarin curtly nodded and then began moving towards the wall. As he drew closer to the edge, he saw a flicker of a forked tongue followed by the tip of a basilisk's mouth. He was briefly taken aback at the size of the snake; its head was slightly larger than a dwarf. Before he could react to the presence of the viper, he heard Syllē's battle cry as she surged past him. Leaping onto the wall, Syllē flat-sided the exposed bottom of the serpent's head, causing it to lose its grip on the wall and hurtle back down to the ground far below where it smashed into and crushed a large group of orc and goblin.

"Show off," Tarin growled affectionately at Syllē as he stood beside her on the wall, looking down at the chaos created by the basilisk's fall.

He was rewarded with Syllē's broad grin before she deftly leapt off the wall, her battle cry reverberating across the mountains. She was closely followed by Trygve and to their left, Finn, Varger, and Flarne leapt into battle. Tarin briskly started to go over the wall as well but was stopped by Halicyon's worried voice calling his name. Turning, Tarin saw the stricken face of the elf, and he understood exactly how Halicyon felt. For once, it was the elf being left behind and not him.

Standing tall, Tarin placed his right fist over his heart while bowing his head slightly at Halicyon. With a serious smile, Tarin saluted his friend, "Aat borthan, Khâzash,"[5] before joining Syllē and the rest over the wall.

The battle went rather well considering the massive force of orc and goblin paired with the remaining basilisk. Kwin and Hil called out enemy locations to the archers and spear throwers, giving much needed coverage to Finn, Flarne, and Varger as they kept the west side clear. Syllē, Trygve, and Tarin battled the remaining basilisk, keeping it from gaining any ground up the wall and knocking out orc and goblin that got in the way. Kwin and Hil both kept a sharp lookout for any opportunity to shoot it, but the snake refused to open its mouth wide enough for an arrow to get through and hit the venom sack.

Since the remaining basilisk was being kept busy by Syllē, Tarin, and Trygve, Akin was able to take a large squad of Drengas and engage many of the orc and goblin on the ground at the base of the stronghold, keeping a large portion of the Dark's army off the walls entirely. Kwin figured

---

5   "Always strong, Brother."

out how to give them some coverage by calling archers to shoot at certain spots effectively mowing down sections of the dark army coming in behind the front guard and keeping the orc and goblin off Akin and his Drengas. Even with these successes, though, the battle wasn't a given, especially with the remaining basilisk free and wreaking havoc upon the walls and lower avenues as it tried to flee Syllē and the dwarves.

Finally, the three had the basilisk trapped on the wall. Syllē had taken her sword and driven it through the side of the basilisk, effectively pinioning its body to the wall, albeit briefly. Trying to force the advantage, Trygve drove straight at the snake's head, trying to get it to strike and open its mouth. Instead, the snake slammed him with its head, sending the dwarf careening across the wall. Thankfully, his ropes held, but he was knocked off kilter and needed a moment to regain his senses and his balance.

Now trying to use its advantage, the basilisk raised its barbed tail and aimed to skewer Trygve into the mountain wall with it. Seeing this, Syllē quickly got in between the dwarf and the barb, knocking it back away from Trygve. Unfortunately, the barb sliced clean through her ropes, effectively detaching her. Falling down the wall, Syllē desperately tried to grab a ledge or handhold before she plummeted all the way to the ground, hundreds of feet below her. About a quarter of the way from the bottom of the wall, she was successful in grasping a small outcrop, but having to hold onto the wall with both hands left her vulnerable to attack—a fact that the basilisk intended to exploit.

The force needed to rip itself free of Syllē's sword caused the basilisk to fall slightly farther down the wall than where Syllē was hanging, but it quickly regained its grip on the stones and almost gleefully headed rapidly towards where Syllē was dangling helplessly. As it neared her, it reared its head up, opening its hood and mouth, which effectively blocked the archers above from the venom of its stare. It was the moment Kwin had been waiting for, and he called urgently to Amarris and Halicyon.

Two well-placed naphtha arrows hit their mark and the basilisk's venom sacks exploded. The percussion of the explosion caused Syllē to lose her grip on the wall and she fell, ricocheting her way to the bottom where she lay unconscious and vulnerable to the orc and goblin in the valley below—a fact that caused Tarin and Trygve to slice their own ropes to descend rapidly down the wall to her. Dwarves were exceptionally adept at traversing any kind of steep incline and the mountain slope of the Drengas wall, while the sharpest incline Tarin or Trygve had ever attempted, with care and caution, wasn't out of the realm of possibility. Tarin was worried, though, that they wouldn't make it down in time as he watched a large party of orc break away from the group attacking Akin and head Syllē's way.

At this point, the flaming remains of the basilisk fell to the ground, setting several orc and goblin on fire and igniting the ground around Syllē, effectively cutting off any attack but also any rescue attempt. The fire was intense and started to spread towards the remaining orc and goblin, who decided that the attack wasn't worth their lives anymore and fled for darker and less fiery ground. Akin and his warriors, unaware of Syllē's fall, followed, causing more orc and goblin to fall as they fled back into the Perdarus.

About fifteen feet above the ground, Tarin and Trygve used their momentum to leap over the fire and to the ground. Once landing, both dwarves hightailed it to Syllē, who was rapidly being overtaken by the blaze. They quickly worked to expand the no-fire zone around Syllē, the savage heat scalding their hands, faces, and backs as they worked. Finally, Tarin moved to Syllē, who hadn't moved or awakened. Carefully gathering her into his arms, Tarin tried to rouse her, but she wasn't responding. Knowing that the fire was too fierce to traverse safely while carrying an unconscious Syllē, Tarin motioned Trygve to his side and settled into the center of the no-fire zone they had created. Soon, though, they were choking on the smoke.

Finding it difficult to breathe, Tarin felt Syllē stir. Opening her eyes and trying to focus on him, Syllē feebly began pulling her cloak over the three of them. Noticing what she was trying to do, Trygve moved closer and finished pulling the cloak up and over them. Immediately, Tarin and Trygve found it easier to breathe.

Her voice almost a whisper, Syllē lovingly scolded the dwarves, "Halicyon is going to be so furious with you two. What were you thinking? Cutting your ropes and running down the wall into such danger." Though her eyes were closed, there was an affectionate smile on her face as she spoke.

Trygve grumbled irritably, "We were thinking that one of our own was in trouble and needed us. Something I believe that elf will completely understand seeing as how he loves you, too."

Syllē's eyes opened wide for a moment before she turned her head to smile up at Tarin. "Tarin," Syllē breathed happily. "Trygve just said he loves me."

As though offended that she could possibly think otherwise, Trygve gruffly retorted, "Of course I do," before brusquely kissing Syllē on the cheek.

Syllē's smile grew wider for a moment before she slowly lost consciousness. Tarin and Trygve huddled close to her under her cloak, waiting with her for the fire to either claim them or die out, which is exactly where Akin, using his great wolf form to leap the flames, found them.

23

While Syllē healed from her fall off the wall, she had plenty of time to consider Merilik's bounty and their coming journey into the Perdarus. The thought of what might await her loved ones as they traveled farther into the mountains did give Syllē pause. When she consulted with Halicyon and Falinor about the possibility of leaving the rest of their party in the Drengas kingdom and simply taking just the elves, Amarris, and Gydion any farther, Trygve overheard their conversation and exploded. They hadn't come this far to simply wait around in safety. No matter how Syllē tried to sell the idea, no one would go for it, and the dwarves, especially, were highly offended she would even suggest it. In fact, Tarin was so offended that he blasted Syllē for her lack of regard for dwarves and then stopped talking to her. Only the twins, who had no desire to be left behind either, seemed to understand her true motives.

King Herald found Tarin sitting on the walls looking out across the Perdarus, stewing over what the dwarf viewed as yet another slight against the worth of dwarves, and what hurt Tarin even more was the fact that it was instigated by Syllē of all people. After quietly watching the dwarf lord stew for a bit, King Herald walked to the wall and, standing to Tarin's right, leaned against it, staring out across the Perdarus as well. He was quiet for a while, letting the dwarf adjust to his presence.

When the Drengas king did speak, his deep voice seemed to resonate across the valley, "You know, she is the best Telimactar I have ever met." Chuckling quietly to himself, King Herald continued, "Of course, the last time she was here she did mention she was raised by dwarves, so I guess that would explain why," King Herald finished with a shrug.

"You would think someone raised by dwarves would place a greater value on their abilities," Tarin angrily muttered, without turning to look at the king.

Still staring out across the valley and the mountains beyond, King Herald calmly continued to speak despite Tarin's cranky attitude, "I first saw her from my hiding place in one of the great trees outside the walls. My mother and I had gone to visit the werelings and returned home to find the kingdom under attack. We were caught outside the walls, my mother and I; and while she probably could have effectively fought her way home—she was ferocious, my mother—she had no real chance while trying to protect a nine-year-old boy. So, she hid us in one of the high trees. I had a perfect view of the wall and the Telimactar, and as a Drengas child, I found the battle on the walls fascinating. That's when I saw her for the first time. She flew across those walls, side by side with a dwarf—a very young dwarf. Maybe a little younger than Kwin and Finn are now. They both fought well, but she was grace and fierce beauty in motion, and I was mesmerized."

Despite himself, Tarin was listening to King Herald—a fact that the Drengas king knew fully. As though he was talking to himself and the valley beyond, King Herald quietly continued, "I remember how they fought together. They never lost sight of each other, it seemed, no matter how fierce or intense the opposition. She fought hard, but I soon realized, she was fighting for the dwarf. She had gone over the wall with him and had every intention of returning with him. Even throwing herself into impossible situations to keep him safe. He did the same for her. It was obvious they loved each other."

Tarin's angst started to abate a bit as he listened to King Herald's story. He knew Syllē had loved Farin, who he was pretty sure was the dwarf in the story. He just couldn't understand why now she wouldn't want him with her. Why would she want to leave him behind? She had promised she wouldn't leave him in the Drengas kingdom and yet, she was trying to do just that.

"I bet if I had been able to watch the battle four days ago, I would have seen even more fierceness in her fighting because she was fighting to protect two whom she loves as they fought to protect her. Am I correct, Lord Tarin?" King Herald finally addressed the dwarf sitting on his wall.

Irritated again by the reminder of how well Trygve and he had fought beside Syllē, Tarin snarled, "If she loves us so much, why is she trying so desperately to get rid of us?"

"Is that what's she's doing?" King Herald's question rankled Tarin even more.

"Yes, what other explanation is there?" Tarin spit out.

"What about the bounty?" Tarin noticed from the corner of his eye that King Herald was now staring sternly and kindly down at him. A situation that only seemed to increase his irritation and anger.

"What about it?" Tarin growled. "I promised her that I wouldn't let any orc or goblin or Vikari harm her, and she repays me by telling everyone I'm not good enough to fight beside her."

Continuing to kindly stare at Tarin, which the dwarf found exceptionally irritating, King Herald calmly asked, "Lord Tarin, if the roles were reversed, how would you handle the situation?"

Tarin answered sharply, "I don't understand what you mean. What roles?"

"If she were the one who had promised to kill you before she allowed anything dark to harm you, what would you do? Would you take her into the Dark's stronghold?"

Tarin found King Herald's stare was almost as disconcerting as Syllē's, and the king's question left him dumbstruck. Swallowing hard, Tarin finally answered slowly and with difficulty, "No, I would ask you to lock her in the strongest cell you had until I had finished the mission." Sighing heavily, Tarin looked unhappily down at his hands.

Halicyon joined Tarin on the wall. "So, Syllē told you she was raised by dwarves, eh?" The elf asked King Herald. At the king's amused nod, Halicyon said almost breathlessly, "Well, that explains everything."

Tarin looked sharply at his friend and curtly demanded, "What does that mean?"

Staring sternly at the dwarf in response, Halicyon admonished Tarin, "Don't act that way with me, Tarin. You know how much I value you and your kin."

Sighing heavily, Tarin responded, "I am sorry, Halicyon." Looking out over the valley and the mountains beyond, Tarin reluctantly continued, "I guess I should find Syllē and apologize for my bullheadedness, yet again." Tarin, however, didn't move from his seat on the wall. Instead, he continued to stare into the distance.

Halicyon watched him, raising an eyebrow with curiosity at the dwarf's reticence. "Tarin?" he finally asked.

Sighing again, Tarin spoke, his voice rife with pain, "What if I can't protect her? Worse, what if I can't keep my promise?"

Placing his hand on his friend's shoulder and locking eyes with Tarin, Halicyon responded, "It will be okay, Tarin. I have no doubt that, if necessary, you will keep your promise; and I promise you to fight to my utmost so that you will never have to keep it."

Tarin nodded almost curtly at the elf beside him. It was all he could manage. Returning to gaze across the vastness in front of him, Tarin became lost in his thoughts again as he tried to regain his composure. Finally, Tarin sighed softly, "I'm in love with her."

As soon as the words left his mouth, Tarin looked with horror at the elf, but Halicyon remained silent. In fact, he didn't respond at all. Taking the elf's silence to mean outrage at the idea of Syllē with a dwarf, Tarin growled sadly, "You don't approve. You think Syllē with a dwarf is disgusting and wrong. Demeaning to her, even."

Fury flashed in Halicyon's eyes as he tersely answered Tarin, "Kindly refrain from putting words in my mouth that I would never think, let alone say."

Tarin was startled by the ferocity of Halicyon's fury, but he blustered, "Well, what were you thinking then?"

Trygve growled rather sarcastically from where he'd been standing in the shadows, keeping an eye on his cousin, "He was trying to think how to say, 'Tell me something everyone doesn't already know,' in a way that wouldn't offend you."

Tarin whirled so forcefully he almost lost his balance. If Halicyon hadn't grabbed him by the arm, there was a good chance the dwarf would have whirled himself right off the wall. Tarin was even more startled to see on the faces of everyone, including King Herald, that Trygve's statement was true. Standing up and looking from one to the other, Tarin finally stuttered, "Everyone knows? How? I didn't even know."

"Well, cousin, you're not the most subtle, and you've never been good at masking your feelings," Trygve shrugged.

Hil continued, "Everything you've done since the day you met her has been for her. Why do you think we knew it was going to be so easy to manipulate you into allowing her to stay in the mountains?"

Still a bit gobsmacked by the revelations, Tarin shook his head as if that would make everything clear, "But I am a dwarf, and she's supposed to be with an elf. With Halicyon. She loves him. I have seen them together repeatedly—after the first meeting in Exulias and when she rode home with him after Kilead and before she left to save the father and son and even before she headed off this wall to fight the basilisk."

"We love each other, Tarin, that is true; but neither of us is in love with the other," Halicyon tried to explain.

"But even Lady Sariel commented on what an excellent couple you two make," Tarin stubbornly continued.

"She only said that to try and spur you into action, Tarin," Hil explained. "She seemed to think if she could stir up your jealousy, you'd tell Syllē how you felt about her."

"Even Sariel knows?" Tarin asked incredulously. He was starting to feel a little sick to his stomach. An even more horrifying thought occurred to Tarin. "Does Syllē know?" he managed, terrified.

"No, you've done an excellent job of convincing her that you could only fall in love with a dwarf, uncle," Kwin responded.

"Well, that's good, and it's going to stay that way," Tarin glared at the group on the wall.

"Uncle…" Kwin began in protest.

Tarin quickly cut him off, "It's for the best. She knows I love and regard her as family. That's all she ever needs to know." Tarin moved down the wall towards a familiar figure sitting far away from their group and staring herself off across the valley and towards the mountains beyond. It was time for him to apologize.

Kwin looked almost pityingly at his uncle's back as he quietly whispered, "Coward."

24

Finn sat with his back to the fire, staring out into the darkness of the wereling tunnel, feeling that its gloom mirrored his own feelings. Finn and most of the group had been surprised by how relatively uneventful and quick the trip to the werelings' kingdom had gone. The most opposition they had faced was various groups of dead, of which Gydion and Syllē made exceptionally short work. In fact, the group had found the mountain passes strangely free of orc and goblin, leading several to think that maybe Syllē's earlier fears were unfounded. Finn had considered that since the battle at the Drengas' walls had claimed a vast number of orc and goblin, perhaps there wouldn't be as much opposition to their party as they had originally thought. Still, Finn couldn't quite believe the battle had killed the greater percentage of that pestilence.

Syllē, for her part, knew that hadn't happened. She also knew that the relative ease with which they traversed the Perdarus was a ruse. Merilik had a plan for them. That was certain. What it was, Syllē was sure, was wrapped up in that bounty on hers and Tarin's heads. The Dark Lord had every intention of making both her and Tarin suffer, and she had no intention of obliging him.

When they had entered the hidden valley that had once been the home of the werelings, Finn had been struck by the silence. It was as if sound had been exterminated from this place, just as the werelings obviously had.

Finn had also noticed that he wasn't the only one in the group unsettled by the silence. Warily glancing around their group, Tarin had slowly crept closer to Halicyon, who Finn had noticed was also warily studying their surroundings. Halicyon had acknowledged the dwarf's presence with a curt nod, while continuing to keep a keen eye on everything around them.

Finn had sidled up to Syllē when he noticed that both she and Gydion had begun to appear weighed down, almost as if a great burden had been slammed onto their shoulders. Syllē had quickly maneuvered them through the outlying village and into the first tunnel—a short path connecting the previous village with another in the next valley. It, Finn had observed, was as disconcertingly desolate as the first; and as before, Syllē swiftly led them through that settlement and into the next tunnel—the one they were currently traversing. It was longer and appeared to have offshoots into the vast darkness that now surrounded them. Syllē had ordered them to stay away from the walls and not touch anything. She had stared quite pointedly at Finn—he believed, which slightly irritated him—when she gave that order.

If he was being honest with himself, Finn was also currently irritated with his brother over this whole Amarris business. He and Kwin had spent their lives always having each other's back, but now it appeared to Finn that his twin had forgotten all about him in favor of Amarris, which was unsettling. Now, for the first time in his life, Finn felt alone. He glanced up as Syllē sat down beside him, handing him his dinner as she did. Smiling companionably at him, Syllē started to eat her own portion while silently staring off into the gloom of the tunnel as well.

Finn sat quietly eating beside her for a bit before venturing to ask a question that had been bothering him since the Drengas kingdom: "Did Athos want the throne? Is that why he did everything that he did?"

Syllē took a moment to swallow her food before answering, "I'm not sure how he thought taking down Akin would get him the throne since Akin is only second in line after Freyda, King Herald and Queen Anya's oldest, who takes after her mother in her battle skills."

"Her?" Finn was curious. "Wouldn't the throne go to the oldest son?"

"Not for the Drengas," Syllē shrugged. "The throne is passed down to the firstborn regardless of gender, which I find very refreshing." She grinned almost gleefully out into the darkness.

"Well, then, why did Athos do what he did?" Finn asked.

Syllē shrugged again, "Possibly to weaken the royal house altogether or stir up distrust among the Drengas and thereby weaken the nation itself." She cocked her head and mused, "Possibly to destroy one of the last remaining werelings. Akin was saved from extermination and safeguarded by the Drengas his entire life. The only way for Merilik to reach him was through treachery and intrigue." Looking thoughtfully at Finn, Syllē continued with a slight shrug, "Possibly a little of all those reasons."

"But I thought that for the Drengas, their honor was paramount," Finn observed. "How could he do something so dishonorable?"

Syllē gazed thoughtfully at Finn for a moment before answering, "You can have evil in any race. Greed, lust, want, hatred, prejudice—these emotions aren't restricted to just one of the races or totally absent in others. They, unfortunately, can be found in anyone; and when just one of them is, Merilik is exceptionally adept at using it to his advantage and purposes."

Finn nodded. He was silent again, quietly looking off into the darkness around them. It wasn't as deep and unsettling as the dark of the Strygoi tunnels, but, if he was being honest, he felt a great sadness—a deep sorrow—permeating the air of the tunnels, which filled him with a dread of what might be coming their way. His trepidation evident in his voice, Finn hesitantly asked, "So, what happened to the werelings, do you think?"

Setting her bowl down beside her, Syllē sighed, staring contemplatively off into the darkness. "I think that the majority have been exterminated. There might be remnants, but if there are, they are mainly Merilik's prisoners—a fate I know from personal experience is worse than death."

Kwin spoke up curiously from his spot beside Amarris at the fire, "But werelings are so fierce. How could they have been destroyed?"

"Being fierce doesn't necessarily make you immune to harm or impervious to annihilation," Gydion observed. "Consider Shara and Cere."

Silence rested on the group, which was broken eventually by Finn's sigh, "I hope that Akin isn't the last. That would be so lonely."

* * *

Using the tunnels and valleys of the wereling kingdom, Syllē and Gydion continued to lead the group through the Perdarus towards the dark lair that Syllē had seen in her laudenium-induced dream. Their trek had been dark but uneventful. In fact, if it weren't for the unsettling feeling that they were being watched, the group may have relaxed. As it was, Tarin and the rest found themselves constantly looking over their shoulders or peering intently down crossroads and side tunnels and always sticking exceptionally close to each other. For her part, the deeper they got into the Perdarus, the more swiftly and quietly Syllē traveled.

Finally, the tunnel dead-ended in a small circular valley with high walls on all sides. Tarin thought it looked like a lava spout, which was entirely plausible. He couldn't understand the markings on the walls, though. They looked like runes, but not any he had ever seen. They were more angular and disjointed than dwarf runes. Syllē, however, understood the runes, cautiously searching the walls for the ones, or one, she needed.

Finn, who had grown bored, meandered around the small clearing looking for a possible spot for a nap. He was careful to remember Syllē's instructions not to touch anything until something twinkling near Syllē's right foot caught his eye. Unfortunately, his curiosity quickly overrode Syllē's instructions.

Syllē heard the trap spring a mere instant before the bolt shot out of the wall, but that instant was all she needed to whirl Finn and herself out of the direct path of the spear. However, the trap wasn't done. The bolt barely grazed her side, but the jolt was just enough to knock her off balance. Exacerbated by the added weight of Finn, Syllē couldn't keep them from falling into a hole that had mysteriously opened almost beneath them after she spun them out of the way of the flying bolt. Kwin almost saved them by grabbing her arm, but the ground suddenly slid out from under him, sending him toppling with them into the dark hole. Before anyone else in the group could react, the floor was solid again.

25

"Finn! Didn't I tell you not to touch anything?" Syllē whisperingly yelled at Finn as soon as she had pushed herself out of the pile that she, Finn, and Kwin had made on the new tunnel floor. "What were you thinking?"

Finn disgruntledly pushed himself off the floor and made a slight show of brushing himself off to avoid immediately answering Syllē. He knew he'd screwed up and that now, because of him, she was injured, and they were trapped somewhere below ground in the wereling tunnels, or he *hoped* they were wereling tunnels. Syllē stood with her hands on her hips glowering down at Finn. Kwin stood beside her, glaring just as ferociously at his brother. Starting to answer, Finn guiltily noticed the blood on Syllē's side.

Ignoring her question and simply acting on his concern for her, Finn stepped forward. "You're hurt. Let me see the wound."

Grabbing his hands, Syllē looked down at Finn, her anger slightly tempered now. "It's just a scratch, little brother. Won't even need stitches. Now, concentrate—we must get back to the others." She turned in a wide circle, carefully surveying the small room they had fallen into.

"What is this place?" Kwin asked as he also studied the hole. The walls were way too smooth, he observed, to be natural—the same for the floor and shape of the room.

"A troll or goblin trap," Syllē tersely explained. "And, thanks to Finn, a dwarf and Valaraii trap as well," she finished rather sarcastically.

Ignoring her, Finn studied the walls around them. "So, how do we get out of here?"

"Wereling guards open the door and let us go, or kill us, depending on their mood," Syllē's sarcasm continued to rankle Finn, but he refused to show that he was affected.

"Why would they kill us? We're not goblins or trolls," Finn retorted.

"Well, werelings were never overly fond of dwarves," Syllē grinned. "In the beginning, your clans fought over some of the same homelands, and werelings have a long memory."

"So, we're stuck here?" Kwin finally asked. "The only way out is if someone opens the door from the other side?"

"Or one of us climbs up there, through that small hole in the corner of the ceiling, finds the hall that leads to this door, unearths the correct door key, and opens the door to let the others out. We could be out of here in under an hour, barring having to deal with anything particularly ugly any-where on the other side of this wall," Syllē explained with an ironic shrug of her shoulders while never seeming to take her eyes off the tiny crevice in the wall above.

Finn turned to his brother to say that since he'd gotten them into this mess then he should be the one to go, but Syllē's words stopped him: "Okay, my brothers, give me a boost."

* * *

Even before the trap had fully closed, Halicyon and Falinor searched the area for the lever to its door. Gydion, in the meantime, studied the wall to try and decipher it. He wasn't as adept at wereling runes, but he felt he knew enough. It just might take him a while. Unfortunately, the wizard didn't have a while.

The searchers were shortly interrupted by Elēandil, who almost hissed at them, "Listen. I believe we are about to have company."

Halicyon and Falinor obeyed, and their hearts sank at what they heard heading their way. Obviously, the noise of the trap being sprung had alerted those they had been trying to avoid to their presence. Their enemies were converging on them fast and none of the elves knew how to get out of the tight valley. Gydion, sensing the elves' alarm, continued to urgently search the wall near where Syllē had been standing before Finn accidentally set off the trap. Soon, the wizard could feel the encroaching darkness, which spurred him to try even more desperately to understand what Syllē had been about to do. Suddenly, the wizard recognized the pattern in the runes, but it was too late. The enemy had found them.

26

Finn felt like he'd been trapped in the hole with his brother for a century, at least. After Syllē had made it through the small crevice and disappeared, Finn had begun looking for other possible exits. Kwin, on the other hand, had taken the time to lecture his brother on his lack of maturity and total stupidity, which had prompted Finn to accuse his brother of disloyalty and treachery. The argument became physical, which, since both brothers were evenly matched, meant they pretty much served each other blow for blow.

They were taking a slight breather from the brotherly battle when the wall Finn was leaning on to catch his breath suddenly disappeared from behind him, causing him to tumble backwards into darkness. Looking up, he found himself at Syllē's feet, who grinned rather gleefully down at him, he thought.

Looking between the two brothers, Syllē asked, "So, you two talk out your differences and make up yet, or did you just spend the time I graciously gave you to beat the tar out of each other?" Neither Kwin nor Finn met her eye. "Fine, here's reality. You were never meant to be joined at the hip for your entire lives. So, you," Syllē said as she pointed at Finn, "should be happy that your brother found someone amazing who loves him back."

Before Kwin could interject some smart remark agreeing with Syllē, she turned to Kwin and continued, "And you should remember that your brother has been in your life and had your back much longer than Amarris." Continuing to look sternly between the twins, she finished, "You're family, and you love each other. That's a gift. Treasure it. Don't trash it." She paused a moment to let her words sink into the twins' brains before bringing them back to their current situation. "We've got to get to the others. Hopefully, Gydion has deciphered the wall and found the entrance, but regardless, we need to find that tunnel and our group and do it without generating any notice from the current inhabitants of these mountains. Let's move."

Syllē grabbed Finn by the front of his shirt and pulled him towards her so that he was standing on his tiptoes looking her straight in the eye as she pointedly instructed, "And don't touch anything."

* * *

The battle in the small valley wasn't going well. Goblins were coming out of holes and crevices in the walls no one had known were there. To Tarin, it almost felt like for every one goblin his group killed, five more popped out of nowhere. He'd already been lassoed four times, but, thankfully, someone had shot or sliced every rope before Tarin's feet even left the ground.

The group had formed a protective circle around Tarin, which is probably why one goblin's lasso only made it around Tarin's throat. Thankfully, Elēandil instantly sliced it before the goblin could pull it taut and, most likely, break Tarin's neck. Gydion, who had figured out the rune pattern, desperately wanted to put his knowledge to good use but couldn't since he had to fight goblins leaping off the cliff face every time he moved towards the rune wall. It was at this point that a goblin caught a break in the form of a dwarf.

Swiftly, before anyone could react, the goblin yanked his lasso as soon as it landed, which, fortunately for Tarin, was around his shoulders, instead of farther down his arms. The shoulder position left his arms free and not pinned to his side. This enabled Tarin to grab and hold onto a small outcropping on the cliff face, which did not make his would-be goblin captor very happy.

Realizing he would not be successful at jerking Tarin free, the goblin sent his cohorts to wrestle the dwarf free of his hold on the wall. Tarin found himself kicking and head-butting goblin left and right, making his precarious position even more so. Amarris, Thēorin, and Elēandil were helping by shooting many of the goblins attacking him, but Tarin knew he had to get off this goblin ride and soon. Flipping himself to the other side of the outcrop, Tarin tried to wedge himself between the ledge and the cliff face, giving himself some leverage against the goblin. Grabbing the rope now in both hands, Tarin pulled hard. It worked. The goblin went flying and landed at the feet of Firth, who quickly relieved it of its head.

Now, Tarin had to figure out how to traverse the cliff face to the ground—a cliff face teeming with goblin. Halicyon found the solution for him. Using his own rope, Halicyon lassoed Tarin's ledge. Meeting Tarin's eye, Halicyon attached the rope to himself and moved backwards a way. Using the handle of his battle axe, Tarin slid down the rope towards his friend. Sensing they were losing their prize, the goblins on the cliff face surged forward and tried to cut the rope. The archers mowed them down, but one sliced the rope as he fell from the wall, causing Tarin to abruptly fall into the goblin horde on the valley floor.

Halicyon fought his way forward to wrest Tarin from the grasp of the goblins. Then the two fought side by side, back to their friends. Such valor and bravery are always beautiful to see, but as Gydion had said earlier, in the face of overwhelming evil, even the fierce bravery and skill of this group didn't stand a chance. As Gydion tried to fight his way to the wall (their only real chance of surviving was making it through that hidden door), the goblins in front of him were felled from behind. As they hit the ground, Gydion saw the twins and Syllē in front of the door he'd been trying to open.

"Move!" the wizard shouted, trying to shepherd the group towards the door.

The final two through the door were Tarin and Halicyon, still fighting side by side. As they entered the door, a large goblin made a frantic grab at Tarin but was stopped by a powerful right hook to its head that sent it flying backwards. "Not today," Syllē growled as she shut the door firmly behind her. Looking around the group, she finished her head count, satisfied they had left no one behind with the goblins. "Let's put some distance between us and this place, and remember, don't touch anything..." Staring directly at the dwarf, she finished, "...*Finn.*"

Syllē started to move to the front of the group to continue leading them towards their goal when she found herself being flipped off her feet. Startled speechless for a moment, she turned her head to find herself face to face with Tarin. "Tarin, what are you doing?" she managed, trying to keep her temper at bay.

"You're wounded," Tarin said. He found Syllē's closeness made it very difficult for him to concentrate.

"I am not. My legs are working perfectly fine," Syllē answered back. "So, thank you, but you can put me down now."

Tarin continued stubbornly, "No."

Feeling her irritation rising, Syllē curtly asked, "Why not?"

"Because," Tarin tried to focus on his words and not Syllē's closeness, "if I hold onto you, then you can't be almost killed by orc or fighting orc without me, or falling through any more trap doors. You'll be safe," Tarin finished as he glared at her.

Syllē understood. Her eyes glowed a soft blue as she leaned her head fondly towards Tarin, who was slightly mesmerized by her eyes. He was so distracted by her eyes that he didn't notice for a moment how close her face was coming to his. Terrified, Tarin did the only thing that came to mind—he let go. With a cry of pain, Syllē slammed unexpectedly onto the stone floor.

Her eyes sparking navy, Syllē looked up at Tarin, who was so astonished that he was frozen for a moment above her. "Damn it, Tarin! What is wrong with you?"

Hastily, Tarin leaned down and helped Syllē to her feet. "I thought you were going to kiss me," was all he could manage.

Syllē irritably rubbed her back as she muttered, "Well, if you don't like me kissing you on the cheek, you should have just told me, instead of slinging me to the ground."

"Well, I didn't think you'd listen to me," Tarin sputtered. He was saying whatever came to mind. "You know, you're not the easiest to tell things."

"Well, don't worry. I won't kiss you again." Syllē glared down at Tarin before whirling away, heading back towards the front of the group. Her forward trek was stopped when she caught a look at Halicyon's face. He was keenly studying Tarin, and he looked concerned. She turned around to see what Halicyon thought was wrong.

"Tarin, you're wounded," Halicyon said worriedly, beginning to walk towards Tarin.

"No, I'm not," Tarin returned, confused.

"Yes, your left side is covered in blood," Halicyon said, pointing at Tarin's side as he drew closer to the dwarf.

Looking down with a shade of horror, Tarin wondered if he could be so badly injured that he didn't even know it. He'd heard of that happening, but he didn't feel weak, and he couldn't remember any goblin weapon really getting close enough to him to harm him. Suddenly, Tarin realized that his bloody side was the side Syllē had been pressed against. This wasn't his blood; it was hers.

"You lied to me," Tarin almost yelled at Syllē.

"What do you mean, I lied to you?" Syllē retorted angrily.

"You are wounded. This," Tarin pointed to his bloody side, "is your blood, not mine." Tarin advanced on her, reaching furiously for her shirt to expose the wound.

Syllē grabbed his hands to keep him from ripping her shirt off her. "Tarin, stop it. Tarin, I am fine. It is only a scratch."

Tarin continued to try and get at Syllē's wound. "Scratches don't bleed like that," he stubbornly asserted.

"Tarin, I promise you that I am fine. It truthfully is a mere scratch, nothing major." Syllē was having a difficult time maintaining control of Tarin's hands, and the dwarf refused to listen to her. "Tarin, if I promise to allow Hil to check me out right here, will you promise to stop trying to strip me in front of the entire group?" She moved her face down so that she was eye to eye with Tarin. "I mean, really, my lord, I would prefer you try and rip my clothes off me when we have much more privacy." Syllē grinned mischievously at Tarin, her blues eyes sparking with amusement.

Startled, Tarin finally focused on Syllē's face. Taking a deep breath, he stepped back and motioned Hil forward. "Have Amarris help you care for Syllē, sister."

"Fine," Hil growled, stepping forward, "if she can take her hands off my son long enough to help me."

27

Tarin was greatly anticipating the what-had-to-be vast chamber Syllē had described as the wereling graveyard. Syllē had explained that werelings didn't live inside a mountain as dwarves did, but rather they lived in the valleys of a mountain range and used the mountain tunnels to connect their villages as well as lead to their ancestral graveyard, which was always hidden somewhere deep within the mountain range. For werelings, the mountains belonged to the dead.

Tarin's anticipation was quickly turning to irritation, which was only a small step away from anger. "Syllē, what's wrong? You're moving slower than a dwarf away from treasure," Tarin grumbled. "Are you actually more wounded than you let on?" Now, the step to anger had been taken.

Glaring slightly sideways at Tarin, Syllē retorted, "Hil confirmed it was only a scratch."

"Well then, why are you moving so slowly?" Tarin's frustration was evident in his tone.

"Because it doesn't make sense." Syllē cautiously continued to move down the tunnel while speaking to Tarin; but to him, it sounded as if she was speaking more to herself. "How did the wereling vanish? How did the Dark defeat them? I can't figure it out, but I feel as though I am missing a huge piece. An exceptionally important piece." Syllē stopped and gazed thoughtfully around her as if searching the very air for an answer.

"Well, we did find the shedded basilisk skin in the first tunnel," Falinor offered, "and the only ones I know immune to the basilisk's stare are dwarves."

"Yes," Syllē nodded offhandedly as she started walking slowly down the tunnel again, "but werelings are adept at battling basilisks. They can sense them coming in plenty of time to set up an ambush and dispatch those worms without even having to take them head on. It's not just basilisks."

"King Herald told us of his battle with a Drēor-led army that almost annihilated them. Perhaps that Drēor had a hand in defeating the werelings," Halicyon shrugged.

"Yes, that's definitely possible, and I would bet that Drēor was Therendē'al." Tarin noticed Syllē almost spat that name. "He was always bragging about his great relationship with the werelings." Syllē paused, cocking her head in thought. "So, betrayal—definitely. Basilisks—there's evidence of them. But Therendē'al would need more than basilisks and subterfuge to exterminate the entire wereling nation." Looking worriedly at Halicyon, she finished, "We're missing something, and it's that part that bothers me."

Suddenly, Finn stopped dead in his tracks at almost the same time as Kwin. The two exchanged a look before Finn caught Gydion's sleeve, and in an extremely quiet voice tempered by fear, said, "Strygoi."

Gydion was startled enough to trip over his robe before catching his balance. Shaking his head, the wizard answered, "That's certainly an interesting theory, Finn; however, there aren't any Strygoi left in MithTerra." Gydion noticed Syllē stop dead in her tracks in front of them when he said "Strygoi."

"No," Finn responded sharply. Moving quickly forward, towards Syllē, Finn asserted softly, "Not a theory. Strygoi—ahead of us—in the tunnels. Kwin senses them, too." As Syllē turned to meet Finn's eyes, he asked, "Can't you feel the ice-cold terror in the air?"

Pulling Finn towards her into a hug and smiling over his head at Kwin, Syllē breathed softly, "The missing piece. Of course."

Halicyon's face blanched with anger as he almost shepherded the group into a tight circle while glaring down the tunnel. "They would use the graveyard as their nursery. Plenty of bones for the newly hatched young to devour."

Syllē released Finn and nodded in response. "It would appear, my friend, that we have a coven to exterminate."

"So it would seem," Halicyon's voice had a steely edge to it, but Tarin also thought he heard a trace of weariness in his friend's voice. Tarin had no way of knowing that this wasn't Halicyon's first extermination of a Strygoi coven. Nor could Tarin know that Halicyon had lost friends and a brother in the previous battles against the beasts. In fact, according to Halicyon, there hadn't been one totally successful coven extermination ever because while they had destroyed each coven, Halicyon believed the losses were too many to call any of the battles a true success.

"Very well," Syllē's voice, while soft, was steely and determined. "We are going to enter that graveyard and move through it to the back wall. There's a door of some kind in it that we must get through. Fight your way there." Turning towards the group, she finished her instructions, "Finn, remind everyone how to kill Strygoi. Falinor, you're in charge of the archers. Use naphtha on the cocoons. Halicyon, you oversee the remaining ground fighters. Tarin," Syllē looked briefly at him as she spoke, "start counting." Then she moved forward down the tunnel.

Tarin was startled by Syllē's instructions. Start counting? What did she mean by that? It wasn't until Halicyon began his instructions to the group after Finn had finished his brief Strygoi explanation that Tarin realized what Syllē was going to do. She was going to be bait for the adults keeping watch over the coven's cocoons. She was going to lead them far away while their group skulked through the burial grounds to the escape door. *Syllē!*

Tarin bellowed. He noticed with satisfaction Syllē falter a moment and grab the side of her head.

Whirling angrily, Syllē harshly whispered, "I told you to start counting."

Tarin quickly made it to her side and said, "Beside me or a step in front of me, Syllē. No more of this putting yourself in grave danger and making me watch. You go beside me from now on. We fight the Dark together. Am I clear?"

Syllē arched an eyebrow a moment. She had never heard such steel in Tarin's voice. It was obvious he meant it. Trying to explain why he had to stay with the group, Syllē calmly and quietly spoke, "Tarin, this fight will be very different than the one on the side of the Rudu Mountains." At Tarin's questioning glare, she sighed, "That fight was out in the open where the Strygoi couldn't use their greatest weapon as effectively—their ability to immobilize you with your greatest fear. Inside, their mental telepathy is extremely difficult to ignore and to fight. Plus, it will be exceptionally close quarters. You won't have much room to maneuver."

"Well, it's a good thing I'm a dwarf. I don't need much room," Tarin growled.

"Tarin," Syllē tried assertively, "you need to stay with everyone else."

"Beside me or right in front of me, Syllē. That's the deal, period."

"Tarin, they use your greatest fear against you. You…"

Tarin grumpily interrupted, "Well, my greatest fear is failing you, which I will do if I stay with the group."

Syllē lost control. Grabbing Tarin by the front of his shirt and pulling him towards her, she hissed, "You are the most frustratingly confusing man!"

"Well, I don't know why that would surprise you. I am a dwarf," Tarin shrugged, not taking his eyes from Syllē's. "Beside me or right in front of me," he calmly reminded her.

Syllē let go of Tarin's shirt, but she didn't stop studying him. The rest of the group had joined them and were quietly waiting a few steps away, trying to pretend they hadn't noticed the altercation. All except Finn, that is.

Grinning up at Halicyon, Finn drawled, "I really hate it when Mom and Dad fight, don't you?"

Before Halicyon could respond, Hil smacked her son hard across the back of his head, not even bothering to look at him. Halicyon shrugged when he caught Finn's disgruntled stare and said, "I would have if she hadn't." Finn just growled to himself and stared sullenly ahead.

28

Tarin and Syllē stood in the darkened doorway of the wereling burial grounds. Tarin couldn't see any Strygoi, but Syllē had warned him that the adults would rest on and in the tombs of the dead, occupying the same space as the bodies of the werelings. She didn't want him to be startled when the shades rose from the graves to confront them as they moved through the graveyard. Grappling to overcome the horrific terror and intense weighty sorrow that slammed into him as soon as they rounded the corner in the tunnel and came to the graveyard door, Tarin reached for Syllē's hand in the darkness and held on tightly.

Tarin? Syllē's voice in his head was tentative and Tarin could hear her breathing rapidly.

Beside me or right in front of me. Tarin tried to calm Syllē and himself. He felt Syllē turn her head towards him as she grasped his hand tightly.

Tarin, I need you to know my greatest fear. Tarin felt Syllē grip his hand even tighter. Looking up at her, Tarin met her eyes, blue-gray pools that filled him with light. He heard her slowly take a deep breath and then release it. *My greatest fear is losing you. I don't believe I would survive your loss.*

Well, when I die, I promise to come back and haunt you forever. That way you'll never lose me. Course, you will probably regret it since you'll never have any peace or time to yourself. Tarin felt Syllē's laugh fill him with warmth and he knew they were going to be all right. *Beside me or right in front of me, Syllē.*

Syllē released Tarin's hand and then slowly and quietly drew her Scylarian long knives while Tarin unsheathed his hand axes. The close quarters made a sword or full-size battle axe more cumbersome and a possible hindrance over the smaller weapons. Tarin felt his breathing match Syllē's as they stepped into the graveyard in unison.

* * *

Finn could hear the customary slithering and rattling of the Strygoi begin soon after Syllē and Tarin disappeared into the graveyard. Soon that noise was joined by a terror chorus of unearthly shrieks followed closely by Syllē's battle cry and his uncle's roar. Then, the sound of fighting could be heard.

Moving together towards the burial grounds, the group split into their squads. Falinor's group was in the center, ready to start burning the cocoons, while Halicyon's group surrounded them to combat any adults on guard or any young successful enough to escape their fiery cocoons. They had progressed almost to the center of the vast chamber without any opposition or finding any cocoons. Halicyon and Falinor were searching the far reaches of the chamber and within open tombs for what they knew had to be there but could find nothing.

It was Amarris who found them. "Look up." The slight tremor in her voice was the only indication of the sheer terror she was feeling.

The group raised their eyes to the ceiling of the chamber to see that most of it was hung with cocoons, which appeared on the brink of hatching. Falinor sprang into action, issuing orders to his archers. Soon the burial grounds were bathed in the light of burning Strygoi cocoons, gaining the attention of the adults who had been drawn completely out of the chamber and partway down a long side corridor by Syllē and Tarin.

Turning, the remaining adults fled down the corridor and back to their young with Syllē and Tarin now chasing them. Only one made it back into the burial grounds before being cut down. The Strygoi hatchlings were on their own, which was a fate that, for a lesser creature, might have been the end; however, Strygoi hatchlings were terrifying and quite capable of fending for themselves as soon as they left their cocoons. Plus, all Strygoi hatchlings were born with an almost insatiable appetite for flesh, and these hatchlings were no exception.

29

As the cocoons lining the ceiling started burning, they started falling, making the group's progress to the back door of the chamber amazingly difficult. The fighters were desperately dodging these living bombs and often having to then dispatch the terrors erupting from them. Many of those terrors clawed their way out of their fiery cocoons before they fell and then launched themselves at the fighters on the ground. Finn found this horrifying. The shrieks of the hatchlings combined with the smoke and fire and burning cocoons dropping left and right disoriented the fighters. Twice, Finn found himself slammed to the ground by a hatchling he had failed to avoid; and twice, Elēandil decapitated the demon before it could do any true harm to the dwarf.

Finn wasn't the only one disconcerted by the appearance of the hatchlings. The archers had calmly shot the innocuous cocoons, but once confronted by a ravenous hatchling, all but the elves had a moment of freezing terror. Amarris had never seen or experienced anything like these hatchlings. The creature that erupted towards her was dark charcoal with a strong, lithe body. Amarris was struck by how almost childlike it initially looked, but that thought was quickly dispelled when the demon locked eyes with her and let out a bone-chilling shriek while powerfully leaping at her from the tomb slab upon which it had landed. Its fangs and long sinewy fingers with razor-sharp talons were ready to rip her to shreds. Kwin deftly spun and removed the hatchling's head before it could land on Amarris, jolting Amarris back into action. Taking a deep breath to steady her nerves, Amarris rejoined the battle and never faltered again.

Thēorin had a similar incident as he moved with the group shooting the cocoons on the ceiling. The first hatchling he encountered erupted from its cocoon just above him. Thēorin froze, eyes wide and unconsciously holding his breath. If Flarne hadn't quickly skewered the hatchling and then slung it towards the side of the group for Firth to decapitate, Thēorin may have been lost to the creature's bloodlust. Each member of the group unfamiliar with Strygoi had momentary lapses before finding their way back to the battle in the burial grounds.

* * *

The chamber was on fire. The smoke and heat made it difficult to breathe and stay together as well as the disorienting cacophony of hatchling shrieks. Falinor and Halicyon tried their best to keep their groups together as they fought their way through the burial chamber. Soon, they were joined by Syllē and Tarin, who, after dispatching the adults, had begun destroying hatchlings as well. It wasn't until they reached the door Syllē had mentioned that Elēandil realized they were missing someone. Swiftly turning, Elēandil glared through the smoky haze and flames engulfing the chamber, desperately searching. How could he have possibly gotten separated? Where was that dwarf?

Having opened the door, Gydion was quickly shepherding others through it when he noticed Elēandil's concern. "What's wrong?"

"I can't see Finn," Elēandil tersely responded.

Brusquely, Syllē, who had overheard, instructed, "Get them all through that door," before she spun and headed back into the flames. Tarin and Halicyon followed closely behind her.

* * *

Finn had been fighting slightly behind Elēandil as they traversed the graveyard when he was hit hard by a hatchling which had hurled itself at him from the tomb it had landed on. The force of the hit sent Finn's hand axes flying out of his hands and into the murky atmosphere of the graveyard. He heard them clatter somewhere off to his right as he flew through the hazy air of the burial grounds. Finn and the hatchling landed inside another room that had not yet filled with smoke or fire.

Reacting quickly, Finn solidly punched the hatchling in the face, breaking its nose and throwing it off him. Before the hatchling could recover and continue its attack, Finn attempted to exit the small chamber but had to rethink his plans as two more hatchlings entered the room either hunting him or simply trying to evade the flames. Changing course, Finn leapt over the altar tomb in the center of the chamber, trying not to disturb the wereling who lay upon it and began looking for an escape; but Finn swiftly realized he was trapped. The only way out was the small crevice he'd fallen through that was now blocked by three rather hungry hatchlings. Finn started to reach for a weapon, but what could he possibly use against those things? His battle axe was too long and unwieldy for the close combat of this small tomb and his knives would allow those things to get way too close for comfort. Their talons would slice him to shreds before he could cut anyone's head off.

Finn searched the small chamber for some sort of weapon, but werelings didn't really use conventional weapons. Finn desperately scanned the walls and floor but found nothing that would help him. His attention was now caught by the cautiously approaching hatchlings. Why weren't they attacking him? Suddenly, he realized that they were waiting for the most strategic time to launch and claim him as their own. The three were about to fight over his body. "I really hate Strygoi," Finn muttered.

As the hatchlings edged cautiously forward, keeping an eye on him and each other, Finn gave another cursory glance around the room, hoping he'd missed a cache of weapons near at hand or anything he could use to defend himself. A glint of metal caught his eye. Peering more closely at the crossed arms of the wereling, Finn noticed that she was grasping what looked to be the hilts of long knives, actually very similar to Syllē's Scylarian long knives. Looking at the head of the wereling, Finn spoke, "I mean no disrespect, but if you could see your way clear to letting me borrow your knives, I would greatly appreciate it." Reaching carefully for the long knives, Finn was barely able to say, "Thank you," to the wereling before the first hatchling leapt at him.

Taking a step back, Finn deftly slashed the chest of the hatchling, causing the beast to divert its frontal attack and land slightly to Finn's left. Swiftly, Finn charged the wounded hatchling and removed its head. Turning, Finn faced the remaining two hatchlings, glaring fiercely at them. Without a second thought, the hatchlings decided to feed on the bones of the wereling on the altar tomb over the rearmed and dangerous dwarf in the corner. Finn realized this was his chance. He could simply leave the hatchlings to feast on the wereling while he crept out of the crypt and rejoined his friends.

There was only one problem with that plan of action; it was dishonorable. The thought of leaving the wereling to be desecrated by the two demons not only felt wrong, but it felt cowardly, too. Shooting forward and jumping onto the altar tomb, trying his best not to disturb the wereling, Finn speared the closest hatchling with his left long knife and then deftly sliced off its head with his right. Sensing Finn was distracted by the other hatchling, the last demon leapt at the dwarf's back. Without even turning to face the beast, Finn speared it with his right long knife before spinning and slicing off its head with the left.

Slowing his breathing, Finn knelt respectfully beside the wereling. Placing his right fist across his heart, Finn bowed his head. "Thank you for the use of your weapons. I am sorry I disturbed your rest. Please forgive my intrusion into your tomb."

Finn was about to replace the knives on the chest of the wereling when movement caught his eye. Standing and turning towards the door to the chamber, Finn's heart sank as two more hatchlings entered the chamber, and one of them was on fire. As the hatchlings careened into the chamber, the first one slammed into two of the oil funerary lamps at the foot of the altar tomb, spewing lamp oil over itself, the floor around the tomb, and the already aflame hatchling.

Finn watched with horror as the entire tomb began to be rapidly engulfed in flames. Standing on the altar tomb, Finn could see the door but knew there was no way for him to reach it. He'd be barbecue like the hatchlings before he could even get two steps off the altar tomb. "I hope you don't mind sharing your tomb with a dwarf," Finn commented ironically to the wereling below him.

Finn crouched above the wereling on the altar tomb. As he tried to shield his face with his sleeve, he heard the most terrifying roar ever reverberate through the crypt. It seemed to shake the entire mountain. Before he could even react, Finn felt something powerful slam into his back and sling him over the flames and through the small door of the crypt. Bouncing across the floor of the main burial grounds, Finn came to a bruised rest at someone's feet. He looked up to see a very relieved Syllē looking down at him with an equally relieved Tarin and Halicyon by her side.

Smiling at Finn, Syllē reached down, grabbed his arm, and hauled him to his feet. From the small crypt came another mountain-shattering roar. Finn looked and saw a huge, brown bear standing within the flames of the small crypt. As he glanced at it, the bear seemed to dissolve into the form of a tall, strong woman, who nodded her head at him a moment, before transforming back into the bear. Her roar reverberated through the mountain again, and this time, Finn thought he could hear answering roars.

"Come," Syllē ordered as she pulled sharply on Finn's arm and headed back towards the exit the rest of the group had already taken. "The dead are reclaiming their mountain. We need to leave them to it."

* * *

Deep within the darkness of his cage, Oran felt a whiff of something shiver through him a moment and raised his head to look around. He could see the other cages and their occupants. Some appeared to be listening intently to some far away sound, and he could have sworn that a few of them were smiling. The orc nearby, however, seemed oblivious. Oran stayed in the middle of his cage. He'd learned quickly that if you wished to survive, you stayed away from the bars and walls, especially the front. Changelings walked these halls, and they were always hungry, as were the orc and goblin. Sometimes, the orc would drag an unwilling victim out of a cage and disappear down a long corridor to the east. Sometimes, the victim would walk back past them, and the orc and goblin would give them plenty of room. The former prisoners never looked right or left, never spoke, and seemed off in a terrifying way that Oran couldn't quite understand. All he knew was no one wanted to go down that hall.

Oran was startled by the sound of metal scraping stone and looked up to see a large orc entering his cage. The orc grabbed him and shoved him towards the door where two other orcs waited, grinning maliciously from ear to ear. As soon as Oran was outside of his cage, the orc started to drag him down the eastern hall.

"Elrohir says you aren't needed anymore," one of the orcs cackled maliciously.

30

Syllē studied the deep crevice below the treacherous rope bridge that spanned it. It appeared to be the only way across and constructed by goblins, who weren't all that adept at building sturdy things of any kind; so Syllē had already ascertained that they would have to cross a few at a time or risk stressing the tensile strength of the bridge, possibly causing it to collapse. She wasn't too thrilled about this, as it would mean time they didn't necessarily have. Time for the Dark to realize they were already within the mountains. Time for their enemies to set an ambush or a full-frontal attack. If Merilik's forces attacked while a few of them were on either side of this bridge and a few were crossing, it would be disastrous for them. They needed to cross now.

Still, Syllē studied the ravine floor. It was as she was about to signal for Tarin to join her in crossing the bridge that she heard it—the slow hissing breathing of a basilisk. Searching for the source of the sound, Syllē's eyes finally pierced the deep darkness below her and just barely made out the outline of the coiled snake in the worst place possible—directly below the center of the precarious rope bridge. Any noise from above, any falling debris, and that snake would make a meal of whoever was on that bridge. Cursing to herself, Syllē tried to come up with a plan.

The only problems they'd had since leaving the wereling graveyard were two small orc patrols that had quickly been dispatched and disposed of down another deep ravine and Finn's sudden insistence they return to the graveyard to return the long knives he'd taken from the wereling's tomb. Finn was convinced he had dishonored himself and his entire family by stealing from the dead. He insisted that he must give back those weapons. Syllē had informed her brother that if the wereling hadn't wanted him to have those weapons, she would have taken them from him before she threw him out of her tomb. He'd been given a gift that, if returned, would be an insult to the wereling. This logic had mollified Finn a bit, but he wasn't entirely happy until his mother informed him that if he was still worried about having the weapons, he could return them to Akin when their mission was over. That way, a wereling would own them. Finn had finally agreed to keep moving forward.

Now, here they were stuck again. They needed to get over that bridge and do it immediately before anyone came looking for those two orc patrols and found her group instead. They were almost to the three tunnels, and Syllē knew that if they had any chance of surviving this and succeeding in their quest, they had to get to those three tunnels before any orc, goblin, Drēor, or troll found them. Unfortunately, Syllē's mind was drawing a blank on how to safely get her friends across that rickety bridge with a basilisk asleep under it.

Tarin crept forward to kneel by her side. Worriedly, he asked, *Syllē?*

Without answering, Syllē simply pointed down to the sleeping basilisk. She heard Tarin suck in his breath in alarm before getting up and heading rapidly down the path away from their group and the bridge. *Tarin? What are you doing?*

Start counting.

Tarin! Alarmed, Syllē got up to follow Tarin, but his response stopped her.

Just trust me, Syllē. I've got an idea.

Syllē took a deep breath and then slowly released it as she began to count. *One. Two. Three.* Tarin's laughter in her head made her feel better, but she didn't stop counting until he returned to stand beside her after effectively getting the basilisk to move down the ravine and far from sight.

He'd had a rather simple plan, which is possibly why it worked. Tarin moved far down the path beside the ravine until it dead-ended into a wall. The ravine continued through a curve and, eventually, out of the mountain. At the dead end, Tarin picked up a rock and threw it hard into the ravine curve. It struck a loose pile of rock which cascaded down the ravine and woke the snake, which decided it was hungry. So, unaware of the large assortment of food right above it, the snake slithered through the ravine and out of the mountain to hunt. Tarin waited several minutes after the basilisk had slithered from view and he could no longer hear its movements before returning to Syllē, who'd counted way past a hundred by the time he returned to her side.

Syllē grinned with relief at him and rested her forehead briefly against his before turning to motion for the rest of their group to join them and cross the bridge as quickly as they could.

31

They'd made pretty good time since the bridge. Syllē had been really pushing them, which was why her sudden stop at the door of a long hall was so surprising. The hall had a strange glow to it in all the darkness as if it had its own personal light source, but Tarin couldn't see any crystals on the ceiling. Where was the light coming from?

"Wow," Finn whistled softly as he stood next to Syllē, gazing at what appeared to be a vast treasure. "Is this a dragon treasure horde?"

"No," Syllē responded tersely.

What Finn thought was a treasure horde was a Drēor's trophy room. The hundreds of objects filling the floors and lining the walls of the room all had their own inner light, their own memory, which was what was reflecting throughout the room. The horde was full of reminders of all Therendē'al had conquered. It was the place where he came to gloat over his greatest victories; and at its center was his greatest treasure—K'tanna. He had been unsuccessful in trapping her spirit in this world. As she lay in his arms dying, she'd laughed at him when he began the incantations to keep her spirit with him. Her final triumph had burned him to his core, so he kept her body always with him.

Suddenly, Finn heard Syllē's sharp intake of breath and felt an intense coldness emanating from her. Finn noticed that Syllē's eyes were locked on something, and her breathing was harsh and quick. Following her stare, Finn saw her gaze was zeroed in on the central altar tomb. Finn's tone as he said his uncle's name alerted Tarin something was wrong.

"What's wrong?" Tarin's concern was evident in his voice as he pushed his way to Syllē's side.

His voice jolted Syllē back to the group at the door. Glancing down at Tarin, she responded, "Nothing I have time to explain." Her voice thick with fury and sadness, she continued, "We need to move. If my memory is correct, the crossroads are right past this hall." Her instructions were interrupted by the muted shrieks of goblins farther back in the mountains followed by signal drums.

"It would appear those orc patrols have been discovered. We need to move fast," Elēandil warned.

Nodding, Syllē turned to Falinor, "Father, start leading them through. Stay on the path, and Finn…"

"I know. Don't touch anything," Finn muttered.

Syllē grinned at her brother, "Yes, but amend it to touch only what I tell you."

"Daughter," Falinor began. His displeasure was evident in his voice. "There's no time."

Syllē curtly cut him off, "Lead everyone to that door and Finn and I will meet you there."

"You mean, you and I will meet them there," Tarin asserted.

"Tarin," Syllē began.

"Beside me or right in front of me, Syllē," came Tarin's growl.

Sighing, Syllē said, "Fine, but stay right behind me."

"That's exactly where I plan to be." Turning to Finn, Tarin instructed, "Go with the others. We'll meet you at the door."

Syllē shook her head, starting to move towards the altar tomb, "No, I need Finn. Both of you follow me."

"Why do you need Finn?" Tarin almost snarled.

"Because I have no doubts about my abilities to toss him onto that tomb. You," Syllē shrugged slightly, "not so much."

32

Syllē and the elves took special care to avoid touching any of the objects in the horde. The last thing any of them needed was to be overcome with a memory attached to an item. The sound of goblin moving rapidly towards them spurred everyone to move even faster. Soon, however, they all could tell that their pursuers had made it to the basilisk's bridge. Their furious shrieks made it apparent that the goblins weren't happy the bridge was down, but everyone knew it wouldn't take long for the goblins to traverse the basilisk's trench and continue to the hall.

For the second time in a very short while, Finn found himself standing on yet another altar tomb, straddling yet another deceased warrior. Swiftly, Finn retrieved K'tanna's war hammer Syllē had requested and a circlet that she had not because as he crouched above the dead woman, he could have sworn she ordered him to take that circlet and run. Her eyes seemed to flash at him, disconcerting Finn even more than her voice in his head.

The taking of the items triggered a trap. The opening in the far wall was closing as a stone door began rather rapidly descending from the ceiling. Falinor's group had already made it through the opening. Syllē, Finn, and Tarin, however, would be trapped; and the goblins were almost to the door of the hall. As they ran, Tarin grabbed a nearby Drengas spear from the horde to jam the door. His throw was accurate, and the door stopped, temporarily.

Within a few yards of the opening, the sound of goblin battle shrieks caused the hair on Tarin's arms to stand on end. Their pursuers had made it to the hall and had no intention of losing their quarry. Finn was almost through the opening, when Tarin deftly spun Syllē off her feet and slung her, causing her to catapult Finn the rest of the way. Tarin made his own almost desperate leap for the door, dislodging the spear as he flew by it, causing the door to crash dramatically behind him, trapping their goblin pursuers and giving them a bit of a breather.

Brushing herself off as she got up from where she had landed on Finn, Syllē ruefully admonished Tarin, "A little warning next time you decide you're going to sling me around, please."

"Well, at least, now you know how it feels," Finn muttered as he stood up, rubbing the small of his back.

Grinning almost maliciously at Finn, Syllē patted her brother on the head. "Attach K'tanna's hammer to my belt. Quickly! We need to put as much distance between us and those goblins immediately." Suddenly noticing what else Finn was carrying, Syllē furiously yelled, "Finn, I swear…"

Finn almost frantically interrupted her, "She told me to take it! I promise! Her eyes flashed and then she told me to take it!"

Syllē studied Finn. "What color were the eyes? Black? Answer me."

Finn shook his head, "Ice blue." Syllē's silence unsettled Finn. "I promise that she told me to take it for you, Syllē." Finn's voice was a plea.

"Ice blue, eh?"

Swallowing hard, Finn nodded, "And terrifying. Even more than yours."

Syllē laughed. K'tanna had had a knack for being terrifying. The sound of the goblins rerouting to pursue them spurred Syllē to decide.

"Fine, give that to Tarin to keep in his bag, attach the hammer to my belt, and let's move."

They ran for the crossroads with an urgency born from the knowledge that their pursuers were almost upon them.

33

The group made it to the crossroads well ahead of their pursuers and split into their three predetermined fight groups, each heading down a different road. They were hoping this would either mean the goblins would pursue one specific group and the other two would elude them or the large army of goblins would split into three, making them more manageable for each group. Regardless, Syllē knew that down those tunnels, they would find the children and Oran as well as the main prison before ultimately coming to the back entrance—or exit, which is how they would use it. Syllē also knew that they didn't have the time to search each of the tunnels together. They had to split up, move fast, and get to the exit bringing whoever or whatever they found with them.

Halicyon's group headed down the far-right tunnel. Hearing the goblins in hot pursuit behind them didn't give him any time to acknowledge who he was leaving or worry at all about them. He had to get his group through the maze and to the central room, hopefully without any major opposition or loss of anyone. With the twins onboard, Halicyon knew that might be a little difficult, since those two, especially Finn, seemed to have a knack for finding themselves in trouble. At least, Amarris was a steadying influence on Kwin, and Thēorin certainly wouldn't instigate any tomfoolery himself.

They had been making pretty good time and weren't hearing any sounds of pursuers when Halicyon abruptly brought them all to a halt. Before anyone could ask what was happening, they heard guttural voices ahead in the darkness. While he couldn't discern what exactly the voices were saying, Halicyon knew those voices belonged to mountain trolls and he wasn't thrilled. Somehow, they'd have to get around those monsters and Halicyon knew it wouldn't be easy. Mountain trolls were the largest of the trolls, greatly outsizing their hill and lowland cousins. They were huge and solid, built like the mountains from which they came and almost as difficult to topple. For all their bulk, though, they were surprisingly agile and brutally strong. One mountain troll was a difficult adversary, but two? Well, two was two more than Halicyon wanted to handle.

As the group slowly crept forward and made their way quietly around the next bend, they could hear that the trolls were fighting over their dinner. They had gotten tired of eating orc and goblin, so they had decided to try and raid the cages guarded by the Black Guard again. This wasn't an easy task, as the Black Guard were orc specifically bred for that unit. They were quite a bit larger than normal orc and stronger and more intelligent than your average orc. They were the elite of Merilik's fighting forces, which is why he always kept a group as his personal guard. They were the only group that wargs respected and rarely attacked. No one, Dark or Light, really wanted to come up against them alone or even at all; and no one would consider a raid on their cages as a smart action, except mountain trolls.

This second troll raid on a Black Guard unit's cages had been more successful than the first as the orc decided to simply let the trolls have their pick. It wasn't worth it to protect their prisoners since the last raid a few weeks ago had cost them three of their own to the trolls' dinner table, instead of any prisoners. After having their pick of the cages, the two trolls were arguing over how best to prepare and eat their prey.

As they drew closer to the trolls, the group did their best to remain in the shadows. Halicyon was desperately searching for a way through that would keep them hidden, not only from the mountain trolls, but also the orcs guarding cages nearby. Finn, however, was intent on the massive trolls dragging a very unwilling man by his arms after them. Drawing the wereling's long knives, Finn crept carefully forward, not really contemplating the tremendous danger he was about to face. Finn didn't even consider that he was engaging two trolls on his own because he was confident that Kwin would have his back and Amarris would have Kwin's, and Halicyon and Thēorin would back them all up. Never having fought mountain trolls, Finn had no real concept of how truly dangerous his situation was and the danger he was about to bring on his friends. Truthfully, though, even if he had known, he still would engage the trolls. No Exulian dwarf could ever stomach leaving anyone to be a troll, goblin, or orc meal just to keep themselves safe.

As the trolls slowly moved forward totally oblivious, it seemed, to the efforts of their prey to get away, they were arguing over what to eat with him. The larger of the two suddenly said, "Dwarf."

His slightly smaller companion retorted, "We're not allowed to eat any dwarf unless Master has seen it first and determined what He wants to do with it. You know that, stupid."

Punching the smaller troll in the shoulder with his free arm, the larger troll roared as he pointed at Finn, who was now standing squarely in front of them, "Dwarf! You stupid!"

Without taking his eyes off Finn and the trolls, Halicyon menacingly muttered to Kwin, "If we survive this, Kwin, I am going to kill your brother."

* * *

Syllē was thinking the same thoughts about Tarin at that moment. Her group had taken the far-left tunnel at the crossroads and had been finding it an easy jog until they heard growling and fighting ahead of them echoing through their tunnel. It was malidaemon fighting each other, and Syllē was hoping that meant their group could use the fracas as cover and sneak quietly by whatever malidaemon were ahead of them. She had no intention of losing Elēandil, Eirik, or Firth to be some daemon's host. Nor did she want any of her dwarves injured in an all-out brawl with a swarm of malidaemons. Motioning to keep quiet and keep low, Syllē started to try and creep forward and past the fighting daemons, sticking desperately to the shadows.

It was working. The daemons were on the other side of a deep chasm, and it was a ferocious battle. Syllē briefly discerned at least five dead or severely injured and possibly five or six more still attacking each other. While the chasm was too wide for any malidaemon to leap, Syllē saw a plank precariously placed across it; so, there was a way for those beasts to get to them. Suddenly, Syllē noticed the sound of fighting had stopped. Crouching in the shadows against the far wall, she looked across at the daemons and became alarmed. The fight was over, and a winner had been decided. The remaining losing malidaemons who could still stand were backing slowly away from a scrappy daemon in their midst, who arrogantly but cautiously, began making its way towards a figure chained near the edge of the chasm. So, that's what the fight had been about—choosing which one got the host.

Sickened, Syllē and the rest watched the malidaemon slowly approach the chained figure. As the daemon was about to leap, Syllē was even more sickened at seeing Tarin swiftly running across the plank. Deftly limboing under the daemon, Tarin used his axe to disembowel it and then decapitated it as soon as it thudded to the ground. Unfortunately, now Tarin was confronted with a slew of other malidaemons ready to kill him. The two closest to him charged, airborne on their final bound. Tarin spun away and used his axe to cut one of the daemons in half. The second, which had turned to pursue Tarin as soon as it landed, was met with a flat-sided strike to its face, dazing it long enough for Tarin to move swiftly beside it and chop it in half. Excellent work, truly, but the only reason the next five daemons didn't leap on him and help each other tear him to shreds was the arrival of Syllē and the rest. Working in teams of Hil and Eirik, Firth and Trygve, and Elēandil and Syllē, the group slaughtered the remaining malidaemons while Tarin worked to release the elf they had been fighting to possess.

Striding furiously towards Tarin after all the malidaemons were dead, Syllē hissed, "What were you thinking? You could have gotten yourself killed!"

"I was thinking that no one, not even an elf, deserves one of those things running around in its body," Tarin retorted as he finally released the cuffs imprisoning the elf. Tarin ordered Hil to put salve on the elf's wrists and quickly bind them as a means of deflecting and ignoring Syllē's fury, but Syllē refused to be ignored.

Grabbing Tarin by the arm, Syllē spun him to face her and bring him closer. Getting right in his face, she jabbed a finger forcefully into his chest. "Fine then. If I must follow the rule, so do you."

"What rule?" Tarin asked angrily, backing up slightly and rubbing his chest.

"Beside me or right in front of me," Syllē glared at the dwarf, almost daring him to contradict her.

Grinning, Tarin gleefully reminded her that rule was his for her and her alone. Truly, there was no way she could follow the rule and be right in front of him at the same time as he was right in front of her. It just wasn't physically possible.

"Fine, beside me or right behind me, and I mean no more than one step behind me, Tarin," Syllē hissed.

As Tarin grinned at Syllē again and nodded, telling her that was something he could do, his attention was caught by a voice coming from some-where in the darkness behind them—an exhausted and weak but painfully joyful voice, "Tarin. I knew you would come. I knew you would find me."

Tarin's eyes widened before he turned to desperately search the dark-ness behind him for Oran.

34

Finn decided to use the fact that the punch from the larger troll had knocked the slightly smaller troll a little off balance to his advantage. The dwarf had noticed what looked like worn down stone steps carved out of the wall to the right of the troll. Swiftly, Finn ran adeptly up the precarious "staircase" until he was basically level with the off-balance troll's head and leapt toward it. One long knife went through the troll's right eye while his other long knife sliced into the troll's neck. The troll blindly struck out at Finn, sending the dwarf flying backwards where he bounced and skipped across the floor a short distance before coming to a slamming stop against the back wall. Fortunately for Finn, who'd had his head a bit scrambled from its abrupt meeting with the wall, the knife through the eye had been a fatal blow and the troll thundered to the floor; but unfortunately for Finn, there was still a very much alive and now very angry troll left.

Amarris got the larger troll's attention by trying to shoot it through the heart, but a mountain troll's hide is so thick it's like chainmail and the arrow barely scratched the surface of the troll's chest. Realizing it had adversaries on both sides of it, the troll checked to see that Finn was still incapacitated before turning its full attention to the rest of the group, who had stepped out of the shadows and were lined up facing off against the behemoth.

Amarris notched another arrow, but Halicyon's voice stopped her from releasing it. "Arrows won't penetrate anything vital. A mountain troll's only weakness is its eyes, which they're exceptionally adept at protecting."

At this point, the troll, who was relishing the thought of the coming annihilation and then consumption of so many delicious creatures he wouldn't have to share with anyone, leaned down on its front fists and let out an earth-shattering, mountain-rocking battle roar before falling forward dead from a well-placed arrow that rocketed through its throat, clipping its tonsils before severing its spine.

Staring rather incredulously at the second dead troll, Halicyon observed ironically, "Or, apparently, a shot through the mouth also works. Nicely done, Amarris. Now, where's Finn so I can kill him?"

"What do you mean, where's Finn?" Kwin asked. "He's right there against the…" Kwin stopped talking as soon as he realized his brother was no longer lying against the far wall where the troll had thrown him. In fact, Finn was no longer in sight. Before Kwin could get too worried, they all heard Finn's battle cry emanating from not too far down the tunnel to the left. However, the answering orc roars spurred them all into a full-on sprint.

"Dammit, Finn!" Halicyon swore as he ran towards the noise of battle.

* * *

Recklessly, Tarin shot forward, looking for Oran in all that darkness but soon found himself walking on air. Before Tarin plummeted into the curve of the exceedingly deep ravine, Hathor, the elf he'd just saved, reached out and grabbed him by his axe sheath's strap, hauling Tarin back onto solid footing. "Your friend is chained to that small pinnacle of rock jutting up in the center there," Hathor quietly explained.

Tarin peered intently across the ravine and could soon make out Oran chained spread eagle to the wall of a tall, thin tower of rock. With a sinking heart, Tarin realized he couldn't get to Oran. It was way too far across for a dwarf to jump. Perhaps he could climb down the side of the ravine and then climb back up the rock tower. Searching for a good place to start descending, Tarin suddenly caught a whiff of something truly foul. "Syllē," Tarin's voice was a warning whisper, "I smell changelings nearby—at least one. Down in the ravine."

Hathor answered quietly, kneeling next to Tarin as he spoke, "Your friend's where they put the victims for the changelings to feed upon."

Eirik whispered furiously, "We have to get him off that tower. We can't leave him to be—"

Tarin's glare stopped Eirik short. So, with changelings in the pit below, climbing down was not an option. Maybe they could use the plank to get across. Tarin quickly dismissed that idea as he couldn't see any truly solid ledge on the other side on which to rest the plank. Tarin noticed the smell of the changeling was getting stronger. He couldn't see it, but he was certain the strength of its smell meant it was getting closer. Swearing to himself, Tarin racked his brain desperately for a solution to save Oran. He had not come all this way only to have to watch his friend be consumed by a changeling.

At that moment, Tarin heard Syllē's voice in his head order him, *Start counting*, before he saw her take a running leap towards Oran and the rock tower, a long knife gripped tightly in her hands. She landed against the tower only a short distance below Oran, her long knife shoved into the rock face like a climber's pick. She grabbed a hand hold with a free hand, pulled her weapon free and then sheathed it before beginning to rapidly climb the short distance to Oran. Releasing his feet first, Syllē carefully climbed up Oran himself until she was precariously standing on a sliver of a ledge with only enough room for her toes to grip. She had gotten the chains around his waist and his right arm undone when the first changeling appeared almost beside them. Its forked tongue licked its lips eagerly at the thought of not one but two tasty victims.

Rolling Oran away from it to the other side of her body, Syllē prepared to dispatch the beast without falling off the rock tower, not an easy thing to do. At least Oran was being held on the rock by his left hand, she thought. She wouldn't have to worry about him falling into the pit. Syllē was reaching for one of her long knives, when a shaft of wood sailed forcefully past her and pierced the changeling—pinioning it to the wall of the tower just out of reach of both her and Oran. Hathor had seen several victims fed to the changelings while chained on this side of the ravine and had noticed how the goblins, orc, and the occasional Drēor had used ash wood staffs to keep the changelings off themselves. He had handed one to Tarin, and yet again the dwarf's throw had been accurate.

Turning her attention back to Oran, Syllē swiftly undid his left hand and caught almost his full weight over her shoulder. Grasping the chains that had once held Oran to the tower, she tried to keep them both from falling into the pit below as she carefully tried to maneuver them to face their friends. "Tarin, Trygve, have Elēandil and Firth hold onto you and climb slightly down the ravine and get ready to catch Oran," Syllē instructed.

Finding a minuscule amount of flat space to the side of the tower, Syllē used it to get a more solid footing, grasp Oran firmly, and then sling him with all her strength towards Tarin and Trygve. Her throw was almost too short, but Tarin and Trygve both stretched out as far as they could and grabbed a hold of Oran, reeling him towards them and then shoving him up the wall towards Hil and Eirik, who dragged him the rest of the way to the top.

Turning back towards Syllē, Tarin and Trygve gagged at the strong stench of changeling. To their horror, another one rose off the tower directly in Syllē's path. "Hathor, spear that thing!" Tarin yelled.

"I can't," Hathor responded. "If I do, the shaft will go straight through it and pinion your friend as well. It's right in front of her."

Syllē had no room to get away from the changeling and it knew it. Grinning maliciously, it started towards her, laughing at her attempt to kill it with her long knife. Its mirth changed when it saw a blue flame erupt down the hilt of the weapon and sear through its skin and into its body. It realized too late that this wasn't an ordinary elf it was facing.

"You are the one Master has been looking for," it managed before falling backwards off the blade and into the deep pit below.

Using the precarious runway to help launch herself, Syllē leapt towards Tarin and Trygve, who stretched out and grabbed her as adeptly as they had grabbed Oran just moments before. Again, they handed their catch up to Hil and Eirik, who helped haul Syllē to the top of the ravine where she met Hathor's and Elēandil's inquiring gazes with her own raised eyebrow, a slightly indolent shrug, and, "A well-placed ash wood stake to the heart works against one of those things every time."

35

Getting slammed into the wall had briefly disoriented Finn. Shaking his head, he tried to rid his brain of the stone-induced fog and concentrate on his situation. A hulking dark figure to his right caught his attention. Turning to look, Finn tried to focus his eyes through the darkness of the narrow corridor. When his eyes finally did focus, Finn almost screamed in alarm. The figure appeared to be the she-bear sitting in the corridor staring at him. Without taking her eyes off the dwarf, she rose and started moving down the corridor. Without thinking, Finn followed her, watching her disappear around a sharp curve.

Quickening his pace, Finn rounded the curve and found himself in a large cavern. Its walls were lined with cages and the floors were strewn with trash obviously from orc and goblins, because much of the trash was bones. Finn didn't even want to contemplate the number of tortured souls who'd passed through this room based on what littered the floors of the cavern. He strained to find the she-bear, but she seemed to have disappeared. Shortly, Finn's eye was caught by a woman tied hand and throat to a rock pillar jutting out of the floor of the chamber.

Finn cautiously approached her, peering into the darkness beyond the chamber for whatever trap lay in wait for him. Why wasn't anyone guarding her? Why was she just there like bait? It seemed too easy. What Finn didn't know was that the Black Guard had abandoned the chamber as soon as they'd heard the trolls lumbering towards them. They had no intention of being on the trolls' menu this time and were giving the trolls plenty of time and room to make their meal choices.

Deciding it was as safe as it was going to get, Finn approached the woman, who appeared to be alive but unconscious, and deftly cut the ropes binding her throat before moving to one side of the rock to slice one of the ropes binding her wrists together. Catching her as she crumpled to the side, Finn gently laid her on her back and then removed the rest of the ropes from her wrists before trying to waken her. His efforts quickly paid off and her eyes opened, widening a bit at the sight of the dwarf in front of her. She had obviously not expected to see him. Finn found her honey brown eyes with flecks of gold mesmerizing. Hearing distant movement echoing towards him from one of the other narrow corridors leading out of the chamber, Finn helped the woman sit up and offered her some water, which she drank greedily.

"Can you move? I have a feeling we need to get out of here and fast," Finn was speaking to her but not looking at her. Instead, he was studying the dark corridor from which he'd heard something rapidly moving their way. "My friends are just down that corridor." Finn absently gestured towards the narrow corridor he'd followed the she-bear down only a few moments before. "Course, they're dealing with a couple mountain trolls, so they'll be a minute. We really should head their way."

The woman rather unsteadily tried to rise to her feet. She got as far as her knees before grabbing her head a moment and swaying slightly. Finn quickly caught her arm and tried to help stabilize her. "If you can move at all, now would be the time," Finn spoke urgently, still surveying that corridor. Whoever or whatever was coming was almost within view.

Using Finn and the rock for balance, the woman stood, swaying again slightly as she gained her feet. Grasping Finn's shoulder, she steadied herself and started to turn towards the corridor down which Finn had come, but her attention was caught by the first Black Guard to return to the chamber. His companions wouldn't be too far behind him.

Finn sighed resignedly, "Of course I'd find Black Guards in here. I mean, we've already run into Strygoi, a basilisk, a couple mountain trolls, and a dead woman with terrifying flashing eyes. Why wouldn't I find Black Guards, too?" Almost angrily, Finn finished, "Next, it'll be malidaemons and changelings with a few Malrauk thrown in for fun." Pointing towards the other corridor, Finn instructed the woman, "Get to my family. They will take care of you." Moving forward as he spoke, Finn continued, "And if you don't mind, send them my way before I get killed."

Finn moved to engage the Black Guard, who was still on his own but not worried. Dwarves were never a problem, especially not a young juvenile like this one. Grinning gleefully at the fun he felt he was about to have, the Black Guard slowly started to charge Finn, who had moved towards the middle of the chamber. Overconfidence spawned from malice caused the orc to pick up its pace as it anticipated the kill. Maybe he'd slice off the dwarf's arm or leg first. He always enjoyed watching a victim writhe and suffer. It enhanced the thrill of the final kill.

Finn had no intention of letting the Black Guard get that close. He would only allow it close enough to spring his trap. At least, right now, there was only the one he had to fight, but Finn knew the rest were coming and coming fast. He stood with his sword in his right hand appearing to wait to engage the orc in hand-to-hand combat; but as soon as the orc came within six feet of him, Finn dropped his sword and swiftly swung his battle axe that he'd been holding in his left hand behind his back over his head and using both hands for force, slung the axe at the orc's head. The Black Guard never saw it coming and, therefore, had no way of dodging the flying axe. It hit its mark, splitting the orc's head in half like a melon.

Finn had no time to run forward and retrieve his axe. The rest of the Black Guard unit had arrived in the chamber and were swiftly bearing down on him. Picking up his sword, Finn tried to find a less out-in-the-open spot from which to fight, effectively limiting the Black Guard on maneuverability and leveling the playing field a bit more. He rapidly retreated towards the cages and the rock pillar. Amarris, who was well ahead of the rest of their group, shot the closest orc to Finn with an arrow to the right eye. Notching arrows swiftly as she strode forward, Amarris made it to Finn's side, taking out four more Black Guards as she did.

"Never thought I'd be happy to see you," Finn grinned at her as she joined him.

Smirking at him, Amarris shot another orc, effectively holding the rest of the unit at bay. They regrouped around the body of their first fallen comrade before deciding to charge Amarris and Finn as a compact group. They knew she'd get some of them, but there was no way she could fell them all before they were on top of her and Finn, and the pair knew it, too.

"Kwin is going to hate me forever if you die, Amarris," Finn muttered in frustration. "So, get out of here, now."

Amarris snorted derisively, "Yeah, like that's going to happen. I let you die, and he'll hate *me* forever."

Both were distracted by a ferocious growl coming from right behind them. It was quickly answered by other unnerving roars and growls emanating from several of the cages behind them. Finn noticed the noises caused the charging orc to check their strides and stop a moment several feet from them, looking with alarm at something behind him.

"Duck!" Amarris yelled as she slammed her hand on his shoulder, forcing him to his knees.

Finn looked up to see something huge and tawny fly over his head and land a few strides in front of the stalled Black Guard unit. In only two bounding leaps, the creature leapt onto the closest orc and tore him to shreds. Finn quickly started forward to aid whoever or whatever this animal was but was knocked roughly to the floor by another huge beast as it leapt into the battle. Soon, the Black Guard were on the run with at least eight or nine beasts that vaguely resembled bears, cougars, or wolves hunting them. The cavern rapidly emptied of all but Halicyon's fight group and a few prisoners too weak to exit their open cages, whom Halicyon was trying to aid with herbs and a little elven medicine.

Finn turned around, looking for the woman he had saved, but she wasn't there. Confused, he asked Halicyon, "Where is she? The woman? I sent her down the corridor to you. Where'd she go?" Finn was worried she may have fallen and been missed in the darkness.

Halicyon shrugged, "There was a woman here when we first entered the cavern. She was opening the cages."

"Where is she now?" Finn asked as he headed to retrieve his battle axe.

Before Halicyon could answer him, Finn noticed the beasts returning to the chamber. They may have resembled bears, lions, or wolves; but their size was at least twice as large as the average bear, lion, or wolf. Plus, their eyes shown with an intelligence and ferocity that Finn found exceptionally unnerving. Against his better judgment, Finn decided hesitantly to sheath his axe and stand weaponless and quietly in the center of the room. It wasn't easy, because as the group of beasts came closer and closer, Finn became more and more uneasy.

Soon, a large lioness was only a short distance from Finn and walking straight at him. The rest of the group parted and encircled him, so he had no escape. "Halicyon?" Finn's voice betrayed his fear, and it killed him.

Enjoying Finn's discomfort more than he should have, Halicyon responded flippantly, "You got yourself into this mess. I can't take on a whole pack of werelings for you. Figure it out."

"Werelings?" Finn was astonished, but then it made complete sense. Finn grinned, "So, Akin's not the only one left." Then Finn remembered what Syllē had told him about werelings and dwarves. "Halicyon, Syllē said werelings don't like dwarves." He was trying to find a way out of the circle and away from the slowly approaching lioness, who was now only a stride or two away from him. "Shouldn't you be helping me now?"

Halicyon responded, still enjoying Finn's discomfort, "Maybe next time you'll remember to be more cautious." He paused a moment before saying ominously, "If there is a next time, that is."

At this point, the lioness stopped directly in front of Finn, her mouth with its extremely large front canines directly in front of his face. Swallowing hard, Finn tried desperately not to faint or turn and run. Then he noticed the lioness' eyes—honey brown with flecks of gold. "It's you," was all Finn got out before she ducked her head towards him and rubbed her forehead against his chest.

Finn heard Halicyon laugh, but the elf's laughter quickly stopped as Finn pulled out the long knives from the tomb. "Finn," Halicyon said, concern evident in his voice. "What are you doing?"

"I'm giving them back," Finn answered. "They're werelings, and these came from the she-bear's tomb. She let me borrow them against the Strygoi and now I can give them back."

To Finn, it was very simple. He'd return the long knives, and no one could ever accuse of him of dishonoring his family or his clan by stealing from the dead. Unfortunately, it appeared that his having the long knives angered the werelings as the lioness caught sight of them and rapidly backed away from Finn, snarling slightly as she did. The others in the circle all seemed to glare at Finn.

Nervously, he continued to hold the knives out to the lioness. "I asked her permission to borrow them to fight the Strygoi. I didn't steal them from her. I would never steal from the dead. When she tossed me from her tomb to save me from the flames, I didn't have a chance to give them back to her."

"Finn," Halicyon's tone was rife with warning, "stop. Stand still. Put those away."

"But I don't want them to think I would steal from their dead," Finn protested, never taking his eyes off the lioness, who appeared to be studying him. Then she turned and disappeared out of the circle. "Hey! Wait!" Finn yelled, trying to follow her, but he was blocked by the circle of werelings, who had absolutely no intention of letting him through. "Halicyon!"

"Hang on, Finn. If they wanted you dead, you'd already be ripped to shreds. Your friend is returning."

Finn's eyes widened as the circle parted, giving Finn a view of Halicyon and his friends. Then, the woman he'd first seen upon entering the cavern returned to stand in front of him, a lioness no more. Finn held the long knives out to her again, but she refused to take them.

Shaking her head, the wereling informed Finn in a deep and silky voice that sounded almost like a purr, "I cannot take those. She gave them to you to use. Only she can take them back."

"But I can't go back there. The way is blocked," Finn protested. "Please, take them."

"Finn," Halicyon's voice was still rife with warning, "you are currently doing something that no dwarf in over five thousand years has been able to do—meet a wereling face to face and survive. Don't blow it."

"But—"

"Finn, I'm serious."

Suddenly, the wereling stepped forward and took a small hatchet out of Finn's waistband. Turning it over in her hand, her silky voice purred at him, "A trade. You now have a piece of us to take with you—my great great-aunt's knives—and we have a piece of you. You have stolen nothing, Master Dwarf." She smiled at him kindly now as she placed his lucky hatchet in her belt loop.

Finn looked around at the circle of werelings before meeting her steady gaze. Taking a deep breath and then slowly releasing it, Finn solemnly nodded at her before bowing slightly. "I am Finn, son of Hil, daughter of

Farin of the line of Asger. I am honored to carry your great great-aunt's weapons."

The wereling smiled warmly back at him before bowing slightly in return. "I am Tasha. Thank you for rescuing me, son of Asger. I am in your debt."

Halicyon began to breathe again. Shaking his head in amazement, the elf could barely believe what Finn had just accomplished. For the first time in thousands of years, a dwarf was not only leaving the presence of wereling alive but as a friend. *It could only happen to Finn,* Halicyon mused.

36

"That's it!" Varger furiously confronted Gydion. "We trust Lord Falinor above all else, so whatever your game is, you won't be able to turn us against him." From slightly behind him, Flarne gripped his battle axe tightly and nodded firmly in support of Varger.

Confused, Gydion turned towards Varger. "Why do you think I am trying to turn you against Falinor?"

"Because every time Lord Falinor takes us in a direction or makes a decision, you ask us if we think that's a wise decision." Varger's temper was rising. "How should we know? We've never been here before."

Calmly, Gydion explained, "This is an ancient dwarf kingdom, long abandoned but still the same format. I just assumed since you were dwarves, you'd have a better feeling with direction in here than an elf."

It was Varger's turn to be confused. Looking briefly at Flarne and then back to Gydion, he responded, "I know of no dwarf kingdom ever being in the Perdarus."

Falinor explained, "This is the remnants of King Asger's original kingdom. Where he began his rule. His people came into conflict with the wereling, and much bloodshed ensued. King Asger brokered a peace with the wereling to stop the violence, and part of the peace was to remove his people from this kingdom."

Varger shook his head, still confused, "I can't believe it's a dwarf kingdom. Those always run east to west. This runs rather haphazardly with a slight tilt from north to south. Dwarves wouldn't do that."

"Regardless, it was a dwarf kingdom at one time, and that is the only reason I was asking for yours and Flarne's opinions," Gydion said, looking directly at Varger and Flarne as he spoke. "I promise."

Varger looked at Falinor, who smiled encouragingly at him before frowning darkly down the corridor they had just traversed. Tersely, Falinor instructed, "We need to move. The goblins are closing in."

Varger heard Flarne clear his throat and then cautiously say, "Er— something has grabbed hold of my arm."

Falinor, Gydion, and Varger all swung around and noticed a small hand desperately gripping the sleeve of Flarne's tunic, emanating from what they all had thought was a solid wall. Striding forward, Falinor peered into the darkness. He realized that the wall had a cage door in front of a deep recess. Peering more intently into the recess, Falinor's eyes widened. They had just found more of the missing children.

"Oran told me the dwarves were coming for us," the young boy grasping Flarne's sleeve stated softly, when his desperate eyes met Falinor's.

37

Tarin hadn't expected the final chamber to be so full of light. He wasn't sure what he'd expected—maybe pitch black with horrid smells and terrifying screams of fear and pain emanating from the darkness. Instead, they cautiously entered a rather well-lit, immense, musty, and eerily silent chamber. The cages in this chamber were few and surprisingly empty. There were three crow cages hanging from the vaulted ceiling. Only one held a prisoner, who wasn't moving. Tarin had the sickening feeling that the elf or man in that cage was deceased, and he didn't want to even try and imagine how lonely and torturous the prisoner's last moments must have been.

Tarin could see an opening at the far end of the chamber and through it, clear sky. Turning to Eirik, who was helping to support Oran, who had only made it this far thanks to Syllē's healing, Tarin ordered, "Take Firth and get your brother through that door. Don't look back. Keep going. We'll be right behind you."

"Wait," Syllē quietly spoke, studying the room around them. "Something isn't right. Just wait."

Soon, Halicyon's and Falinor's groups joined them. There was no time for joyous reunions as they could all hear the rapidly approaching goblins. Tersely, Syllē started barking orders rapid-fire: "All of you, move towards that door. Carry the slow if you have to, but get out of and off this mountain now. Don't look back until you are safely in the Indili's valley. Don't stop. Just move." Looking almost angrily at Tarin, she asked, "I assume, due to our rules, that you will not be leaving my side, my lord?"

Tarin's derisive snort was really all the answer Syllē needed. "Fine then. We're going to make sure that Merilik's forces can't spring their trap and slam that rock down to block the door before any of us can get out."

Tarin's eyes grew wide as he finally noticed the huge rock leviathan above the far opening tucked up in the darkness of the vaulted ceiling. If that fell, it would not only block their exit but most likely also crush any number of their party. The empty and limited number of cages now made sense. They were never supposed to make it out of this mountain alive, and those few who did survive the rock fall and the ensuing battle would inhabit those cages.

The goblins weren't far from the end of the tunnels now. The sound of their rapid approach echoed ominously through the chamber. Syllē, with Tarin right behind her, began to move in a diagonal line through the chamber and towards the far corner wall. Halicyon grabbed Tarin's arm and said, "I made you a promise, Tarin, that you would never have to keep yours to Syllē. Go with the others. I will stay with her. We'll meet you in the valley."

"Halicyon," Syllē's anger was evident in her tone as she spoke, "you know Tarin would never go without either of us, and forcing him into the other group will only cause him to do something stupid and get us all killed or captured." Hugging Halicyon fiercely, she almost whispered, "We will meet you in the valley, my friend. I promise." Then she practically shoved the unhappy elf in the direction of the door.

Looking at Tarin, Halicyon placed his right hand over his heart and bowed slightly to the dwarf as he said, "Aat borthan, Khâzash." Halicyon had no idea what he'd said, but he felt it had to be the right thing since Tarin had said the same to him before going over the Drengas wall. Hopefully, he hadn't just insulted the dwarf. His fears were allayed when Tarin sincerely returned the salute. A goblin arrow flew right past Halicyon's head and embedded in the wood of a nearby ladder, ending the nice moment and sending both parties flying in opposite directions.

The goblins, thankfully—for the children and Oran—chose to follow Syllē and Tarin; they were the bigger prize anyway, and there was no way the group could survive the trap. As they ran, Tarin tried to slow their pursuers by slicing the chains holding the three crow cages up near the ceiling. The two empty ones rocketed down, effectively squashing a goblin or two and slowing the progress of their pursuers. The third, which was occupied, slammed into, and then rolled over several more, hindering the goblins immensely. It was enough to give Syllē and Tarin the time to occupy the high ground and prevent anyone from disengaging the chains holding the rock above the door. As they'd been running, Syllē had already shot several Black Guards whose job it had been to spring the trap. Now, she and Tarin used their advantage to keep the goblins and other Black Guards off them and away from the chains.

Their defense was so effective that many of the goblins decided they had a better chance of survival against the other group, which had almost made it out of the cavern. They were within the trap striking distance and in a very good spot to get out of the cavern if no one stopped them, especially since Tarin and Syllē now controlled the access to the door chains.

Syllē noticed their flight. "Tarin, cut the first chain. The one closest to you," she ordered as she deftly cut the head off a Black Guard, who had made a grab for the dwarf from behind. Shooting another Black Guard as it charged her from a nearby hallway, Syllē measured the progress of their friends versus the goblins. Her eyes narrowed slightly as she saw Halicyon stop just shy of the door to dispatch the advance group of goblins before they could overrun the children and Thēorin. Successful, Halicyon turned and started through the door, his eyes catching Syllē's as he exited the mountain. "Now, Tarin, cut the last two!"

The massive rock wasn't the only one being held aloft, and its crash coupled with the rockslide that swiftly followed was deafening. When the dust and noise cleared, Tarin could see that their exit was totally blocked and that the rocks had annihilated most of the goblins. Those who remained were regrouping and heading their way. Syllē swiftly surveyed the chamber. She could hear the enemy coming down the various corridors. If she didn't find another way out for them, she and Tarin would soon be prisoners—an experience she never wanted to revisit.

Just then, Syllē heard a formidable, deep, and terrifying otherworldly yell echoing from the corridor where Falinor's group had found the children. The power of the call caused the cavern to shake, freeing rocks to crash to the floor of the chamber. It also caused the remaining goblins and orc to flee the chamber through whatever exit was closest to them. Taking advantage of their flight, Syllē started to lead Tarin to another exit not far from where they had started. If she was right, with a little luck, it would lead them to the roof of the mountain. Not the easiest of exits, but an exit nonetheless.

As the pair passed the fallen crow cages heading for Syllē's choice of corridors, Tarin's ankle was grabbed, causing the dwarf to crash roughly to his knees. Turning his head, Tarin found himself meeting the very blue eyes of the elf who was imprisoned in the cage. Another ground shaking call caught Tarin's attention. The Malrauk was coming closer. Tarin jumped up and used his axe to release the door of the crow cage. Grabbing the elf's arm, Tarin hauled the elf to his feet and started to help him across the cavern after Syllē, but she had changed direction. There were too many orcs down their escape route.

Desperately, Syllē searched for a way out. She could sense that the Malrauk was almost upon them. Choosing a different corridor, she started to head that way when she was grabbed from behind by strong arms and dragged inside the wall. Ferociously, Syllē used the wall as leverage to flip herself up and over the head of her captor. Landing on his back, she drove him viciously into the floor of the narrow hallway.

Before she could harm the man beneath her any further, Tarin caught her arm. "I believe the werelings are actually trying to save us," he smugly informed her.

Startled, Syllē looked up to see they were surrounded by a small group of werelings. Quickly, she helped her savior up off the floor, trying to dust him off a bit in apology. She refused to look at Tarin as his grin was irksome to her.

The trampled wereling lumbered over to a woman with honey brown eyes and a dwarf hatchet in her belt. Rubbing his back, he ruefully informed her, "The rumors about that one are true. She is a formidable opponent."

Tarin noticed the hatchet and recognized it. "How did you get my nephew's lucky hatchet?"

Tasha smiled at him. "We traded—his hatchet for the long knives," she shrugged. Hearing their enemies converging all around them, she continued, "Come. We're short on time." Then, she and the werelings escorted them through the mountain halls to a back corridor that would lead them to a door, which led out just below the roof of the mountain.

Tarin was surprised the werelings weren't coming with them. Turning to Tasha, Tarin bowed slightly, "Thank you for your help, but why are you not coming?"

"We have more of our own to find and free," was Tasha's terse reply.

"Well, if you ever need sanctuary, the Drengas will take you in," Tarin mentioned helpfully. Tarin's next statement caused Syllē to whirl around and stare at him in amazement. "Or if you wish, you can rest and regroup in Exulias. If you can stand the presence of dwarves, that is."

Tasha and the other wereling must have been as surprised as Syllē, but they didn't insult the dwarf. Reaching out, Tasha grasped Tarin's hand and bowed slightly over it, smiling. "Thank you, Master Dwarf. Some of my people might just take you up on that offer."

Tarin nodded uncertainly in return—finally realizing the offer he had just made. Grasping the elf's arm to help steady him as they exited the mountain, Tarin heard Syllē gasp in surprise. Looking up at her, he read disbelief and shock in her eyes as she caught a good look at the elf at Tarin's side.

Before Tarin could ask what was wrong, Syllē stepped forward and placed her hands on either side of the elf's face, raising his eyes to hers. "Thranulas," her heartache filled her voice as she spoke, pulling the elf forward to rest his forehead against hers. After a moment, she took a step back and smiled at Tarin. "Tarin, you saved Thranulas, King Thallan's eldest."

For a very brief moment, Tarin contemplated throwing the elf back in his crow cage. He did almost let go of Thranulas, which would have caused the elf to crash to the floor, but Syllē's glare stopped him. Swallowing the bile that had risen in his throat at the identity of the elf on his arm, Tarin moved forward, following Syllē and helping the elf out of the mountain.

38

"As you get off the mountain, head towards the Indili Valley. Don't hesitate. Keep going and stay wide to the left."

"But the fog."

"When you see the fog approaching, slow down and let the orc gain on you. It will then target them, and if you are wide enough, will reach them first. Watch the fog carefully because as it stalks our enemies, it will show you a pathway into the safety of the valley. Once you see that path, fly. It will only be open a short time, and once through, keep going. Don't look back or allow anyone to stop."

"And what about you, my daughter? Will you not be with us?"

"If I am, I will lead us through, Father. If not, I will meet you within the Valley of the Indili."

* * *

Falinor hadn't liked Syllē's instructions, but he trusted her. If she said there was a safe way through the fog, then one would show itself if he only followed her orders. Heading off the mountain, Falinor led the group far to the left and kept an eye on the fog that permeated the ground of the far tree line. As their group drew closer, Falinor's sharp eyes could see it slowly creeping towards them, stalking them like a predator stalks its prey, almost playing with them as it rolled forward to their right, getting ready to flank them and cut them off. Falinor could sense Hathor's and Elēandil's hesitation, and he was pretty sure Gydion wasn't too happy about where he was leading them either, but none of them hesitated or tried to turn back.

Falinor also kept tabs on the proximity of their pursuers. As soon as the orc cleared the tree line and headed towards the mountain's base and into the short meadow beyond, Falinor slackened his pace, letting the orc gain on them. Again, he could sense the others' uneasiness with his actions, but still, no one questioned him about it. Trygve, though, did look a little slant at him, but even that dwarf trusted him. Falinor let himself smile at that realization.

Soon, Falinor noticed the fog changing course as it seemed to sense more lethal and dark prey. He kept a close eye on the fog in front of him, which obscured the tree line behind it. As the orc bore down on their prey, Falinor spotted a thin break in the fog and headed swiftly for it. "Move! Get to that path at the tree line! Carry anyone who slows down! Fly! Now is our chance!" Falinor shouted at everyone.

Grabbing children, the elves and dwarves did just that. Firth and Eirik helped Oran before Thēorin simply threw his friend over his shoulder and flew towards the opening. The group barely made it, but thanks to the fog's preoccupation with the orc, Falinor successfully led them into the Indili Valley. Seeing their prey eluding them through the deadly fog, the orc tried to turn back to the safety of the Perdarus, but many were not that lucky as the fog wrapped around them, choking them and consuming them almost at the same time.

Syllē, Tarin, and Thranulas watched the attack of the fog on the orc. Tarin wasn't sure what he'd seen since they were so far above the valley floor. It was enough, however, that he understood the fog had done something to the orc, because when it slowly wended its way back towards the tree line, Tarin could discern no orc, not even bodies, left on the valley floor. Thranulas watched the demise of the orc with a little more pleasure than was truly appropriate for an elf and was almost loathe to turn away and follow Syllē, which was what actually got their trio back into hot water, as he was spotted by a captain of a Black Guard unit and the race was on again.

Syllē, Tarin, and Thranulas made a pretty good escape of it from the Black Guard, even with the elf's diminished state. As they ran down the mountain trails, either Tarin or Syllē helped Thranulas stay on his feet and with them. They were nearing the start of Ontari, the life-giving river of all the elven kingdoms in MithTerra as well as the water-bearer for much of MithTerra's lands. Its seven waterfalls, each getting more massive and powerful than the one before it, cascaded out of the Perdarus foothills, cutting through the Indili Valley and branching off into seven different rivers that traveled through the three eleven realms and the rest of the kingdoms of MithTerra before erupting into the great ocean waters beyond.

Ontari's start in a small pool in the foothills of the Perdarus had always been one of Syllē's favorite places, but there was no time to sit and enjoy its calming tranquility. The trio had outdistanced their Black Guard pursuers, but Thranulas was nearing his breaking point. Tarin was impressed the elf had made it this far.

"We have to get to the third waterfall," Syllē quietly informed them as they took a quick rest break for Thranulas. "There is a sanctuary within it where we can all rest and regroup before making our way into Indili territory." Looking with concern at Thranulas, she asked, "Can you make it?"

Leaning against Tarin's shoulder trying desperately to catch his breath, Thranulas managed a slight nod. Syllē wasn't convinced. Looking from Syllē's concerned face and then up into the shattered face of the elf on his arm, Tarin made a decision. Straightening to his full height, he looked up at Thranulas and said, "No one gets left behind. That's my clan's motto, and it includes you." Grasping the elf's arm firmly, Tarin promised, "You will make it if I have to carry you across my back the rest of the way."

Thranulas caught Tarin's stare. Meeting the dwarf's gaze with all the strength he had left, Thranulas nodded, gripping Tarin's shoulder tightly for a moment. Syllē smiled at the two before turning to continue their race to the third waterfall sanctuary. Her plan was to follow the rapids from the riverbank to the third waterfall where she would help them gain entrance to the sanctuary. It was a good plan. There were no orcs between them and the waterfall, and the only orc or goblins to harass them were far behind and not likely to catch them. There was just one thing she wasn't thinking about—that last basilisk from the mountain.

39

Syllē's plan was to follow Ontari's descent out of the foothills from the river's bank, staying high and dry and away from the rapids until reaching the third waterfall, but she wasn't counting on that basilisk. The disturbance of all those feet running through the mountain trails and the guttural calls of orc and shrieks of goblin had caught its attention, and it was rapidly zeroing in on the trio, its hunger for something other than orc, goblin, or troll driving the snake towards the beginning of Ontari. It reached the flat outcrop over the Ontari pool just after Syllē had passed through to start her descent to the riverbank. The basilisk was moving so fast that it almost overshot the ledge. Basilisks are extremely adept at controlling their large bodies, so as soon as the snake realized its mistake, it whipped its body back over itself and landed squarely in Tarin's path on the ledge.

Thankfully, dwarves were also exceptionally adept at quick maneuvers and changes of pace, so Tarin was able to stop himself and retreat swiftly back to Thranulas without a problem. It did not escape the elf's notice that the dwarf could have ducked under the neck of the basilisk and escaped down the mountain without him. Unfortunately, Tarin's actions were also not lost on the basilisk, who swiftly went to swing its tail at the dwarf and skewer Tarin with its barb, but the basilisk was surprised to find that its tail had been pinned to the side of the mountain. Syllē hated to waste her sword in that way, but she had no choice, not if she wanted Tarin and Thranulas to survive. Unsheathing her Scylarian long knives, Syllē vaulted over the snake, using its writhing back as a springboard to get to her friends on its other side. Alas, its jerking caused her to softly ricochet into the mountain wall, disorienting her for a moment.

Meanwhile, Tarin tried to find a safe way to get Thranulas past the snake without the elf falling victim to the venom of its glance, but the snake had no intention of losing its delicious meal. Unable to kill the dwarf with its barb and not wanting to ruin its elven meal with the taste of dwarf in its mouth, the basilisk whipped its head towards the dwarf and sent Tarin flying off the outcrop and towards the pool below. The last thing Tarin saw before he smashed into the water below was Thranulas leaping off the outcrop after him with the furious basilisk striking at the elf from behind.

Tarin hit the waters of the pool so violently that he was knocked unconscious and sank like a boulder to the bottom. Thranulas found some hidden strength and dove down to Tarin. Digging deep within himself, Thranulas pushed off the bottom and dragged the dwarf back to the surface. When the elf's head broke the surface, he heard Syllē's call from the outcrop as she battled the snake, "Ride the rapids down to the third waterfall. I'm right behind you!" Following her instructions and holding tightly to the unconscious Tarin, Thranulas desperately kicked his way out of the pool and into the opening rapids of Ontari.

Seeing it had lost Thranulas, the basilisk concentrated on the she-elf in front of it, giving her its best venomous glare, waiting for its prey to sway and fall; but to its great surprise, its opponent simply stared back, laughing. Shaking its head incredulously, the snake reared backwards, opening its hood and towering over the she-elf below it. No, not a she-elf. It couldn't be, not if she was surviving its venom. Its eyes swirling with anger and confusion, the basilisk hissed at Syllē, "You are not an elf."

Smirking, Syllē sarcastically responded, "And you are smarter than the average worm."

Enraged, the basilisk struck blindly at Syllē, who drove a long knife through the roof of the snake's open mouth and into its brain. Jumping deftly to the side to avoid the snake as it crashed to the ground, its head flopping over the outcrop, Syllē muttered, "I stand corrected. You are as stupid as the average worm." Briefly, Syllē searched the rapids for her friends before adeptly leaping over the dead snake, retrieving her sword, and continuing her run. She quickened her pace, knowing she must catch them before they reached the third waterfall.

The dead basilisk aided her in her escape as the orc and goblin had almost caught up with her. As they rounded the corner in the trail, though, the sight of the snake stopped them in their tracks. None of them wanted to be a meal for a basilisk. Their hesitation gave Syllē the head start she needed. She was past the first waterfall heading for the second before any of her pursuers realized the snake wasn't breathing. Still, it wasn't until after the snake slowly slipped off the outcrop and crashed into the pool below that any of the orc or goblins found the courage to continue down the trail. Their hesitation gave Syllē, Tarin, and Thranulas the lead they needed, and she wasn't about to waste it.

Syllē strained to catch sight of her friends in the rapids as she raced along the bank of Ontari. She was rewarded with the sight of Thranulas' head, bobbing towards the second waterfall. Just before Thranulas went over the second waterfall, Syllē saw him turn in the water to take the fall backwards. With a major sigh of relief, Syllē was able to discern the dark head of Tarin pressed against the elf's chest before they both fell over the falls and into the rapids below.

It had taken almost everything Thranulas had left to get Tarin back after that first waterfall. The force of the water driving them deep into the next pool had ripped Tarin away from him and Thranulas had barely been able to drag Tarin back off the bottom and into the flow of the river. He knew if he lost Tarin again, he most likely wouldn't have the strength to get him back to the surface; so Thranulas spent the next section of the river desperately trying to find a way to attach Tarin to him so the second waterfall wouldn't dislodge the dwarf from his arms. He was still working on it when they entered the second set of rapids and began ricocheting from boulder to boulder.

The elf finally got Tarin jerry-rigged to him using the dwarf's belt and axe straps. Seeing the second waterfall almost upon them, Thranulas wrapped his arms tightly around Tarin before turning his back to the falls. He was hoping that if he took the brunt of the drop, the straps attaching Tarin to him would better hold. He was right, but the weight of the dwarf drove them both almost to the bottom. Thankfully, the force of the current sent them spinning forward as well, and soon the pair was bobbing through the ever increasing current on their way to waterfall number three.

Syllē picked up her pace. She had to reach the third waterfall before Thranulas and Tarin. The orc and goblin were too close for her to haul them out and get them to the land entrance to the sanctuary; therefore, they'd have to enter via the waterfall, a trick she'd have to coordinate herself. If they fell into that third set of rapids, they'd be in trouble with no way to outrun their pursuers before reaching the safety of Indili territory. Her concern spurred her forward, dodging a few stray orc and goblin arrows as she ran.

Thranulas looked behind them as they bobbed along the swift current. He could see their pursuers, but he couldn't see Syllē. Searching the bank, he flipped around to face the waterfall and found Syllē standing on a boulder near the very edge of the drop. His eyes caught hers and she grinned just before launching herself into the river current right beside him. Locking her right arm around him as tightly as she could, the three fell over the third waterfall together.

40

Tarin awoke from an unsettling dream to someone gently shaking him by the shoulder. He could hear someone ask, "What's the matter with him?"

As he opened his eyes, he heard Syllē's voice respond with concern, "I don't know, but he's been screaming for me in my dreams. He must be having some sort of nightmare."

Looking up, Tarin met Syllē's worried gaze and without really thinking reached out to squeeze her hand on his shoulder. She smiled down at him with relief and said, "I was worried about you, Tarin. You were searching rather desperately for me in your dreams."

"I needed to find you to tell you I would live. That I was fighting, and it wasn't your fault," Tarin explained.

Syllē's eyes widened a moment. Bending closer, she searched his eyes, looking for weakness or any injury she may have missed earlier when they entered the sanctuary, but she could find nothing amiss. Relieved, she moved back. Lying back down to return to sleep, Syllē stretched languidly and yawned. "Well, you've told me, and you appear none the worse for wear after your battle with the basilisk and ride down the rapids. So, just take this time to rest up. We have quite the race ahead of us tomorrow."

"I remember," Tarin breathed, almost under his breath, but it was enough to catch Syllē's attention.

"What do you remember, Tarin?" Syllē's voice was muffled against her arm.

"I remember kissing you," Tarin almost whispered to Syllē's back.

At that revelation, Syllē rolled over and looked at Tarin with concern. "You're not going to start shunning me again, are you?"

Tarin shook his head, but if he had to admit, he was definitely a little more uncomfortable in her presence thanks to the memory.

"You promise?" Syllē prompted, sitting up and facing him, a very serious look on her face.

Swallowing hard, Tarin nodded again, "I promise."

Syllē smiled with relief, but her grin quickly turned mischievous. "So?"

Warily, Tarin responded, "So, what?"

Grinning even more mischievously, if that was possible, Syllē leaned slightly forward as she asked, "Was it a good kiss?"

Despite himself, Tarin laughed outright. "Yes, Syllē, it was a good kiss." Shortly and with mounting horror, Tarin realized he wasn't wearing any clothes. As he looked around the small chamber, he saw his clothes hanging near the back wall, and with them were clothes he recognized as Syllē's, and then some that must have been Thranulas'. Turning his mortified eyes back to Syllē, Tarin noticed that she was only wearing her underwraps and resting exceptionally close to him near the fire. "Syllē, what did you do?" Tarin finally managed, his voice tinged with anger.

Sitting up straighter, which made Tarin swallow hard as he watched her blanket drop down to cover only her lap, Syllē's eyes flashed navy. "What do you mean, what did I do?"

"I don't have any clothes on!" Tarin almost shouted.

"Of course not. We were all soaking wet, and you were turning grey from the cold. We had to get warm and get our clothes dry." Syllē's response was sharp.

"But you are at least wearing your underwraps," Tarin sputtered.

"You weren't wearing any," Syllē's eyes flashed mischievously at him again.

"Well, why didn't you have Thranulas…"

"Leave me out of this," Thranulas' weary reply from just above them cut into Tarin's tirade. "I learned centuries ago never to get in the middle of any of Sylēmar's arguments with one of your family. To do so is simply suicide." Thranulas remained with his back to them above the fire, refusing even to turn over and face them.

Tarin started to complain more but stopped when he noticed Syllē's left arm was wrapped in a gauze bandage. His concern overriding his discomfort, Tarin asked, "What did you do to your arm?"

Looking down briefly, almost as if she'd forgotten about the wound until Tarin mentioned it, Syllē tried to shrug nonchalantly, "Oh, it got sliced while on the outcrop above the first pool."

"Sliced by what?" Tarin pressed, getting irritated that Syllē was obviously dodging his question.

"One of the basilisk's fangs." It was Thranulas, who still refused to roll over and face them, who answered as Syllē remained infuriatingly silent.

Syllē was trying to find a way to explain it to Tarin without causing the dwarf to go into a panic, so she wasn't too thrilled by Thranulas' response. "What did you just say about 'suicide,' old friend?" she tersely addressed Thranulas.

Tarin roared in alarm. "The basilisk bit you! Its venom will kill you!"

Sensing Tarin's alarm, Thranulas rolled over and wearily sat up. He now understood Syllē's earlier reticence. "No, it won't. As you can see, she's very much alive in front of you," Thranulas tried to calm Tarin. "The worst that could happen is Syllē falling asleep for up to a thousand years, but that would only be if she had been bitten by the basilisk, which she wasn't." Thranulas shrugged.

"You just said she was bitten by the basilisk!" Tarin yelled, about to spring up and grab Syllē's arm to look at the wound himself, when he suddenly remembered his current state of undress and remained exactly where he was.

"No, he didn't, Tarin," Syllē tried to keep her voice calm and almost monotone as she spoke. "Thranulas said that my arm was sliced by a basilisk fang. So, some poison has made it into my blood but not a lot. I might get a little extra sleepy, but I certainly won't sleep for a thousand years." She smiled encouragingly at Tarin. "It's what happens when you must use your long knife against a worm, instead of your sword. I will be fine. I promise."

"Of course, she'll be fine," Thranulas picked up the note of encouragement. "She'll probably only sleep, at most, five hundred years, and think of all the peace and quiet you'll have while she slumbers," Thranulas grinned a tad wickedly at Tarin as he finished.

Tarin, unfortunately, didn't get the joke. Before the dwarf could go into a panic and anger-induced tirade, Syllē quickly interjected, "He's just kidding, Tarin. I might get a little tired and lethargic, but I won't go into some eternal sleep. When we get to the Indili, they or Father or even Halicyon can create the antidote and draw what little poison there might be in my blood out of my body. I will be perfectly fine." Syllē gazed steadily at Tarin as she finished speaking.

"Why can't Thranulas create the antidote and heal you now? He's an elf," Tarin said and glared at Thranulas.

"Because we don't have the correct herbs here," Syllē quietly responded. Before Tarin could get any more upset, she swiftly continued, "Tarin, I am tired, but not really from the basilisk's poison. I am tired because it feels as though I have never had a real chance to rest and recover since even before I was put in that tomb. So, how about I make you a deal?"

"What kind of deal?" Tarin asked warily.

"I promise that if I feel myself becoming overpowered in any way from

the minute amount of basilisk poison in my blood, I will tell you immediately and accept whatever your help might be." Syllē looked steadily at
Tarin.

"Even if it means I have to carry you?" Tarin's voice had a slight edge
to it from his concern.

Laughing slightly, Syllē nodded, "Even if it means you have to carry
me."

Seeing Tarin had calmed, Thranulas lay back down and turned his
back to the pair again, but Syllē sat gazing at Tarin for just a moment
longer, making sure the dwarf was truly calm. Satisfied, she leaned her
forehead against his briefly before turning her back and lying back down,
pulling her blanket up under her arm. Tarin lay on his back staring at the
ceiling of the small chamber and listening to her softly breathing next to
him. The sound eventually lulled him into a fitful sleep. He just couldn't
let go of the fact that she had basilisk venom running through her veins.

41

"So, tell me about the fog," Finn, who was tied back-to-back with Trygve, asked of Falinor, who was fastened to a tree facing the dwarf.

The group had made it far into the valley and safely away from the fog, only to be faced with the drawn bows of the very fierce Indili. Finn and the rest of the dwarves had been rather intrigued by the descendants of the first humans to walk MithTerra when they'd seen them, intrigued enough they were almost happy to be disarmed and tied up in the middle of the Indili's village. The elves were not so happy. Finn, who was always full of questions anyway, decided to take the time to find out all he could about the Indili and that terrifying killer fog that protected the borders of their lands.

"It's a weapon that should never have been unleashed on MithTerra," Falinor answered disapprovingly. Seeing Finn's expectant face, Falinor sighed, adjusted his feet to try and find a slightly more comfortable position, and began to explain. "Towards the beginning of the creations, Merilik's jealousy and desire for power caused the Deceiver to create seven dragon lords to rival the seven lords of the Lēas, who served the Creator. It was his first bid for power, and it was effective. His dragons were almost indomitable and were destroying most of the kingdoms and peoples of MithTerra, bringing them under the dominion of Merilik. To save themselves, the Indili worked with the wizard Saing to develop a weapon that could combat the dragon lords, but it came at great cost. When the weapon was unleashed on the dragons as the beasts approached this valley, the life essences of all four of the Indili elders and Saing were drawn into the weapon, and as the fog spread across the valley and engulfed the dragons and their armies, it did not differentiate between friend or foe. Many elves and Indili warriors were caught in the destructive fog along with three of the dragon lords and all their armies."

"So, the fog is a weapon? That's cool," Finn breathed in awe.

Falinor gazed sharply at Finn. "No, it is not cool, Master Finn. It is a weapon that never should have been created, and for many ages now, those who remain have had to deal with the consequences of its creation. It pollutes MithTerra and preys on all—innocent or evil, dark or light. The fog cares not. It simply destroys all who come across it. No one is safe."

"But it did what it was created to do," Kwin responded thoughtfully. "It protected the Indili and killed three dragons."

"Yes, it did, Kwin—but at great cost. The Indili lost all their elders and almost half their population, and we elves lost a quarter of our warriors. Plus, that fog has ravaged the borderlands and everything and everyone who is unfortunate enough to face it for ages now." Shaking his head, Halicyon finished sadly, "Instead of salvation, the Indili and MithTerra received eternal damnation."

Finn thought for a moment, but he was never good at prolonged silence. Soon, he asked, "So, what happened to the other four dragon lords? Where did they go?"

Sighing, Falinor responded, "Merilik had made his creations too powerful—imbued them with too much of him. They banded together and decided to unseat the king and put themselves on the throne. It took everything that Merilik had and came very near to killing him to defeat and imprison his creations. Once the dragon lords were defeated and his realm was again his to command, Merilik rested and MithTerra was safe from the Dark for fifteen hundred years."

"The time of the Great Peace," Kwin answered.

Falinor smiled at him and nodded, "The greatest time of light and beauty and innocence in the history of MithTerra. The time before the darkness reawakened."

"Are the dragons all dead?" Finn asked curiously.

"Yes," Halicyon responded. "Merilik killed one and imprisoned the remaining three when they tried to take control of his realm, but he released those last three and unleashed them on Lumenas where they all met their deaths, but not before completing their mission to destroy the Valaraii."

"Merilik sent the dragons to kill the Valaraii? Wow, no wonder…" Finn stopped himself.

Finn was pretty sure he was the only one who heard Trygve mutter under his breath, "Well, that explains why she's so damn tough." Finn couldn't agree more.

* * *

Tarin, however, wasn't too confident in Syllē's toughness at that moment. His worry had awakened him from his restless sleep, and he found himself scooting slightly closer and closer to her trying to decide if her breathing was normal or some basilisk venom-induced coma. He was so intent on listening to her breathing that her slightly testy voice made him jump.

"You need something, Tarin?" Even though he could tell by her tone that she was upset with him, Tarin was relieved to hear Syllē's voice. "Stop hovering, Tarin, and get some sleep."

"I can't sleep," Tarin replied honestly.

Syllē sighed wearily, "Why not?"

"Because I'm worried about you." Tarin couldn't think of anything to say other than the truth.

Sighing deeply again, Syllē responded, her back still turned towards him, "I'm truthfully fine, Tarin, just tired; but I can't sleep because you're breathing down my neck." Her tone turned sharp. "So, lie down and go to sleep."

Tarin tried, but almost immediately popped back up. Making a decision, Tarin grabbed his blanket and found a spot right next to Syllē where he was able to sit against the wall. Wrapping his blanket around himself, Tarin crossed his arms and stared down at Syllē, watching her breathing carefully. Sighing heavily, Syllē rolled onto her back and looked up at Tarin. Her eyes questioned him, but she said nothing.

Shrugging irritably himself, Tarin answered, "I can't help it. This is what I do now. I worry about you, and I look after you. Deal with it."

Syllē studied him briefly before rewarding Tarin with a quiet smile. Reaching up, Syllē gently touched his cheek with her fingertips. "All right, my lord," she admonished him affectionately, "worry away. Just make sure to get some rest yourself."

42

Tarin did rest a bit, but he didn't sleep much. Instead, he found himself studying Syllē as she slept and letting his mind wander to dreams of things that he knew would never be. She was Valaraii. She would never choose to align herself with someone like him—a dwarf—but his daydreams were definitely sweet, and she was more than beautiful lying there beside him.

As he studied her, Tarin noticed a long scar faintly etched down Syllē's left shoulder. It looked almost like an axe blow, but it was so faint, almost invisible. Tarin leaned down to get a better look. Caught up in his musings, Tarin found himself reaching out to trace the scar before he could stop himself. As his fingertip traced the line of the scar, Tarin noticed Syllē's arm erupt in chill bumps. Tarin reached out and started to pull Syllē's blanket further up and around her, trying to keep her warm. Maybe he should move her closer to the fire?

Before he could decide what to do, Tarin noticed Syllē had rolled over onto her back and was gazing steadily at him. Her eyes were a brilliant blue-grey and they seemed to draw him forward. Again, without really realizing it, Tarin found himself drawing closer to Syllē. Her voice stopped him.

"What are you doing, Tarin? I thought you were going to try and rest?" Tarin thought Syllē seemed amused, but her voice didn't sound amused.

"You were covered in chill bumps, so I was pulling your blanket up to warm you." Tarin was embarrassed at how plaintive his voice sounded to his ears. Making an effort to deepen his voice, Tarin continued, "And I was trying to figure out how to properly get you closer to the fire to keep you warm."

Syllē studied him quietly but said nothing. Tarin found her eyes almost hypnotic and desperately tried to find a way to distract himself from their light. "Is that scar on your left shoulder from Da?" Tarin saw her eyes cloud over and then close as if she was in pain.

Syllē nodded. Opening her eyes and gazing steadily at him again, she asked, "How did you hear about that?"

"Falinor told me about it that day I injured you on the roof. He was trying to make me feel better." Tarin shrugged slightly. "Halicyon also told me that Da shot you in the ankle or foot with a crossbow bolt."

A slight chuckle from Thranulas reminded Tarin that the elf was there. "I had forgotten about that. Farin took one look at Syllē's face and started running and didn't stop until he was safely locked within his own room in Shara." Still chuckling, actually, almost giggling, Thranulas finished, "Farin ran sixty miles straight that day."

Glaring at the back of the elf, Syllē snapped, "Farin did not abandon me. I sent him back to Shara for aid. He never abandoned me. Ever." The force of Syllē's anger reminded Thranulas that it would most likely be to his benefit to go back to sleep or at least pretend sleep.

"So, why did Da hit you with his axe?" Tarin tried to change the subject. Syllē briefly met his eyes before rolling over. "Syllē?"

Syllē sighed sadly, "Someone, possibly Therendē'al, laced his food or beer with methone, waited for it to take effect, and then convinced him I was a Drēor come to kill his parents." She paused, swallowing hard and trying to control her voice. This time it wasn't just the memory. Tarin had taken to tracing the scar with his fingertip again.

"But how did you survive the attack? Was Da able to overcome the effects of the methone?" Tarin found the feel of the scar mesmerizing.

"He heard me laugh just as he was about to land his strike, and it caused him to shank the blow. It was enough to save me." Tarin noticed Syllē's voice sounded strange and thick. He also noticed her chill bumps were back.

"You're chilled again," Tarin murmured. He caught her elbow gently. "Come, move yourself closer to the fire. I am warm now."

"I am not cold, my lord." Syllē's voice still sounded strange to Tarin's ears.

Not convinced, Tarin spoke softly but more firmly, "Syllē, come closer to..." Tarin's voice trailed away as Syllē rolled over onto her back and looked up at him. Tarin found himself unable to resist the pull of her eyes and before he could stop himself, Tarin gently cradled the side of her face in his hand, leaned down, and softly kissed her. Briefly, Syllē was lost in that kiss before Tarin felt her gasp and rise up against him until she was sitting directly opposite him with her forehead pressed against his and his face cradled in her good hand. Tarin tried to move his head to kiss her again, but Syllē stopped him.

The stricken tone of her voice hurt his heart, "No, Tarin. I cannot. I am not free to..."

"What? Love a dwarf?" Tarin sat back angrily and glared furiously at her. "Too demeaning for you," Tarin ferociously spat his words at Syllē.

"That is how little you think of me?" Her voice matched the gray of her eyes.

The sound and the look cut Tarin deeply, but he refused to let go of his own self-righteous anger. He continued bitterly, "It's obvious you don't want to be linked with a dwarf."

Syllē's tone had turned biting now, "And why is that?"

To Tarin's horror, his voice broke as he answered forcefully, "Because I just offered you my heart and…"

"You already have mine!" Her interruption was almost a roar, which startled Tarin, but what she did next absolutely shocked him. Grabbing Tarin's face in her hands, Syllē pulled him to her and kissed him with more passion than Tarin had thought even existed before she let go and sat back.

Dazed, Tarin was able to notice her eyes were sparking navy as she stood up, grabbed her blanket, and walked past him to the other side of the fire where she almost threw herself on the ground before turning her back to him. For a moment, all Tarin could see was Syllē and the way she looked as she rose before him and walked away. By Asger, she was beautiful. He was so caught up in her image, it took him a moment to realize what she had said, and then, it took him another moment to process that she had moved away from him to the other side of the fire.

"Syllē—" Tarin began. His tone was more astonished than furious now.

She curtly cut him off, "Go to sleep."

"Well, that's not happening after…" Tarin struggled for the right words. "After everything…I mean, if it was hard for me to sleep before, it's impossible now," Tarin finished, obviously frustrated.

"Just think of the malidaemon queen or King Thallan. Obviously, you think I am just like them," Syllē's tone, while still biting, was warmer. Tarin wished he could see her face because he had the distinct impression that she was laughing at the effect she had on him.

"I do not," Tarin asserted angrily.

"You accused me of feeling demeaned by an association with you, Tarin." Her voice grew hard again.

"I just…I meant…" Tarin sighed heavily. "I'm an ass."

"You'll get no argument from me." The anger in Syllē's voice dissipated, but she still wouldn't turn towards him.

"Syllē?" Tarin hesitated, but he had to understand. "When you said I have your heart, did you mean that you love me?" Tarin held his breath, truly afraid of her answer.

"Yes, Tarin. Now go to sleep," she said and pulled her blanket tighter around herself as if to emphasize the idea of sleep to Tarin.

Tarin, however, still had questions that needed answers, but he also needed Syllē close so he could keep an eye on her. She had been bitten by a basilisk and now that he knew she loved him, he wasn't about to lose her to some five-hundred-or-more-year nap. Rising on his knees, Tarin tried to see where he could go to be close enough to watch over her, but he quickly discerned that there was no room on that side of the fire. She was almost kissing the wall it was such a small space.

"Syllē," Tarin took the authoritative tone with her that had seemed to work in the Dark's lair recently. "You have basilisk poison in you. Come back over here so I can better watch over you."

Instead of making Syllē obey his commands, the tone of Tarin's voice seemed to amuse her. "I'm comfortable. You're not breathing down my neck anymore either."

Sharply, Tarin ordered, "Syllē, either you come back over here right now, or I am coming over there." He wasn't sure where he'd sit, but he was more concerned with keeping an eye on her. Hopefully, she wouldn't call his bluff.

Rolling swiftly over and sitting up, Syllē looked at Tarin, alarmed. "There isn't enough room here for both of us. You'd be on top of me."

Tarin tried to shrug nonchalantly, "Well, that's not much of a deterrent. Based on our recent interactions, I'd say I would rather enjoy that position."

Syllē's eyes widened and for the first time since Tarin had met her, the Valaraii seemed at a total loss for words. Pressing his advantage, Tarin continued, "Syllē, please return to this side of the fire so that I can look after you."

She still said nothing and studied Tarin. Her head was cocked to the side and her eyes glowed a bewitching crystal blue. Finally, Syllē smiled at Tarin and reached for her blanket. "Fine, my lord, but keep your hands and your lips to yourself." Her amused affection filled every syllable and warmed Tarin all over.

Seeing her start to rise, Tarin quickly held out his hand and pleaded, "Be kind. Wrap your blanket around you."

Syllē's laugh sent shivers through him, but she did as he requested. Soon, she was back in her original spot, and he was sitting beside her, his back up against the wall. Now that she was back on this side of the fire, she didn't seem too interested in sleep as she gazed with intense affection up at the dwarf lord. Tarin found her gaze hypnotic again and found himself having an extremely difficult time keeping his hands and lips to himself.

Trying to divert himself from his thoughts, Tarin asked, "Why?"

Thranulas, unable to ignore the two any longer, answered for her, "Because she is pledged to another. I can't speak for dwarves, but elves take those vows seriously and would shun anyone, husband or wife, who chose to ignore their pledge and take another lover."

"But she's not," Tarin started but then stopped as he caught Syllē's warning shake of the head.

"Yes, she is," Thranulas responded wearily. "Unfortunately, she is married to my brother."

"Unfortunately?" Tarin bridled at the use of that word in regard to Syllē.

"Yes, unfortunately for her," Thranulas explained. "You, Master Dwarf, are three times more a match for Sylēmar than my brother ever was, and you certainly care more about her. In fact, I believe Granulas only married her to spite Father, but regrettably, marry her he did, which makes her unable to act on her feelings for you. Well, unless she wishes to risk shunning."

Unable to stop himself, Tarin blustered, "But she needn't risk shunning. She isn't pledged to anyone, not anymore."

At that, Thranulas rolled slowly over and sat up. His eyes flashed angrily as he looked past Tarin towards Syllē, who had risen to a sitting position near the dwarf. Speaking deliberately, trying to handle his fury, Thranulas asked, "What does the dwarf mean, Sylēmar?"

Tarin was about to answer, but Syllē's hand gently resting on his arm helped him keep his mouth shut. Gazing sadly at Thranulas, Syllē answered softly, "Granulas asked to be released from his pledge."

Tarin saw intense pain and then fury cross the elf's face. Swallowing as though he had bile in his mouth, Thranulas continued, still speaking with that deliberate tone, "When?"

"When I was entombed after escaping Merilik's realm," her soft answer caused more pain to cross Thranulas' face, but the elf said nothing. He simply gazed steadily at Syllē, waiting for more. Sighing heavily, she quickly explained how she had desperately tried to contact Granulas, but to no avail. So, she had used what little strength she had left to force her way into his dreams. She explained how Granulas had not received her presence well and told her he did not wish to be pledged to her anymore. "So, I released him from his pledge," Syllē finished quietly.

Thranulas said nothing and gazed furiously at her. Finally, he spoke, the bitter tone of his voice grated through the small room, "So, have you confronted him?"

Syllē shook her head. "I tried to leave Exulias to do that, but Tarin refused to allow me to leave without a contingent of warriors, including himself, accompanying me. Either that or stay a few months longer recuperating from the Drēor blade in my leg. Then, Helmfirth asked for Tarin's aid, and the hive took over Kilead, and it's been one dark event after another." She shrugged. "I plan to go as soon as we get home from this adventure."

"You had a Drēor blade shoved into your leg?" Thranulas' voice was angry and sorrowful at the same time.

Syllē nodded. "Courtesy of Therendē'al."

Thranulas closed his eyes a moment, gathering and centering himself. When he opened them again, the fierceness of the blue startled Tarin, but Thranulas ignored the dwarf. He only had eyes for Syllē. "So, the divorce is not complete."

Syllē shook her head. Tarin was confused. He asked, "What does that mean?"

"It means, Master Dwarf, that Sylēmar is still technically married to my brother, and for her to be totally free, she must publicly confront him and release him from his pledge. Until then, she's a married woman." Thranulas' voice grated through his obviously clenched teeth.

Tarin's alarm grew. "She can't publicly confront him. He is in your father's realm and that kingdom has been cut off from the rest of MithTerra since shortly after the fall of Shara. No one can get into the kingdom, and no one can get out. To try is utter suicide." Turning to Syllē, Tarin incredulously demanded, "You can't be seriously thinking about trying to gain access to Aelgalad. You can't."

Syllē smiled sadly at Tarin and nodded, "I must go publicly confront Granulas and return his ring or I will never be free."

"No, no, you don't have to do that. We can take his ring and throw it down the deepest trench in Exulias. We'll never speak of it. No one ever need know," Tarin desperately tried to bargain with her.

"I would know, Tarin," was Syllē's soft answer. Sighing heavily, she looked down at her hands for a moment before she continued, "I made a deal with the Limnades, Tarin. They will watch over and protect Exulias if I will release their people imprisoned with Aelgalad. I gave them my word that I would try. I will be dishonored in more ways than one if I do not go."

"But you'd be alive," Tarin countered. "That's the most important thing. Nothing is worth your life. Nothing."

Leaning forward, Syllē gently pressed her forehead to Tarin's and placed her hand against his cheek before leaning slightly back and gazing directly into his eyes. "Yes, there is." At Tarin's questioning look, Syllē softly answered, "You," and pressed her forehead against his again. When she finally sat back, her eyes glowed with such a fierce warmth that Tarin was transfixed. "You are worth it, Tarin. The chance of a life with you is worth it, and knowing that the Limnades will keep you safe is worth it."

Tarin couldn't think of anything to say. No one had ever loved him like this, and he had never loved anyone as he loved Syllē. The thought of her trying to break through the wall of darkness that surrounded Aelgalad, the realm of King Thallan, filled him with utter terror and dread. It was a feat that not even the greatest elven warriors had been able to do, and several expeditions had tried, sending many of the Fair Folk to their graves or worse.

"Syllē," Tarin's voice was a growl and a plea combined as he slowly shook his head back and forth before leaning forward and wrapping his arms tightly around her. Maybe if he just didn't let go.

"It will be okay, Lord Tarin," came the strong yet still angry voice of Thranulas. "She will not go alone. I promise you."

Tarin said nothing. He simply held even more tightly to Syllē.

43

Despite his uncomfortable position, Halicyon found himself falling asleep several hours before sunrise. It was a deep and restful sleep—the kind he used to have when Dol'kah was lying beside him. As his slumber deepened, Halicyon felt his head resting in someone's lap and he could have sworn someone was gently stroking his hair just like Dol'kah would sometimes do. Slowly, Halicyon opened his eyes and looked up into the beautiful amber eyes of his wife for the first time in an eternity. His love caught in his throat and caused his chest to hurt almost to bursting.

When she smiled down at him in welcome, Halicyon was undone. A single tear slid silently down his face as he hesitantly reached his hand up to run his fingers through her silky raven hair. To his astonishment, her vision didn't disappear like usual. Instead, her smile broadened as she leaned forward and placed a soft kiss on his lips. Wrapping his arms around her, Halicyon pulled his wife to him, breathing in her scent deeply and hungrily. Her laugh filled him with a joyful ache.

Holding her tightly to him, Halicyon murmured against her hair, "Nin'emel,[6] I have missed you."

Dol'kah raised her head. Her amber eyes smiled lovingly into his. "I am always right here." She placed her hand on his heart.

Pushing her hair gently back from her face, Halicyon relished the feel

---

6   My heart

of his wife against him and breathed her scent deeply. "You want something or need something."

Dol'kah sat back slightly and looked keenly at him. "Can't a wife just want some time with her husband?"

Her pout made him laugh, but he knew that time was short. He would waken to a world in which she no longer lived, and the thought brought such devastating pain that he almost couldn't breathe. Dol'kah noticed and lightly brushed his face with her hand, smiling sadly at him.

"You must save them. They need you," she responded simply.

"Syllē and Tarin?" Halicyon's concern was evident in his voice. "What's wrong?"

"There are several units of Black Guard hunting them and blocking their way to the valley. To add to their troubles, they are saddled with an elf who has been imprisoned and tortured for several hundred years, and Syllē killed a basilisk but did not leave the fight unscathed," Dol'kah explained.

"She's been poisoned?" Halicyon's concern again shown through.

Dol'kah nodded. "The dwarf will never be able to get all three of them through to the valley safely. Although he'll give it a valiant try." Dol'kah laughed softly as she looked at Halicyon, "I like him, my love."

Halicyon laughed in return. "Yes, he definitely grows on you."

Dol'kah lovingly placed her hand on Halicyon's cheek and leaned forward to kiss him gently. Halicyon wrapped his arms around her again and just held on to his wife. He would hold her as long as he possibly could, until the very last moment, because he knew at some point, this magnificent dream would end.

Her head buried against his neck, Dol'kah eventually murmured, "It is time, my love. Wake up. Your friends need you. Wake up."

Halicyon felt Dol'kah's presence slowly slip away from him. He held on tightly through the very last devastating, "Wake up, my love."

Reluctantly, Halicyon opened his eyes and tried to adjust to a world without Dol'kah in it again. When he had sufficiently shoved the pain deep within his heart, Halicyon raised his head and looked around. He found Trygve studying him with concern, his eyes full of questions.

Halicyon brusquely said, "Syllē and Tarin won't reach the valley without help. There are too many Black Guard in their way. Plus, Syllē killed a basilisk but was poisoned in the battle." Halicyon struggled with his bonds, trying desperately to get free.

"Syllē's poisoned and Tarin's got to take on a bunch of Black Guard alone?" Trygve repeated. Halicyon nodded as he continued to struggle. "Well, then let's go help them," Trygve responded firmly.

Frustrated, Halicyon almost yelled, "That's my intention. Don't you see I am trying to get free?"

At that point, Trygve stepped forward and calmly cut Halicyon's ropes with a knife. Finn and Kwin had already freed Falinor and Hathor, who were both standing and stretching their rather sore muscles, and had moved on to helping Hil free Amarris, Thēorin, and the rest. Halicyon's eyes narrowed.

Seeing the look on the elf's face, Trygve shrugged and grinned rather mischievously for him, "You elves and men never search a dwarf thoroughly. You always leave us a knife or two to work with."

Halicyon growled at Trygve, "You mean to tell me you could have gotten us all free long before this?" Trygve nodded. "Then why did you leave us tied up all night?"

"Because I didn't want to start any kind of a fight with the Indili. She made me promise I would not hurt any of them," Trygve explained.

Trygve couldn't decipher Halicyon's disgruntled muttering, but he had a pretty good idea that it wasn't too flattering to himself or any of the other dwarves. Trygve shrugged again and then frowned. He hadn't enjoyed seeing the elves all trussed up as much as he should have, and Trygve found that immensely troubling. What was he becoming? Trygve didn't have long to ponder because they were quickly surrounded by Indili, who didn't look very happy at the fact that their prisoners were now free. Trygve sighed. He hoped he wouldn't have to break his promise to Syllē.

Stepping forward, Trygve addressed the nearest Indili, "We need to leave the children and the injured boy with you while we go to help our friends. We'll need our weapons, which are right behind you."

Trygve started towards their stack of weapons, but the Indili warrior would not move, nor did his friends appear to be willing to let them pass either. Sighing, Trygve tried again, "I promised her I wouldn't harm any Indili, but if you do not let me through, I will have to break that promise, starting with you."

The stony face of the Indili did not change. Trygve shrugged, "Okay, but you're going to tell her that I tried to keep my promise."

Trygve started forward to move the Indili warrior out of his path. Out of the corner of his eye, he saw Halicyon moving right beside him, protecting his flank. The thought oddly comforted him.

Before he had completely laid the Indili warrior in his way out, Trygve was stopped in his tracks by a commanding voice. "Who is this 'she' you keep mentioning who is so concerned with my people's safety?"

Trygve looked to his right to see the Indili warriors surrounding them part, and a tall, lithe man, who was obviously an authority figure, approach them. It was difficult for Trygve to decipher the figure's age. His hair was silver with streaks of brown, indicating someone older, but his skin was smooth, and his hazel eyes were clear and obviously amused. His voice also bore no mark of age as it was clear and strong. Haleth Vadi, an elder of the Indili tribe, stopped in front of Trygve and waited imperiously for an answer.

His attitude rankled Trygve, but he remembered his promise to Syllē and tried to remain polite. Not an easy task for him to accomplish. Standing tall, Trygve looked the Indili leader straight in the eye and answered,

"She is a member of my family and the leader of our expedition to save the children of Helmfirth and the boy Oran, who were kidnapped by Merilik's forces and imprisoned in the Dark's stronghold in the Perdarus Mountains."

Looking rather incredulously at Trygve, the Indili asked, "A dwarf, then? We don't have dealings with dwarves."

Trygve almost saw red and seriously contemplated knocking the Indili's head off his shoulders. The only thing that kept him from doing so was his promise to Syllē.

Halicyon, surprisingly, spoke and his tone was far from courteous, "I don't believe Trygve said she was a dwarf. Perhaps you should have listened to him better."

Crossing his arms and staring even more imperiously at the group, the Indili asked again, "So, who is she? What is her name?"

Before Trygve could answer, Hil moved forward and spoke just as imperiously as the Indili, "My father, Farin, called her Syllē, and there are those who call her Sylēmar." Pausing briefly after noticing the unsettling affect her words had on the Indili, Hil continued even more imperiously, "She and my brother need our help, so either help us or get out of our way."

Halicyon felt that Hil's glare at that moment could have stopped a wild boar in its tracks. The thought made him chuckle, which brought a furious glare his way from the Indili leader and several of the group around him. Trygve, on the other hand, grinned right back at him.

"Of all the elves who might travel with dwarves, I find it hard to believe that you would, Halicyon." A tall, powerful warrior to the leader's right stepped forward. When he spoke, he seemed to spit Halicyon's name. "After all, they did murder your wife. Or have you simply forgotten about that?"

Halicyon's eyes narrowed and flashed a brilliant green. Trygve had the unsettling thought that the elf was about to attack and probably kill the Indili, but before Halicyon or Trygve could react, Hil stepped in. With a sweep of her leg, she knocked the Indili on his butt and then slapped him hard across the back of the head. Hil's eyes were sheer blue fire as she stared the Indili down.

Kwin had the distinct impression that his brother was enjoying watching someone else get disciplined by their mother, but thankfully, Finn kept his glee to himself. Several warriors started to rush forward at Hil, but their leader held up his hand and stopped them.

Looking at his warrior on the ground, the Indili spoke to him sharply, "That was unwarranted. Get up and get behind me." Turning back to his prisoners, his eyes appeared to have a spark of admiration as they gazed at Hil. Finally, he smiled, "So, our friend is fighting Black Guard, basilisk poison, and our fog." Hil nodded. Without taking his eyes from Hil's, Haleth ordered his warriors, "Get ready. We have a battle to fight."

44

Syllē awoke to fog. Her head felt heavy, and she simply wanted to lay it back down and succumb to the lethargy that flowed slowly like molasses through her veins. She knew Tarin was talking to her, but his voice was so far away that it wasn't penetrating the thick buzzing sound in her head. *Apparently, I got more basilisk venom in me than I had realized,* she mused to herself. *That's not good.*

Syllē desperately tried to fight the lethargy and fogginess in her head and focus on Tarin's face. She had to fight the venom because she had no intention of taking a long nap. She'd already done that once after the dragons almost destroyed Lumenas and then again when someone imprisoned her in that sarcophagus. A third time was not the charm she wanted right now.

"Thranulas, something is wrong with Syllē," Tarin's very worried voice caught the attention of the elf. "Look at her eyes."

Tarin moved to the side as Thranulas knelt in front of Syllē, who couldn't seem to get herself dressed or out of the sitting position. The elf quickly saw what had alarmed Tarin. Her eyes had a distinct dark ring around the iris. Turning to Tarin, he instructed, "Get some water boiling now."

While Tarin rushed to follow his orders, Thranulas began searching through Syllē's things. Very shortly, he found what he wanted. Turning to where Tarin was heating water over the fire, Thranulas crumbled the dried herb into the heating water. Tarin recognized it as some of the same herb Syllē had used to heal him on the Drengas walls. Soon, the pungent odor of the steeping herb filled the room and Tarin's senses. He'd never been so aware of himself or his surroundings in his life. It felt as though he could hear his blood moving through his veins.

"What is that?" Tarin asked wonderingly.

Startled, Thranulas looked sharply at Tarin. "Go stand at the door. Breathe in fresh air. Do it now," Thranulas ordered. "We call it Saeneld, or Queen's Bell. It's toxic in most of its forms but can be an extremely powerful healer, as well," Thranulas explained as he watched Tarin carefully move to stand at the door.

Once Thranulas was satisfied Tarin was safely out of danger, he brought the brewed liquid to Syllē. Tarin noticed that just the steam from the bowl wafting into her face appeared to waken her a bit. Before Thranulas could even get the bowl to her lips, Syllē grabbed it and downed its contents. Soon, she was standing and dressed and Tarin could tell she was ready for their race. However, he was not happy to see that the dark rings in her eyes had not faded.

"I thought you were curing her," he growled at Thranulas. "Her eyes are still bad."

Thranulas calmly informed Tarin, "Saeneld is not a cure for basilisk venom. In fact, it doesn't affect the toxin at all. It is merely a very strong stimulant when the leaves are brewed."

Smiling down at Tarin, Syllē tried to soothe him, "I am awake now, Tarin. I will make it to the Indili's valley. I promise."

"You remember your other promise," Tarin continued to growl.

"Which one, my lord," her affection was evident in every syllable of her voice.

"That if you need my help..."

She fondly interrupted him, "I will let you know and accept whatever aid you wish to bestow upon me." Leaning towards him, Syllē reached out for his right wrist but strangely wouldn't meet his eye. "Here, Tarin. I want you to have this," she said softly as she began to fasten something around his wrist.

Tarin noticed her hands were shaking slightly. Looking down, he noticed it was a bracelet, but not like any he'd ever seen before. The straps were braided mithril and leather, intricately woven in a manner that no dwarf or elf could ever do. The weaving wrapped not only around the wrist but also around a smooth crystal pendant that had been polished to such a high intensity that Tarin was pretty sure this crystal would glow in the dark. Studying it more closely, Tarin saw veins of silver blue light flickering within the crystal's depths, and deep, deep within the crystal, barely discernible, Tarin could just make out the symbol of the Lēas, a spiral fern.

As Syllē fastened the cords of the bracelet and secured it on Tarin's wrist, she softly said, "Let this always be a light for you in any darkness." Meeting Tarin's gaze, she smiled warmly at him. *And may it remind you that there is one in MithTerra who loves you with all her heart.* Tarin desperately wanted to kiss her, but stopped himself, and instead pressed his forehead to hers briefly before reluctantly stepping back.

Tarin found Syllē's voice and smile were making his knees weak and his head swim a bit. Maybe it was the effect of the Queen's Bell, or more likely, the memory of her lips against his and the feel of her skin under his hand. Oh, these thoughts weren't helping. Shaking his head to clear it and get on a firmer footing, Tarin moved to strap on his weaponry and gather up their supplies. Thranulas doused the fire and helped Syllē gather up their bedrolls.

Soon, the three were ready. Taking the lead, Syllē headed out the opposite door from the one they had used to enter the sanctuary and cautiously emerged from the land entrance to begin their race towards the valley of the Indili and their friends. She could tell Black Guard were nearby and probably regular orc and goblin, as well. Tarin could smell them on the crisp air, but that didn't tell him much. Their smell could travel for a couple miles through clear air so their enemies could be anywhere. Briefly and without looking at her, Tarin intertwined his fingers with Syllē's and gazed at the world around him. He realized he had never had so much to lose before in his life, nor so much to fight for.

45

The three were making good time and had been able to avoid or sneak by several orc and goblin patrols as they traversed their way through the foothills where Ontari rapidly flowed. At their current pace, they would make it to the back side of Indili country well before the Queen's Bell's effects wore off Syllē. Tarin kept his eyes peeled for the frightening fog, but so far, none had appeared. Thranulas had explained that at one time, the Indili's fog had inundated the entire area, making it fairly impossible to gain access to Indili territory; but as the years passed, the fog started to dissipate, leaving a revolving entrance to Indili territory. That was probably why the orc and goblin were more willing to venture this close and possibly even make a few incursions into Indili lands as well.

"We'll be in the valley when we get through those trees ahead," Syllē called quietly behind her, moving rapidly forward. "Stay on the path. It's not much farther."

The three hadn't gone too far into the trees when they smelled smoke and could hear the gleeful, cackling singing of goblins coupled with the guttural laughter of orc. Tarin could tell that the sounds and smells were coming from the same place, somewhere forward and left of their position. Syllē slowed her pace and moved off the path, motioning Thranulas and Tarin to follow her closely. *Stay close, Tarin, and keep an eye on Thranulas. He's not as sure-footed as he should be yet.*

Following orders, Tarin placed himself right beside Thranulas and closely behind Syllē and followed her deeper into the woods, following the smells and sounds of their enemies. Shortly, she held up her hand for them to stop and then crouching low to the ground, crept carefully forward. Tarin and Thranulas followed suit. Using the underbrush as camouflage, the three were able to get a good look at what was going on in the clearing beyond the trees, and it wasn't pleasant.

Apparently, this raiding party had been successful in capturing a large group of Indili and were preparing to roast and eat twelve of their prisoners. The chosen had been stripped down and were tied to stakes placed in brush piles. The orcs were preparing the final three and then they would light the bonfires. Tarin didn't like the idea of taking on so many orcs and goblin. He was pretty sure the idea was suicide, especially with Syllē's and Thranulas' diminished physical conditions. Not wanting to watch and hoping to be far enough away that the Indilis' screams wouldn't give him nightmares for years, Tarin slowly started to edge backwards, away from the clearing.

Syllē's whisper stopped him, "Tarin, what are you doing?"

"There's no way we can take on all of those orc and goblin," Tarin gestured sharply at the clearing.

"You're willing to leave them behind? What about your clan's motto?" Syllē whispered incredulously.

"It'd be suicide and we'd be in those fires," Tarin shot back. "I hate it, but we have no loyalty to them."

"Not even the one fourth from the right?" Syllē responded, raising an eyebrow at Tarin as she whispered. "The one with his father's green eyes?"

Tarin's heart sank. Cursing to himself for getting involved with elves, Tarin got ready to engage the orc and goblin. If he didn't, he would never be able to face his friend again.

* * *

The orc had finished securing the twelve prisoners to their stakes. A large orc with a lit torch started towards the center of the line of prisoners, readying to light the fires. Goblins gleefully danced around him, getting in his way and impeding his process, which was a good thing for the trio planning to attempt a rescue. It gave them just enough time to get into position.

As the orc approached the first victim, he slowly crumpled to his knees and his torch set a few of the nearby dancing goblins on fire as it fell from his hand. Several of the flaming goblins were beginning to threaten the prisoners tied to the stakes. They were quickly shot down as well before they could get close enough to ignite the wood stacked around the prisoners. Seeing this, the orc and goblin turned furiously in the direction of the archer and found themselves faced with the she-elf their master wanted so desperately. Growling and shrieking viciously, the orc and goblin began to charge her and several more fell to the ground with arrows to the front and back as Thranulas entered the fray from the other side of the camp, using an Indili bow and two quivers of arrows that he had found discarded in a pile of weapons against one of the far trees. Caught between the two archers, the orc and goblin weren't quite sure who to charge or where to run.

It was at this point that the Indili who could and even those who shouldn't, joined the battle. While the archers diverted the attention of their enemies, Tarin had started to free some of those who were set to be roasted, starting with Lukon, the Indili fourth from the right with his father's green eyes. Lukon heard and felt something embed into his stake right between his hands. Immediately, his bonds loosened. Almost before he could react, Leona to his right and Drego to his left were freed by a well-placed hand axe thrown perfectly between their bound hands as well. Swiftly, they had all used the weaponry that had freed their hands to cut themselves the rest of the way free and join the battle against their captors.

Lukon was startled to see that their savior was not another elf but a dwarf, as the dwarf entered the fray beside him for a moment to help him defeat two Black Guard orc before continuing down the line of stakes, freeing Indili and sending them towards Thranulas for safety and weapons. For the first time in his life, Lukon found himself admiring a dwarf.

Shortly, the group had effectively fought their way out of the camp and were following Lukon's lead towards the Indili valley. Tarin was rather surprised at their progress. When he'd first seen the large raiding party, he couldn't imagine just the three of them even surviving the plan—let alone escaping the clearing. There had seemed to be so many more orc and goblin in that clearing than they'd had to fight. Shrugging his shoulders as he ran, Tarin decided not to question his good fortune, but his calm didn't last long. Looking around their group as he helped shepherd the wounded forward, keeping several on their feet as they ran, Tarin noticed that he wasn't seeing Syllē.

"Thranulas!" Tarin yelled across the group at the elf. "Where's Syllē?"

Startled, Thranulas looked around, thinking Syllē was just on the fringes of the group or hidden by an Indili she was possibly helping, but there was no Syllē. Thranulas stopped and looked intently behind them to see if she was simply covering their rear, but all he could see through the trees were their orc and goblin pursuers. Now he was alarmed, but there was no time as their pursuers were rapidly gaining on them. Granulas' eyes widened further with alarm as he caught sight of another pursuer sinuously threading its way along the ground through the trees towards them. The Indili's fog was coming.

Whirling, Thranulas grabbed Tarin's arm and started moving back towards the fleeing Indili. Drego and Leona joined them and helped Thranulas move Tarin along as the dwarf was not very willing to go with them. The struggle was helping the orc and goblin gain even more ground on them—a situation Leona was quick to perceive.

Trying to look Tarin directly in the eye as she helped shove him after their fleeing group, she asserted, "You will not help her by going back and being killed by orc or our fog, but you can help my people get to safety. Some of us won't make it without your help."

"I cannot leave her behind. I cannot. I promised her I would never abandon her. I promised." Tarin didn't even look at her, but Leona could tell from the stricken and desolate tone of his voice that the dwarf had no intention of giving up.

Speaking softly but firmly, Leona answered, "You cannot help her this way, but you can help my people." Pausing just a moment for the right words, Leona continued, "I give you my word that as soon as my people are safe, I will track her for you. I will not stop until I find her even if I track her to the throne room of Merilik the Beast himself."

Tarin raised his tortured eyes to hers and studied her for a moment before nodding in acceptance. With one last desperate glance behind him, Tarin turned around and headed in the direction of the fleeing Indili and away from their pursuers. As he ran, Tarin's tortured call was filled with anguish: *Syllē!*

What did I tell you about bellowing at me? You almost made me fall off this tree, came her very welcome but, to be honest, slightly testy reply. Before Tarin could say anything else, Syllē continued, *Get to the meadow, Tarin. I'm right behind you.* With those words, the race was on.

Soon, Lukon led the group clear of the trees and into the meadow beyond. It was the last obstacle between them and the knoll that marked where the elders and the wizard Saing had stood and unleashed the fog upon the battling armies in the meadow below. The fog never ventured farther into Indili territory than the meadow, and the orc and goblin hopefully wouldn't either, but that wasn't really guaranteed. Lukon and the Indili picked up speed.

Tarin noticed movement out of the corner of his eye. His heart sank as he recognized a large group of orc led by Black Guard coming out of the trees to their right, moving to flank them and cut them off. "Thranulas," Tarin started to warn the elf.

"I see them, Tarin," came Thranulas' terse reply. The elf called forward, "Lukon, we're about to be flanked. Have the wounded keep going and have those who can still fight protect the wounded's flight."

Before Lukon could comply, Tarin heard a familiar battle cry, and then Syllē came rocketing from the treetops and adeptly landed amid their pursuers to their right. Almost immediately, Tarin could discern orc and goblin parts being rapidly separated from their bodies. The gleam of Syllē's labrys was almost blinding. Grinning, Tarin quickly joined the fight with Thranulas, Leona, and several Indili right beside him. Soon, Tarin found himself standing in front of Syllē as she mopped up the last of their enemies before turning to look warmly at Tarin.

Tarin heatedly scolded her, "Stop disappearing." Syllē's only response was an infuriating grin as she cocked her head and affectionately gazed at him. This only provoked him further. "I mean it. Stop disappearing. Stop making yourself bait. Stop or we won't work."

His last statement wiped the smile off her face. "What do you mean, my lord?" Her voice was guarded.

"I won't survive your loss." Tarin's voice was filled with pain fueled by frustration.

Syllē's eyes glowed as she gazed lovingly at Tarin. Taking a step towards him, her attention was caught by movement at the tree line behind the dwarf. Tarin saw Syllē's eyes narrow with fury. Striding forward, she angrily muttered, "I really hate orc."

The rest of their pursuers had cleared the trees and rapidly cut their small group off from access to the knoll. About a quarter of the orc and goblin headed after the wounded while the rest started towards the extremely small group of fighters, grinning with the anticipation of a quick and easy kill. The fighters readied themselves for the battle that was coming.

Tarin grabbed Syllē's arm and whirled her towards him. Staring seriously into her eyes, Tarin asserted, "I mean it, Syllē. I won't survive losing you."

"You can never lose me, Tarin," she softly answered him, "for no matter what, I will always be right here." She gently placed her hand on Tarin's heart.

Tarin drew himself up to his full height. "Beside me or right in front of me, Syllē," he growled.

Smiling almost joyfully at him, she agreed, "Yes, my lord."

Unfortunately, they had no chance against the overwhelming numbers of their enemies. If Halicyon hadn't ridden over that knoll with their original company escorted by a force of Indili cavalry, well, it would have been a valiant but futile fight. Indili cavalry were the most adept and brutal cavalry in all MithTerra, but they hadn't fought outside of their valley since before the fog, which was a tremendous loss for the Light. Seeing the cavalry bearing down on them, the orc and goblin chasing the wounded began a speedy retreat towards the rest of their force. As they did, Tarin noticed tendrils of fog creeping slowly into the meadow from the trees. Before he could really worry about that, the cavalry swept past the wounded and slammed into the retreating orc and goblin, fighting their way to Tarin's small party of fighters.

Tarin watched Hil skillfully launch herself off the back of an Indili mount and into the battle. Trygve, Flarne, Varger, and the twins quickly followed suit. Tarin chuckled at the look Amarris gave Kwin's back as he leapt off the mount they were sharing. His nephew was going to pay for that when this battle was over, Tarin was very sure. Soon, the dwarves had reunited with Tarin and Syllē, but Tarin kept an eye on the creeping fog. The orc and goblin were aware of it now as the fog had cut off two avenues of their retreat. If they weren't careful, the fog would soon have them all surrounded.

Before Tarin could voice his concern to Syllē, she was lifted out of the battle and onto the front of a powerful chestnut horse, ridden by Halicyon. The elf briefly met Tarin's eye as he rode past. Immediately after, Tarin was grabbed and lifted onto a horse by Hathor and found himself heading full speed back to the knoll, away from the battle and the fog. In rapid succession, all the fighters were grabbed by a rider and everyone, including orc and goblin, were trying to outrun the fog to the knoll. The riders were successful. Their enemies, not so much. Soon, nothing but remnants of fog remained in the meadow.

46

As soon as they made it safely back to the Indili village, Falinor and Haleth adeptly healed Syllē of the basilisk poison and then placed her under the care of Hil. It was a good thing Syllē loved Hil, because the dwarf drove the Valaraii crazy with her order of three days of bedrest. Tarin rather smugly reminded Syllē that she herself had told him only a day ago that she hadn't truly rested in several hundred years, so she should appreciate the opportunity to stay in bed. She muttered something under her breath in answer that Tarin quickly wished he hadn't heard.

"That was unkind," Tarin whispered fiercely at her before turning on his heel and leaving the room, heading somewhere—anywhere—he hoped would help get the images out of his mind that Syllē's words had planted. Her laugh followed him into the night.

"Syllē sounds happy for someone who's been ordered three days bedrest," Halicyon commented as he joined Tarin.

"She's happy because she's torturing me," Tarin muttered irritably.

Halicyon chuckled, "Ah, that does sound more likely."

"I am not going to survive this relationship," Tarin sighed heavily.

Halicyon did a double take. "Relationship? You told her, did you?"

"I assumed Thranulas had already told you," Tarin answered bitterly.

It was now Halicyon's turn to sigh. "Tarin, Thranulas may be Thallan's son; however, do remember he was only in that crow cage because he chose to follow Falinor into battle to fight for your people."

Tarin found Halcyon's pointed stare rather uncomfortable. Gritting his teeth, Tarin shook his head before nodding curtly at the elf. The two were silent for a bit as they walked. Tarin finally broke the silence, "She told me she loves me, and she gave me this." Tarin held up his right wrist where Syllē's bracelet shone in the darkness of the night. "She said it would be a light in any darkness for me."

Halicyon nodded but still didn't speak. After a moment, Tarin sorrowfully continued, "She said she wasn't free. That if she wanted to be with me, she had to confront Granulas who is trapped in Aelgalad, a kingdom no one has been able to access in over two hundred years." Tarin's voice rose as his frustration and his fear mounted. He felt Halicyon place a hand on his shoulder, which slightly helped to calm the dwarf. Continuing more softly, Tarin forlornly looked up at Halicyon, "I told her it wasn't worth it. That nothing was worth her life, but..." Tarin paused, swallowing with difficulty. "She told me I was wrong. She said I was worth it." Tarin's voice was now a wondrous whisper.

Leaving his hand on Tarin's shoulder, Halicyon smiled warmly at his friend. "They're amazing gifts the Creator gave us, aren't they?" At Tarin's questioning glare, Halicyon explained, "Love—the ability to love another being with all we have and then the ultimate gift of them loving us back. I was blessed with those gifts, and now, so are you." Halicyon's smile did help Tarin feel a little better, but the fear still wouldn't go away.

"But she is going to put herself in more danger because she says she loves me," Tarin's voice was rife with his fear. "I cannot allow her to go to Aelgalad. I cannot. I am not worth her life."

Turning to face Tarin straight on, Halicyon placed his other hand on Tarin's shoulder and gazed calmly into his friend's eyes as he spoke, "If the roles were reversed..."

Tarin snapped irritably, "Don't use that Drengas logic on me right now.

Just let me hate the situation for a while."

Halicyon smiled understandingly at Tarin. "All right, Tarin. I am sorry. Just know that I understand. I totally understand."

Tarin met Halicyon's gaze. "How did you do it, Halicyon? How did you survive losing your wife?" Tarin quickly regretted the question when he saw the flash of intense sorrow in his friend's eyes. Quickly, the dwarf apologized, "I am sorry, my friend. I never should have asked that. Please forgive me."

Halicyon shook his head and stared off somewhere above Tarin's head for a moment. When he spoke, his voice seemed as far off as wherever he was looking: "I'm still trying to survive." Laughing silently to himself, Halicyon continued, "I don't agree with that saying about time healing wounds." His eyes resting back on Tarin, the elf finished sadly, "There are some wounds that no amount of time will ever heal, but even if I had known how short my time with her would be, I still wouldn't have traded a single magnificent minute."

Tarin turned and started walking again. Halicyon walked by his side and for quite some time, both elf and dwarf were quiet, appreciating the company of a good friend. Halicyon led Tarin to a large outcrop that looked out across the village and the valley beyond. It had been one of his and Dol'kah's favorite places. The two sat companionably side by side on the rock ledge, silently staring out across the valley.

Finally, Tarin broke the stillness, "I met your son today. He is quite a warrior, like his father."

It took a moment for Halicyon to answer him, long enough that Tarin was concerned he may have said the wrong thing again. "Yes, Thranulas said you saved him from the orc fires. Thank you."

Remembering how he had almost left Lukon to the fires, Tarin rather shamefacedly admitted, "If it hadn't been for Syllē, I would have left him behind. I am sorry, Halicyon."

Halicyon smiled at Tarin, "But once you realized he was my son, you were all in for the rescue, even freeing him first and fighting beside him against several Black Guard who had ganged up on him."

"Thranulas talks a lot," Tarin muttered.

Halicyon laughed, "Yes, but he was only giving credit where it was due, Tarin." There was silence between the two again briefly before Halicyon said sadly, "Actually, I believe my son is much more like his mother, which is probably a good thing."

"So, your wife was Indili," Tarin commented. "What was she like, if I may ask?"

Halicyon's voice went far away again as he answered, "Fire and ice. Strong and ferocious. Much more intelligent than me and absolutely beautiful," Halicyon's voice trailed off wistfully. "I was never more amazed than the day she told me her heart had chosen me. Never more amazed nor more grateful. I still don't know why she chose me," Halicyon laughed sideways at Tarin, "but she did, miraculously, even against her father's wishes."

"Against her father's wishes?" Tarin blurted the question before he could stop himself.

"Yes," Halicyon sighed. "When her father found out his daughter was falling for an elf, he decided to put a stop to it immediately. He informed his daughter in front of the entire tribe that he had procured an advantageous alliance for her with someone in the tribe. I guess he thought she wouldn't dare defy him in front of everyone, but she did." Halicyon laughed quietly. "She stood up and informed the tribe and her father that she was already pledged to me, so while she appreciated his offer, she couldn't take it."

Halicyon grew quiet again, lost a moment in a memory. Unable to stop his curiosity, Tarin asked, "Then what happened?"

"Her father made her choose: me or her family," Halicyon replied quietly.

"Obviously she chose you," Tarin said. He realized he was acting a bit like Finn at a time when he should be more reserved and respectful, but he just couldn't fight his curiosity. Plus, the story was helping him forget about Syllē's upcoming harrowing quest.

Halicyon nodded. His voice was full of wonder as he explained, "She showed up at my door in Aelgalad and said that she had chosen me. She never told me of her banishment. When she found she was pregnant, her separation from her mother weighed on her heavily, so I told her we should return for a visit. That's when she told me she was no longer welcome in the valley and that I was her only home."

The dwarf and elf looked out into the night for some time again without speaking. Tarin knew there was more to the story and desperately wanted to hear what it was, but he overcame his inner Finn and gave his friend some peace. Eventually, Halicyon continued his story, telling Tarin how Dol'kah's brother had shown up in Aelgalad when he was away hunting Ragdgard with Syllē and King Thorunmilé. It was rumored that Ragdgard knew the Drēor in the region and could give them much needed information. Plus, the vile dwarf was wanted for the murder and betrayal of at least forty-five souls—dwarves, humans, and elves—including a party from Cere, Aelgalad, and Shara who had been trailing a Drēor and his orc pack.

Dol'kah's brother had convinced her that her father had lifted the banishment, and her mother was desperate to see her. Wishing to see them, too, especially now that she was pregnant, Dol'kah had headed home with her brother, leaving a note for Halicyon explaining everything. They were betrayed and ambushed as they travelled through the Perdarus. Her brother fought valiantly but he had no chance, and Dol'kah was slaughtered by Ragdgard.

"Syllē and Farin buried Dol'kah somewhere," Halicyon's voice was almost devoid of emotion it was so raw. "I told her never to tell me where, because if I knew, I would entomb myself with her and never leave. King

Thorunmilé and I brought Dol'kah's brother's body home and told them what had happened. Her father never forgave me for not bringing Dol'kah home to be buried, but as he'd banished her for marrying me, I didn't think he wanted her back."

"I thought your son was dead," Tarin said, a tad confused. "You said you had lost him."

Halicyon chuckled darkly, "I did lose him. I gave him to his grandmother to raise, and I left this valley and never returned."

"Why? Did you not love your son?"

Halicyon's voice grew ferocious, "I adored Lukon. I carried him the entire way here, close to my heart because his warmth and smell and life gave me light in a very dark time. I had no wish to leave him here, but King Thorunmilé thought that Dol'kah's murder had been deliberate. That someone was trying to use the pain of her loss and my son's loss to turn me to the Dark. The thought was that Lukon was safest as far away from me as possible."

"Well," Tarin began thoughtfully, "you're here with him now, and I noticed that you two sat as far away from each other at dinner as you possibly could."

"My son has no desire to know me, and I would never impose myself on him unwanted," Halicyon's voice was the most haunted Tarin had ever heard it.

Tarin took a moment to gather his thoughts. "If I had a chance to speak to my father again for just a second, I would jump all over it. For just a second." Tarin turned and looked long and hard at the elf beside him, willing Halicyon to meet his gaze. When the elf finally and rather reluctantly did, Tarin continued kindly, "I would give anything to have a moment in my father's presence—anything. You and your son are in the same place again. Take the chance you have been given. Don't waste it."

Halicyon leaned forward and pressed his forehead to Tarin's for a moment before turning and staring back out into the night. Neither spoke again. They just companionably sat together, gazing out across the valley until the sun rose.

47

The group stayed with the Indili for a week, resting and recuperating. Tarin wasn't sure when Halicyon and Lukon talked, but when it came time for them to leave, there was one more in their party walking tall beside his father. When they made camp that first night out from leaving the Indili valley, Tarin smiled at the pair sitting side by side by the fire, comfortable in and relishing in each other's presence. Soon, though, the pair caused his own heart to ache for Farin, and he had to turn away. Getting up from the fire, Tarin called, "I'll take first watch," as he moved away from the group by the fire and found a high rock to use as a sentry post.

Staring off into the night, Tarin wondered about Farin. Where in MithTerra was he? Was he still alive as Therendē'al had insinuated? Or had the Drēor just been playing with all of them to try and stay alive? Shortly, he was joined by Syllē, who sat down beside him and stared off into the sky herself. Tarin felt her interlace her fingers with his and pull him gently up against her side, erasing the distance between them. It was as if she had sensed his thoughts and was simply letting him know that he was no longer alone. She was with him. If only he could forget what she was planning on doing. Syllē gripped his hand tighter, willing him to look at her. When he did, her smile filled him with a heartbreaking joy and an equally magnificent wonder. She loved him. Syllē loved him. How in Asger's name had he managed that? She had to be reading his mind somehow, because with that thought, her smile became a wide grin.

* * *

It took them three weeks and a few days to make it to Kuaryll, but thankfully, the trip was rather uneventful. Only a few half-hearted skirmishes with orc and goblin. After facing changelings, wraiths, malidaemons, Strygoi, and basilisks, orc and goblin didn't seem so difficult or scary. The only issue they faced in those skirmishes was keeping the children together and safe in the middle of their group to make sure none of them were lost again. When the group finally trudged through the west gates of Kuaryll, they were ready for baths, good food, and a safe place to rest their heads before making the final three-to-five day trek to Helmfirth and Exulias.

They rested and recuperated at Kuaryll for only two days before heading home. King Thorunmilé and Queen Athenéal did not try to force them to stay longer, although the queen was pretty sure they needed more time to rest. After hearing about Syllē's incident with the basilisk, the elf queen did insist on Syllē reporting to her healing room for a thorough check, which the Valaraii begrudgingly did. Tarin had a feeling that things would go massively downhill if Athenéal ordered bedrest for Syllē. She'd barely made it through Hil's order without seriously injuring someone; so, he was understandably worried when he was summoned to Kuaryll's healing room. He found Syllē standing in the middle of the room tightly holding a war hammer in her right hand. Reaching out, Tarin grabbed Syllē's left hand. He was startled by its icy coldness.

Syllē's gasp caught Tarin's attention. Tarin tightened his grip on her hand. Athenéal had been right. Tarin's presence was the urging Syllē needed to bring her back to Kuaryll's healing room. Meeting Tarin's concerned eyes, Syllē smiled before leaning her forehead against his. She could feel the weight of the hammer in her hand and that was all. The memory was cleansed.

* * *

The king and queen of Kuaryll did insist on one thing: sending a bodyguard of elves with them on their final trek. No one thought to argue with that, not even Trygve, who spent the journey comfortably riding with Elēandil. He said it was simply to save his feet after so many months of walking. Syllē simply smiled and nodded at that. Finn, however, openly laughed and called the dwarf "a decrepit old man," and then ran for it as Trygve grabbed a wooden staff and came after Finn. It was a good thing for Finn that he was infinitely faster on his feet than Trygve. Tarin completed the journey sharing a mount with Halicyon, who kept his mount between Syllē's and Lukon's the entire way.

Helmfirth was waiting for them. The surviving five from the ill-fated rescue mission, Hern included, had finally made it home to tell their tale, and they had all regaled the town and anyone who would listen of the feats of Tarin and his dwarves. The alliance between Exulias and Helmfirth had never been stronger. As they entered Helmfirth's gates, they were given a hero's welcome that lasted long into the night and the next day.

At some point during the festivities, Kwin screwed up the courage to ask Brandt for his daughter's hand in marriage—and his request was readily granted. It should be known that Amarris had already told her father that she was marrying the dwarf whether he said yes or no, but Brandt did really like Kwin and thought the dwarf a solid match for his daughter. The elven bodyguard, including Halicyon and Elēandil, returned to Kuaryll but would return and escort the king and queen to Exulias for the wedding.

The prospect of a wedding meant that Syllē would have to put off her trip until after the celebrations, which for dwarves lasted two weeks. This was something that had Tarin half-seriously looking for a mate for Finn and anybody else he could think of whose nuptials would delay Syllē's journey even further. His cousin, a confirmed bachelor with absolutely no time for "such nonsense," refused to cooperate with Tarin's plan. Not all that surprising.

It was after a particularly long day of wedding planning forced upon him by his sister since he, as Hil reminded him, "was that boy's only uncle," (in reality, Tarin figured it was simply a ploy by Hil to keep his mind off Syllē) that Tarin finally found himself exhausted and dejected, but at least totally alone in his own chambers. Throwing himself down in his favorite chair by his fire, he almost immediately sprang up as he sat on something hard and a little sharp. Turning around, he saw his shoulder bag from their journey lying in the chair. He must have thrown it there the other night when they were finally allowed to return from Helmfirth. Curious, Tarin flipped the bag over to see what he had felt when he sat down. K'tanna's circlet fell out into the seat of the chair. Tarin stared at it for a moment before he suddenly grabbed it and headed out into the mountains in search of Haldor.

Twelve days later, Tarin stood at his front gates in full formal attire awaiting the arrival of Amarris and her father. Kwin stood next to him, as dressed up and uncomfortable as he'd ever been in his life, but Kwin wasn't even aware of his discomfort. He was too terrified of everything that was to come. What if he said the wrong thing? What if Amarris didn't like the ring he'd designed for her? What if he did something to offend her father? The list of his possible goofs went on and on in his head. He probably would have worked himself into a fainting frenzy if Finn hadn't stepped in.

"You can run now. After this," Finn shook his head sadly, "you're stuck with that ball and chain for life."

Startled into anger, Kwin whispered furiously at his brother, "What are you talking about? I love her."

"Well, then, why do you look as though you've been given a death sentence?" Finn ironically observed.

"I do not," Kwin stated emphatically.

"Do, too," Finn laughed at his brother. "I thought you were happy about this wedding, but you look like you'd rather be anywhere but here right now."

Kwin took a deep breath and slowly released it, trying to steady his nerves. "What if I say the wrong thing? What if Amarris suddenly realizes she made a major mistake and she doesn't really want me? What if…"

"What if you stop being an idiot and remember that no matter what you do, that crazy woman is still going to love you?" Finn finished for his brother.

At this point, Tarin stepped in. "I agree with Finn—something I truly thought I would never say," Tarin ruefully shrugged.

Trygve continued, "Here's something I was convinced I'd never say: Kwin, your brother is right."

"Hey!" Finn was insulted.

Kwin, however, laughed, loud and long—and the laughter calmed him. Syllē's laughter echoed Kwin's. She was standing behind them with Falinor and Hil, who simply shook her head in mock disgust. Nothing more was said, as at that moment Brandt with Amarris and their Helmfirth friends, including Hadrin and Sariel, rounded the last bend and came towards the gates.

"Wow!" Kwin breathed as he caught sight of Amarris. "How did I possibly get her to love me?"

His brother, not wanting to miss out on any gibes, leaned forward and grinned, "Well, Syllē did say that Drengas beer was potent. Ouch!" Finn stepped back, rubbing his ribs where his brother had elbowed him.

Both twins suddenly felt a lethally powerful presence towering over them from behind.

Before they could turn around, the twins heard Syllē quietly promise, "If either of you embarrass your mother, I will make you regret your actions for the rest of eternity."

48

Several days later, Kwin found himself, thanks to the machinations of his twin, sitting on the roof, magnificently all alone. He'd been about to be dragged into yet another dwarven ritual—the endless bachelor party where everyone drinks a lot of beer and makes a lot of crude comments about the wedding night, and even more outlandish comments about married life. Kwin had never truly enjoyed those parties when they'd been for others and was not looking forward to several days of that when he was the center of all the jokes and ribaldry. So, when Finn had entered the Great Hall with news that Kwin's presence was demanded elsewhere, Kwin had never loved his twin more. It had been exceedingly funny to see the expressions on everyone's faces when they demanded to know who had the audacity to call for the groom at such a time, and Finn had answered as deadpan as ever, "His mother." No one wanted to cross Hil. Not one single dwarf in that room.

Kwin heard the roof door opening and turned to see Finn. Getting up, Kwin resigned himself to his fate and gathered himself to head back down to the Great Hall. He had known his respite would be for only a brief time anyway. One can't just buck traditions and expect to get away with it. Kwin stopped, as he saw who was following Finn through the door.

As soon as Amarris reached the roof, she kissed Finn on his cheek. "Thank you, Finn."

Finn bowed deeply to her, winking at his brother as he did before he exited the roof, closing the door firmly behind him. Amarris managed to smile at Kwin before he launched forward and began rather hungrily kissing her. He hadn't been allowed a moment alone with Amarris since they'd returned, and Kwin had found it to be torture—so close to her and yet never able to even hold her hand.

When Kwin finally let them both come up for air, Amarris laughed and brushed her hair out of her face. Grinning happily down at Kwin, she sighed with relief, "Well, that answers my first question." Sitting down on the roof edge, Amarris looked lovingly up at Kwin.

"What was your first question?" Kwin asked as he sat down next to her, reveling in her closeness.

"Whether or not you still loved me," Amarris answered with a smile. "You've been so morose and silent these past few days that I was beginning to worry. You haven't even tried to hold my hand or sneak a kiss or anything," she finished with an exaggerated sigh.

"It's forbidden," Kwin moaned. "I don't want to ruin anything or cause anyone to challenge this marriage, so I've been playing by all the rules." Suddenly, panic filled Kwin. "Speaking of rules, if anyone finds out we're up here without a chaperone…"

"Calm down, Kwin," Amarris said as she leaned over and softly kissed him. Smiling into his eyes, Amarris continued, "Finn's on the other side of that door and promised to keep any and all off this roof for the foreseeable future."

Kwin grinned as he kissed Amarris. "Sometimes I do love that twin of mine," he murmured.

"Hmm, yes, he does grow on you," Amarris laughed back.

* * *

The elves from Kuaryll arrived three days later. Tarin was pacing the parapets above the gates in anticipation of their arrival. He'd never been so anxious to see an elf before, but he desperately needed Halicyon's help. He hadn't been able to spend much time with Syllē since arriving back at Exulias; every time they were together, Falinor called her away for one reason or another. Tarin found that helpful, as every time he was in her presence, all he could think about was how it had felt to touch her and kiss her, and that made it very difficult for him to keep his hands and his lips to himself as she had requested. As soon as his eyes met hers, he was lost.

Reaching the end of the parapet, Tarin turned to pace back the other way and found Syllē sitting on the wall staring at him. As soon as their eyes met, she smiled and Tarin felt himself come undone. Cautiously, he approached her. His caution caused her eyes to darken slightly. Did Tarin not want to see her? Had he had a change of heart? It was only a few days ago that he had found her sitting next to the Ioneir Pool and asked for her Shara crystal and the necklace he had given her at the Fall Festival, and he hadn't returned either. Maybe he was rethinking his feelings for her.

Stopping and standing near her, Tarin looked out across the foothills near the gate and into what he could see of the valley beyond. Sighing heavily, Tarin admitted, "Being in your presence is torture."

"So, what would you rather be doing, my lord?" Syllē murmured.

"I'd rather have you in my bed and—"

"Tarin!" Syllē's rather shocked voice interrupted him.

"Well, you asked," Tarin shrugged.

I love you, Tarin.

Unable to control the grin that spread across his face, Tarin reached down and grabbed her hand. *I love you, Syllē.* Her joy filled him.

They were both jolted back into reality with the horns sounding a welcome. The elves had arrived. Tarin squeezed Syllē's hand before heading down to greet his guests. Hopefully, the accommodations Sariel and Hil had created would meet the elves' requirements comfortably and everyone would be content.

As soon as Halicyon laid eyes on Tarin, the elf knew something was up. Halicyon waited patiently for Tarin to finish the formalities of greeting and welcoming them to Exulias. Once Tarin had passed the elves off to Sariel and Hil, Halicyon drew Tarin aside.

Before Halicyon could say a word, though, Tarin blurted, "Halicyon, I need your help." Then they were off to Haldor's workshop, and Syllē didn't see Tarin again until the next evening at the wedding ceremony.

49

Three days of feasting, drinking, and all out partying followed every dwarf wedding. Dwarves loved parties and had no problem coming up with any excuse to drink and carouse; so, when an actual reason to celebrate like a wedding came around, dwarves always went all out. The wedding itself was calm and formal as all dwarf ceremonies always were, but once the couple were declared officially married, the festivities began in the twin mountains and didn't end for three whole days. Syllē saw almost nothing of Tarin during that time. He was at the ceremony and opened every feast and conducted his leader of Exulias duties with graciousness and great poise, but once his job was done, he seemed to disappear, much to Syllē's disappointment. She was leaving two days after the wedding festivities officially ended and had hoped to spend as much time in Tarin's presence until then that she could, but it would appear Tarin did not feel the same way.

The night before she was to begin her journey to Aelgalad, Syllē found herself sitting alone on the roof of Exulias staring at the stars. A clear night like this had always calmed her soul, but this night, the stars seemed cold and lonely and so very far away. A bit like a certain dwarf lord who had been avoiding her lately. Hearing the roof door open, Syllē quickly turned, hoping to see Tarin come to keep her company; but it was Falinor, who came out the door and joined her on the ledge. Trying to hide her disappointment, she looked back out at the stars and remained silent.

Shortly, Syllē leaned her head on Falinor's shoulder. Still saying nothing, the pair stared off into the night, relishing the calm before the massive storm their journey would be. Both knew that their chances of success were very slim, whereas their chance of death was exceedingly high. In fact, Syllē had tried to convince Falinor to stay behind in the safety of Exulias by asking him to be an advisor to Tarin while she was gone, but the elf wouldn't hear of it. There was no way Falinor was going to allow his daughter to try to infiltrate Aelgalad without him—absolutely no way.

Well into the night, the pair sat silently on the roof together. When it finally came time for them to retire to their rooms, Falinor walked Syllē to her door and gently kissed her forehead. She stood in her door for a moment watching Falinor walk away before she slowly retired to her own bed for some much-needed sleep. She was totally unaware Tarin was watching. Coming out from his hiding place as soon as her door closed, Tarin quietly walked forward and placed his forehead against the cool stone.

Placing his hand on the door, Tarin softly whispered, "Sar Asger akvel othok nar undivar othok, mot amoruk."[7]

In the morning, Exulias and Helmfirth were still recovering from the revelry so very few were at the gates of Exulias to bid Syllē's small group farewell, which was for the best, as their greatest chance for survival was based on the fewest number who knew their plans. Still, Syllē noticed two from the company who she thought above all others would be at the gates, but Tarin and Halicyon were noticeably absent. She lingered over her goodbyes longer than she should have, waiting for the elf and dwarf to appear, but they never did.

Finally, Falinor admonished his daughter, "Syllē, we must go."

Nodding sadly, Syllē gave Trygve one last hug. "Keep him safe, please,"

---

7   "May Asger guard you and protect you, my heart."

she murmured into Trygve's hair before pulling away and turning to follow Falinor towards Elathnora and beyond.

Athenéal reached for Syllē one last time. Placing her hands on the Valaraii's cheeks, the elf queen smiled warmly into Syllē's eyes and blessed her, "May the light of the Lēas flow within you and all around you, especially in your darkest hour." To Syllē alone Athenéal murmured, "And never forget the immense love that follows you wherever you journey." Stepping back, Athenéal grasped her husband's hand as she watched Syllē turn and catch up to her father before disappearing from their sight. Silently, she sent a prayer up to High Queen Sedivar that the High Queen would see to it that she, Athenéal, would lay eyes on her friend again.

As Syllē cleared the mountains and headed into the valley, she turned with a smile on her face and gazed up at the roof of Exulias. Her smile faded as she realized Tarin wasn't there either. Closing her eyes against the hurt, Syllē sighed deeply before calling Tarin. *I will see you soon, Tarin. Please be safe.* She had tried to keep the hurt out of her voice, but she wasn't sure how successful she had been. Turning back around, she continued to follow Falinor and the rest away from Exulias.

So caught up in her own dejection at Tarin's absence, Syllē almost tripped and fell when Tarin's voice, warm and rich, flowed through her. *Right beside you, Mot Amoruk.*

Her heart leapt. Out of the corner of her eye, Syllē saw Tarin followed by Halicyon and the rest of her loved ones emerge from the trees to her right and start towards her. The only indication she had that Tarin wasn't happy was his guarded eyes. Trying to steady her breathing and her fluttering heart, Syllē quickly closed the distance between them, wanting desperately to reach out and touch him and kiss him—but any of that activity would be highly inappropriate, especially in front of all these witnesses.

Tarin noticed Syllē's hands clenching and unclenching as he moved towards her; and her eyes were a mesmerizing blue gray. Stopping right in front of her, Tarin almost awkwardly held his gift out to her and was appalled to notice his hands were shaking slightly. He tried to swallow his nerves to keep his voice from cracking before saying, "I am sorry I have been absent for the past few days, but I needed to finish this. I wanted you to have something to take with you on your journey."

Pausing a moment, Tarin stared keenly at Syllē. She was standing with the necklace lying in her hand as she gazed almost wonderingly at it. Now she knew why Tarin had not returned her crystal or necklace. He had used them to construct this one, as well as K'tanna's circlet. Someone had melted the circlet enough to weave the silver with leather into an intricate dwarven braid. The leather and silver wrapped around three blue-gray stones that had been highly polished to the point they each had a star of Sedivar shining in the center. The stones were then positioned in a slight horseshoe shape around the Shara crystal, which had also been shaped and polished to such a degree that it almost mimicked the crystal in the bracelet Syllē had given Tarin. Etched delicately into the surface of the crystal was a spiral fern.

Worried about Syllē's continuing silence as she gazed at her gift, Tarin hurriedly continued speaking, "I crushed the other stones or they'd have been in it, too. Halicyon helped me with those last three. I wanted you to have something to remind you that your home is here with me in Exulias. Her people love you, as do I, above all else. Please don't ever forget..."

Syllē's voice, full of love, stopped him. Still gazing at her necklace, she almost breathed, "Damn it, Tarin," before she grabbed him by his shirt and pulled him right up against her and kissed him deeply.

Falinor was about to step in when Finn spoke up with a knowing grin, "I knew she'd like it."

Falinor sharply smacked Finn on the back of the head. Rubbing his head, Finn glared reproachfully at the elf. Shrugging, Falinor informed Finn, "Your mother instructed me to keep you disciplined while on this journey. She did not want you returned to her unruly and unmanageable."

Turning angrily to his father, Bearn, who was standing on his son's other side leaning nonchalantly on his battle axe, Finn complained, "Don't you have anything to say about an elf disciplining your son?"

Not even looking at his son, Bearn wryly responded, "I have had a long and happy marriage by never countermanding your mother, and I see no reason to break that streak now."

Syllē laughed. Her emotions under control again, she tried to take a step back but found that Tarin had her arms in a death grip. "Don't go. Stay with me. I will make no demands on your heart. Just don't go. Stay with me."

Leaning forward, Syllē softly kissed Tarin's lips. She felt his grip on her arms loosen slightly. Resting her forehead against his, she traced his cheek with her finger. "I will come home, Tarin. I promise."

Tarin's hands fell from her arms. Stepping back, Tarin looked directly into Syllē's eyes. "Say that again," he demanded.

"I promise I will come home, Tarin," Syllē repeated as she fastened the necklace around her neck.

Tarin nodded and said, "I will hold you to that, my lady." Stepping away from her, he rejoined Halicyon, who put a supporting hand on Tarin's shoulder.

Smiling sadly and lovingly at her family, especially Tarin, Syllē slowly turned and rejoined Falinor and the rest. The small group was soon completely out of sight. As she disappeared from his view, it was the comforting support of Halicyon's hand on his shoulder that kept Tarin from falling to his knees in despair.

Read an Excerpt from
VALARAII RISING TRILOGY BOOK 3, THE DEAD

Tarin stood at the end of the road and waited. He soon noticed small ripples on the water as if something huge was moving his way just below the surface. Tarin felt the fear rising, but he stood his ground. He hadn't told anyone where he was going or what he was going to attempt to do, because he had a pretty good idea they would have tried to stop him. He had to try, though. He needed to get out of this swamp. He needed to get home.

Halicyon, who had been told by a worried dwarf from the swamp gate where Tarin had ventured, caught sight of Tarin just as Boris, the largest of the swamp gators, erupted from the waters to Tarin's left and grabbed the dwarf in his jaws, slinging him towards the pool where Cletus leapt out of the water and caught the terrified dwarf. Racing to the edge of the dwarf road, Halicyon screamed Tarin's name just before Boris's tail knocked him far out into the pool. Halicyon surfaced to find himself surrounded, and Tarin gone. Suddenly, something grabbed the elf from below and dragged him down into the depths of the dark pool.

Thank You

I truly hope you enjoyed *Valaraii Rising Trilogy, Book 2: The Lost.* Thank you for taking the time to read my work. If you're new to the trilogy, I recommend you also check out *Book 1, The Forgotten,* as well as stay tuned for the final book, *The Dead.* Regardless, I do hope you found the world of MithTerra to be engaging, exciting, and full of fantastic creatures and peoples.

To find the entire trilogy, or to sign up to be notified by email about new releases, please visit www.jancarolpublishing.com.

If you have the time and the inclination, I would love to hear your feedback in the form of a short book review. Post your review on your favorite book vendor site or share a message with your friends through social media. Or drop a note to me on my Instagram, @valaraiirising. Please let me know what you think—your favorite character, your favorite scene, or favorite monster. Let me know.

ABOUT THE AUTHOR

Kristen Johnson lives in Jonesborough, Tennessee, with her husband, daughter, two dogs, and a bunny. She has been a high school teacher for over 20 years—the best job in the world; so, Kristen Johnson is usually found in her classroom or working with her students in some capacity. Recently, that work has involved volunteering with her students to help their neighbors who were victims of Hurricane Helene.

When not working, Kristen Johnson enjoys riding, especially a simple hack through the fields of her and her parents' farms. Those rides are an amazing way for Kristen to forget about everything but the lovely horse, nature around her, and let her world slow down for a few hours. In the classroom, Kristen tries to pass her passion for reading and writing on to her students and recently had the amazing experience of discussing her first book, *The Forgotten,* with her school's high school book club. Readers can connect with her through Instagram @valaraiirising.